# Asylum

## Jack Adams

Atlas Productions

**Asylum**
Copyright © Jack Adams 2019
All rights reserved. No part of this book may be reproduced, stored in a retrieval system, or be transmitted by any form or by any means, electronic, mechanical, photocopying, recording or otherwise, without the prior written permission of the publisher.

Jack Adams asserts his moral rights to be identified as the author of this book.
First published 2019
Publisher: Atlas Productions
Greenslopes QLD 4102
Web: www.atlasproductions.com.au

 A catalogue record for this
book is available from the
NATIONAL National Library of Australia
LIBRARY
OF AUSTRALIA

ISBN: 978-0-9941822-0-3

Edited by Joanne James.
Cover design by Helen Goltz.
Photograph by Twilightzone, Pixabay.

Dedicated to Joanne James.

You can't pick your relatives, but I got lucky.

# Prologue

Something happened here.

Behind these walls, in these rooms, on the grounds, at the river.

The inmate sketched it all – fine lines.

See there, in the negative space, the truth in the pencil strokes.

Then he was gone.

# Chapter 1

**Then...**

Nathan looked back over his shoulder to make sure his best friend was following; Adam usually followed. They journeyed to where the river met the border of the lunatic asylum – or to give it its full name, the River Park Lunatic Asylum. Here, spotted gums towered above them, rainforest fronds covered the ground, and the earth smelled perpetually damp – their favourite spot and a regular haunt.

'Mum said if she catches us here I'm grounded for a week, and she'll call your parents,' Nate said with a glance behind to where in the distance, his house—along with a row of new, formula suburban homes—gleamed in the River Park estate; their neutral-coloured tiled roofs and neat yards fulfilling the great Australian dream of home ownership. The estate wound around the river, and as the distance increased so did the size and value of the properties. Adam's house was a few suburbs away, in 'rich row' – waterfront with a jetty.

'It's not like we're going to catch something,' Adam

said as they scampered across the old timber bridge.

'Can you catch madness? I thought you could be driven mad,' Nate said, kicking a stone off the edge of the bridge into the water below. He looked down to see it splash; Adam stopped beside him.

'That's different. Your mum's just worried that one of the inmates will try and strangle you, *Natty*,' he said, wrapping his hands around Nate's throat in a pretend strangle. Adam knew his parents wouldn't have cared less where he was, as long as he wasn't underfoot.

Nate pushed him off and winced at the use of his mother's nickname. 'C'mon.'

They left the bridge and disappeared into a row of large ironbark trees that formed a guard of honour along the riverbank. Nate wedged his foot into a groove on the lower trunk of one of the trees he'd climbed many times before and pushed himself up on the first branch. His hands and feet habitually sought out the best branches and grooves to a mid-level branch, he swung himself over it and sat.

'He's there,' Nate said, his voice raised as he looked across at the asylum grounds.

Adam swung himself onto the branch opposite. 'I told ya he'd be back.'

A man with clipped brown hair flecked with strands of grey sat in a chair in the sun. He leaned flush against the wire fence as if by sitting so close, it didn't exist. The light bounced off his white pants and loosely-fitted shirt.

Nate squinted from the glare. 'He missed two days, I thought he'd died. He's got to be pretty old, forty or so, I reckon.'

'Yeah at least,' Adam agreed. 'You got it?'

Nate responded by patting his pocket.

2

'Let's go,' Adam said and swung down from the tree. He waited until Nate landed near him, and followed. They ran along the river's edge until they neared the man and then Nate called out.

'Joe, it's us,' he said. He turned to Adam and lowered his voice. 'Don't want to scare him big time.'

They watched as the man looked up, recognised them and a smile formed on his face. He raised his hand in a wave; the boys went to the fence and dropped down beside him onto the grass. To a stranger, it would look like a father talking with his two sons, except for the ten-foot wire fence between them and the asylum looming in the background.

'We were worried you'd—'

'... been sick,' Adam cut off Nate in case he said the 'dead' word.

Joe tapped the wide timber arm of his chair and smiled at the boys again.

'You're good to worry about me young fellows, but no, just a few days that I had to stay inside. Sometimes it's good to have some time in solitary, for reflection, you know?'

The boys nodded. They didn't know.

'We brought you a present,' Nate said with a look to Adam.

'A present,' Joe's eyes lit up. 'Well, that's thoughtful.'

'You said you liked those cigarette lollies, those musk ones... when you were a kid...' Nate said.

'You can't get them now,' Joe said, 'I've been told, they don't make them anymore.'

'We got some,' Adam said, his face lit up with pleasure.

Nate pulled them out of his pocket and slipped them between the wire; Joe hesitated before taking them.

'Well look at that, look at that,' he said, reaching for the pack and turning it over in his hands. He looked up at them. 'My, well, aren't you two lads thoughtful. Thank you, thank you both.'

Nate and Adam beamed with pleasure.

'We must smoke one now then,' Joe said, gently prying open the pack of musk candy cigarettes and offering one to each of the boys. When they all had one, Joe made a pretend show of lighting them, and the three sat back, sucking and faking the smoking of their candy cigarettes until they were gone. Joe chuckled at the sight.

'Can we ask you a question, Joe?' Nate asked.

'Of course, anything.'

'What do you do... you know, for a job?' Nate asked.

'Well, today... I am an artist. Yes, I like to draw. What do you two lads do?' Joe asked.

Nate and Adam glanced at each other.

Adam shrugged, pulling at his T-shirt. 'Nothing. We're kids.'

Joe's eyes widened. 'Oh, no, you're at a very important stage in your life. When I was a kid, I was a pirate for at least a year. Then I became an inventor when I was about ten, and for a while, I was a writer. But I found my true calling when I was about fourteen; I became an artist. I'm still an artist. How old are both of you?'

'Ten,' they said in unison.

'But I'm the eldest, by two months,' Nate added.

'We're not brothers,' Adam clarified.

Joe nodded; he briefly studied Nate with his handsome Aryan features and then turned to Adam noting the boy's finer features—the blue eyes and dark hair. 'Hmm, I see. So, what do you do then?' Joe asked, turning to Nate first.

Nate frowned as he thought about it. 'I like to explore.'

'Then you are an explorer, and I suspect you are very good at it. And you, young man?' He turned to Adam.

Adam answered without hesitation. 'I like to work out how things work.'

'Ah yes, I can see that,' Joe said, 'a student of life.'

Adam flushed and smiled, pleased with the title. He mumbled the words so he would remember them later. Someone was coming through the grounds and he nudged Nate.

'We better go,' Nate said, 'but we'll see you soon Joe, maybe tomorrow.'

'I look forward to it, and thank you, lads. A happy memory, most kind,' he said, holding up the cigarettes and studying the packet. He slipped it into the wide pocket on his shirt front.

The boys hunched over and scurried to the river bank, losing themselves behind the canopy of trees. When they were out of sight, they stopped to look back.

'You know there really are mad people in there, lunatics!' Nate said, circling his fingers near his temple.

Adam nodded. 'Mum said they should move them further away.'

'What do you think is wrong with Joe?' Nate asked. 'He seems pretty normal.'

Adam shrugged. 'Nothing, probably in there by mistake.'

'One day, we'll ask him,' Nate said, before turning and heading towards the river.

# Chapter 2

**Now...**

Nate put his shoulder against the stubborn, rusted iron door and gave it a shove; it opened with a groan. He looked behind to make sure Adam was close by—Adam usually followed—then he stepped into the abandoned building of the River Park Hospital, or as it was unofficially known, the Lunatic Asylum. The locals knew it as the loony bin.

'Christ,' he muttered, grimacing as the stale air assaulted them – a stench of urine, decay, and misery.

Adam covered his nose with his hand, trying to filter the smell before giving up and breathing it in. 'I can't believe I let you talk me into coming here. Why did we have to come at night? It's not a bloody ghost tour,' he said, doing up his jacket and trying to get the collar high enough to cover his nose. It wasn't a cold night—Autumn in Brisbane was equivalent to a Tasmanian Summer—but the abandoned building gave him a chill.

Nate rolled his eyes. 'Because I called in a favour with the security guys; they're turning a blind eye to us.'

'What? You mean we're illegally...' Adam sighed. He ran

a hand through his dark hair that was due for a haircut last month. 'Forget it, don't tell me,' he shook his head.

'C'mon, if I went through the normal approval procedures to get in here it could take us months, and there's no guarantee they'd let us in any way. Besides,' Nate continued, 'I thought we'd get a better feel for the place at night.' He felt a strong desire not to go any further, but he wasn't going to admit it. He reached for the torch in his jacket and turned it on. 'Are you chicken?' he asked Adam.

'You think I still fall for that line?' Adam asked, and pushed past Nate.

'Apparently,' Nate said, as Adam took the lead, then stopped suddenly a few metres inside the door.

Adam retrieved his torch and listened; in the distance was a faint tapping sound.

'Hear that?' Adam asked.

'Yeah. Old pipe dripping?' Nate suggested.

'Maybe.'

The two men walked a few more steps past the entrance, allowing their senses to adjust to the smell and shadowed room. Nate ran his torchlight down the hallway of the abandoned west wing. A thump sounded upstairs and both men looked above their heads.

'Let's get a move on, it stinks in here, like a public lavvy.' Nate wrinkled his nose in disgust.

'I feel like I'm in an episode of *Ghost Hunters*,' Adam said, staying close to Nate.

'Wouldn't have thought you'd be the type to watch *Ghost Hunters*.'

'Steph used to watch it, only during the daytime though,' he referred to his ex-wife. He felt a stab of pain at the mention of her name; the pain was raw, recent enough – a blend of betrayal, anger, failure and loneliness… a classic mix.

Nate nudged him to follow as he took the lead and moved down the hall. He glanced into the second room; Adam stayed close by, breathing down his neck and not letting the blond head in front of him out of his sight.

'Can't you just feel the misery of this place?' Nate said. 'I wonder what Joe was in here for, how he came about being in here. He never did tell us.'

'You almost asked once, remember?' Adam said. He flashed his torch into a large empty room and checked out the four corners.

'Yeah, but you wouldn't let me.'

'Like you ever did anything I told you,' Adam scoffed. 'So, are we there yet? What's the note say?'

Nate fished a folded letter out of his pocket and directed his torch to it; it was written on official letterhead from a solicitor who claimed to be representing his missing client, Joe O'Connell.

'Says Joe's diary was left in the ward he slept in… he wanted us to have it… blah, blah, blah, might still be hidden there… yadda, yadda, that's the gist of it.' Nate turned it over and looked at the hand-drawn map. He looked up and then back at the map. 'This is the treatment wing, not Joe's room.' He turned and led the way down the hall, letting the light from his torch chase the edges of the high ceiling, reflecting off rooms he passed.

Sour white paint peeled from the walls, plastic flapped in the windows where glass had once been, and graffiti artists had worked their magic on the walls. He glanced into a large room where broken beds with loose straps leant against the wall as though in casual conversation with the rusted, folded steel-frame chairs stacked nearby.

'Miserable,' Adam muttered, looking over Nate's shoulder.

A door slammed and they wheeled around; no-one was there.

'For the love of God,' Nate muttered, and breathed in deeply, patting his heart through his jacket.

Adam grinned. 'Getting a feel for it?'

'Yeah, maybe the daytime might have been better.' Above them, they could hear boards creaking, again.

'Want to go check that noise out?' Nate asked.

'Hell no.' Adam said.

Nate grinned. 'Let's find Joe's wing.' He exited the doorway, with Adam close by and flicked his torch left then right. 'This way,' he said. 'Three doors up on the right, supposedly.'

'What a miserable old place,' Adam said, almost to himself.

'Should demolish it,' Nate agreed. 'Along with all its memories.' He stopped outside the third room and consulted the map again. 'This is it. If we're going to find it at all, it should be in here.'

They stepped into the room and Adam let out a low whistle. 'It'll be a miracle if anything is here; I'm guessing the place has been cased a few times.'

The room was a shell: snapped single iron bed-frames were scattered around the room like broken limbs; a makeshift fireplace was set up in the corner, deserted now even by the squatters; a row of chipped basins lined half of the opposite wall; windows were broken and stuffed with plastic or newspaper, and the few remaining cupboards were missing their doors, their shelves bare. The room smelled damp, and the floorboards felt unstable as the men tested their weight on them.

Nate looked around. 'The solicitor said Joe's bed was closest to the window in the left-hand corner if you stood at the door looking out to the field.'

Both men took in the instructions and turned towards the empty corner. They moved towards where Joe's bed would have once been. Nate pointed – a small, faded pen-drawn portrait of a man was on the wall – a self-portrait of Joe; they were in the right area. Adam shone his torch along the timber boards. He glanced back at Nate.

'Six along, bottom row,' Nate said, consulting the map again.

Adam counted and found the board; he tapped it lightly at the top, it was secure. He started from the bottom and felt it give slightly. He prised it up and moved the board slightly to the right, shining his torch into the cavity. There was something there, wrapped in an old cloth. Adam hesitated, then reached in and pulled it out.

'I think we've found it.' Adam unfolded the cloth—a large blue and white checked tea-towel—and found a leather-bound book with a faded gold inscription that read 'Diary'.

He looked up at Nate standing over him. 'Ha, I can't believe after all these years Joe's diary is still here.'

'It wouldn't be if squatters had pulled the floorboards up for firewood,' Nate said, 'we're just lucky I guess.'

Adam returned his attention to the book and gently prised apart the pages. The first few were full of pen drawings and small, handwritten notes – impressive etchings of the building's façade and detailed faces.

'Look!' Nate laughed, shining his torch on a drawing of two boys in the corner of the page. 'I'm guessing that's us.'

Adam smiled and nodded. He read aloud the words written underneath: '*My two young friends*. Wow, look at that.'

Nate sighed. 'Well, we've got your diary, Joe, but where are you?'

## Then...

'If you're an artist, Joe, what do you draw?' Nate asked the man dressed all in white, sitting in the timber chair. The two boys lay on the grass nearby – the wire fence a tenuous barrier between the sane and unbalanced.

'Ah, lots of things young Nate – you see I write a bit of poetry, prose, short stories, and then I do illustrations to accompany them. But sometimes, I just draw the world around me; the things I see every day... and of course, the things that we don't see.'

'How do you draw things you can't see... do you mean like spaceships and stuff like that?' Nate asked.

'Yes, like that. I sometimes draw angels, places I dream of going, faces of people I remember. Want to see one?'

'Yes please,' Adam said, and sat upright.

Joe leaned down and reached for the note pad that lay on the grass beside his chair. He winced as he leaned over. 'This is just a little drawing I've been working on today... it's a work in progress,' he said. 'An etching.'

The boys studied the line drawing of the external façade of the hospital.

'Wow,' Adam said, 'so like it.'

'Wish I could draw like that,' Nate said.

'Thank you, lads,' Joe said, closing his book again. 'I love to draw.'

'We do art at school, but it's kind of boring,' Nate said.

'Do you go to the same school?' Joe asked. He was comfortable asking questions; deflecting them drained him.

Nate shook his head. 'Adam goes to the rich school and I go to the State school.'

Joe chuckled and Adam rolled his eyes. 'It's not the rich school; it's just... well, Dad went there and so did his Dad, so I have to as well.'

'Ah tradition, I understand,' Joe nodded. 'So how did you meet?'

'Here, near the creek,' Adam continued. 'We were riding our bikes around, we live kind of near each other, and we've joined the same football club.'

Nate pointed down the river. 'Adam lives around there and I'm over there,' he said indicating the suburban sprawl.

Joe nodded. He ran his hand down his face and across his clipped beard. He sat thinking and the boys waited. He often did this.

'You could draw us, Joe, maybe...' Adam suggested.

Joe looked at the boys. 'I think that's a wonderful idea; I'll give it some thought. You see, you have to have a passion, lads, and when you find what that is, then no matter what else happens in your life, you have to pursue it. It can save you.'

'From what?' Adam asked.

'From the world, from yourself,' Joe said, waving his arms around, 'and if it is your passion, it will be your best work.'

'Are you famous, Joe? Are your drawings in museums and shops?' Nate asked. He flicked an ant from his arm and squinted up at Joe.

'They might be lads... anything is possible.'

# Chapter 3

**Now…**

Small, slim and wearing a black knit fitted-top, a vintage houndstooth skirt, and black court shoes, Jessica Johnson suited the two-story, Art Deco building she was about to enter. She stood at the bottom of the stairwell and glanced up. It felt better than the chrome and glass environment of her current position in the city. Here there was no lift and no fire-drill down twenty flights of stairs.

She didn't want to admit it, but she was nervy. Her friends' social media feeds boasted that terrorist attacks weren't going to stop them from living adventurously, from travelling and doing everything they normally would. A bus driver killed by a random act of violence; people run over as cars plunged into the public sidewalks; no siree, get out there and live! Jessica joined in the bravado, but it wasn't how she felt under her skin, where the blood flowed, where the heart pumped. The city, her city, was safe… until it wasn't. Now, she stood behind the steel light posts on street corners before she crossed so she couldn't be mowed down by a car; she avoided crowds; found excuses not to go out to crowded nightclubs; hated working in high rises since the September 11 attack in the USA; and she wasn't ready to travel. It was an insidious fear she couldn't shake.

The chance to work outside the city fringes in this village-like place, in a private office in Stones Corner, Brisbane, felt right, and she felt confident about this job interview—after all, she knew Nate—and she was the first candidate to be interviewed. Jessica took the stairs to the office on the second floor; at the top of the flight of stairs she could see a frosted door with the lettering:

Nathan Delaney, *BA (PsychCrimnlgyJust)*
Private Investigator
Adam Murphy, *DPsych (Clinical), MSc (Psych), MAPS*
Psychologist

Nathan Delaney... she ran the name through her memory banks – time had not made her like him anymore; he was a charming pain in the butt. As a cocky, young cop he had annoyed the hell out of her with his flirting and getting her in trouble with his late reports. She had covered for him to her boss, the Deputy Commissioner, so many times. But at twenty-eight, single, and wanting a change of job—a life shake up—the call from her old colleague wasn't entirely unwelcome. Jessica wondered what he would think of how she had weathered in the years since they had seen each other. She'd heard he had married and had a kid; he was a step ahead of her.

She made her way up the stairs and went to knock on the door as it swung open. Nate—five years older than when she had last seen him and better looking than she remembered—stood there.

'Jess! You're here.' She noted his eyes ran over her before returning to her face. 'Looking good too, in a purely professional manner,' he said, with a grin, and moved aside for her to enter.

'Hi Nate and thanks, in a purely professional capacity,' she said, narrowing her eyes at him as she passed. He was broader than he had been in his early twenties. His blonde hair had outgrown the crew cut and was shaggy and full, and he looked good; damn him. Jessica looked at the only other person standing in the room.

Nate did the introductions. 'Jessica Johnson meet Adam Murphy, my new partner... well, we're sharing office space. So, are you going to take the job?'

Jessica frowned at Nate and turned to greet Adam. He moved like a man comfortable in his own skin, and his dark suit, and she took his extended hand in a shake. She noted, like Nate, Adam was tall, a head taller than she was in heels, but darker and leaner – he looked like he needed a sandwich.

Nate continued, 'We've just finished unpacking boxes and we're going to go downstairs for a drink if you've got time... consider it part of your interview!'

'I feel like we should be cutting a ribbon or something,' Adam said as he stood, hands on hips, looking around the reception area of their new office.

'I'd rather take the top off a beer,' Nate said. He perched on the end of the reception desk and folded his arms. 'It's going to be alright, isn't it, going out on our own... sharing these digs?'

Adam grinned. 'It's going to be great. Although my name should have gone above yours on the door, alphabetically you know...' He ribbed his best friend and looked back to the front glass door where the sign writer had done his work. 'Don't you think Jessica?'

15

'I'm not taking sides already,' she said, with a smile, 'but alphabetical is usually the go—Adam should have gone first—unless one partner is paying more than the other.'

'There's an idea,' Adam brightened.

'You're costing me money already, Jess,' Nate frowned at her. 'Besides, my name should be on top; I'm two months older.' The words rolled off his tongue with familiarity; Adam had heard them a few thousand times in their boyhood.

'So, this is where I *might* be working?' Jessica asked and walked around to look behind the reception desk.

'Right there, ready to greet the future rush of clients,' Nate confirmed with a nod.

Jessica sat and tried out the chair. The reception desk faced the front door; at least no-one could creep up behind her. A bench ran behind her desk where a printer took up a fair bit of space, and to the side of the office, there were quite a few windows; the drop to the lower level wouldn't kill her if she had to… she stopped that train of thought. To the right was Nate's office, to the left of the reception was where Adam would see his patients – both rooms appeared similar in length with frosted glass windows. She swivelled around and to the left, behind her was a large room with scattered empty boxes on the floor, and a set of weights in the middle – *Boardroom* was written on the door. A small room next to it featured a kitchenette with a bar fridge in the corner and Nate pointed out a closed door that led to a shower for future employees who liked to exercise before work.

'Will you be doing that?' she asked him.

'Don't be ridiculous,' he shot back. Jessica laughed.

Jessica turned back to face the waiting room that allowed for about twelve people – six people on both sides if they chose to be segregated.

'See yourself here?' Nate asked again, and Jessica pursed her lips as she took in the area.

'You're not going to separate the waiting room with a partition or something?' she asked. 'A private investigator and a psychologist… some of Nate's clients might be a bit shady and yours, Adam, well they could be nutso.'

'I bet you won't tell them apart,' Adam said, giving Nate a wry look. 'Besides, I might need the overflow into Nate's area if I run a group session.'

'Might be good to mix them up anyway, could be entertaining for you, Jess,' Nate said.

'Are you going to take the job?' Adam asked.

Nate glanced at his watch. 'Sure she is. Come on, let's celebrate with a drink… it's happy hour.'

*****

Sitting opposite Adam, Jessica studied him as they waited for Nate to return from the bar with their drinks. Adam seemed lost in thought, comfortable in silence, and not concerned about making small talk. She sat back in the half-circle booth.

'So how do you know Nate?' she asked.

'We were neighbours, grew up together,' Adam said. 'And you met him in the police service. You're small for a cop, no height restrictions then?'

'I was only ever in administration, no desire to be a cop,' she said, with a glance to Nate to confirm she didn't ever want to go down that path. 'They had a restructure a few years ago and a lot of the admin staff was let go, me included. I've been contracting around the place ever since.'

Adam nodded and waited – occupational hazard. Jessica continued.

'I'm working in the city now… in the public service, Department of Communities,' she said. 'So boring… it's comatose stuff. Anyway, I want to buy a unit and I would prefer to have a full-time job if I'm going to have a home loan.' She realised she was raving… filling in the silence that Adam artfully left for her to bridge.

Adam smiled. 'I get it, I've got one of those too.'

She turned the spotlight back on him. 'And this is the first time you've worked together, you and Nate? Or are you going to do some work *on* Nate?'

Adam laughed. She noticed how it changed him; lit up his face, made him more handsome.

'There are not enough hours in the day to work *on* Nate, but yeah, he might get a case that I can get involved with. That's why we need someone who can manage appointments, files, banking, phone, especially manage people – an office manager. I get some highly-strung clients and Nate gets a lot of desperados.'

'That's cool, I've worked for the cops… I know how to pacify the stressed and manage egos. So, what has Nate told you about me?' she said with another glance to Nate leaning against the bar. He must have sensed he was being talked about and looked their way, frowning slightly.

'Just that you're the best he's ever worked with and you'd be better than anyone else we're bound to interview,' Adam answered.

Jessica involuntarily raised her eyebrows, surprised, and accepted a glass of wine as Nate slipped into the booth beside her. He pushed a beer in front of Adam. Nate raised his beer in a toast.

'To the new business and Jess joining us, yeah?' he said, with a glance at Adam, trying to read if he had got her across the line. The three clinked their drinks.

'Can I ask how many applications you had?' Jessica asked.

Nate and Adam exchanged looks.

'We haven't got around to running an ad yet,' Adam said. 'It's kind of a unique job. There are some weird hours and...'

'Weird clients, especially Adam's,' Nate added. 'But c'mon, we worked well together when I was a cop... this will be great.'

'We didn't work well together then,' Jessica rolled her eyes. 'You drove me nuts. You never did your paperwork; I was always chasing you and getting my butt kicked by the Deputy Commissioner because the reports were never in on time – actually all of the reports except yours were in on time. You'd call at all hours for contacts, and...'

'Yeah we get the picture,' Nate cut her off, 'but you'll find Adam is very organised.'

She looked at Adam, who nodded in agreement.

'Hmm, I have something to say before I accept the job, if I accept the job,' she said, feeling braver than she actually was... she wanted this job; she was mentally gone from the other one.

'Sure,' Nate invited her to speak.

She took a deep breath and sat upright. 'I know you are the boss or bosses, but here are my terms and conditions: I will arrive at the office sometime before eight-thirty and finish at five unless we've got a situation, and that's fine, working back or odd hours is not a drama. I don't want to be micro-managed, or clock watched; I'll do work after hours and on weekends that you guys probably won't be aware of, so just trust me that I'm doing the hours you pay me to do.'

The men nodded, and she continued.

'I will come into the office before I do a coffee run and if you are in, I'll happily get your coffee or if you're AWOL, I'll text you to check if you want one. Once I get back from the coffee run, I'm not running out again to get yours if you miss the latte train. I'm happy to get your lunches, at the same time, and another coffee round in the afternoon but I don't make tea or coffee for clients or pick up dry cleaning. I'll enter all appointments into your online diaries and give you a print out in the morning. Shall I continue?' she asked, pushing a strand of her shoulder-length brown hair behind her ear.

'Sure,' Nate answered on behalf of them both. Jessica sensed he'd break every one of her rules anyway. She continued, 'I can keep the books for the business or provide notes to your accountant, but you need to remember to give me all the receipts regularly. I don't want to get to the thirtieth of June and be landed with hundreds of dockets,' she said directing her gaze to Nate. 'Adam, I'm guessing that I charge your clients before their appointments… most psychologists do that?'

Adam nodded his agreement and Jessica continued.

'… and Nate you'll need to tell me your procedure, I'm assuming I take an initial deposit once the client agrees to your rate? Again, don't get months behind and create a mountain of paperwork for me. I would like you to provide a car park for me, and I don't want a second mobile phone, I'll use mine, but I will charge any work-related calls to you. That's it. Are you still interested in hiring me? Actually, take some time, you can get back to me later if you want to chat about my terms and conditions.'

'I'm good,' Adam said.

'Me too,' Nate agreed. 'Can you start Monday?' He dug the receipt for the drinks out of his wallet. 'There's the first receipt… call that one the weekly staff meeting.'

## Chapter 4

He'd often wondered if there was something wrong with him, really wrong with him... other than all the things he had been told were his fault from people who wouldn't really know... but, was he really a nutcase?

Ron 'Mac' McIntyre cut another wedge of cheese and stuffed it in the folds of his breadstick. He sat back and taking a large bite, chewed and thought about his situation. Even in the darkness of the top floor room, he knew this place... could find his way around blindfolded. He knew every corner, hallway and room, and what went on there, once. How many people would live in a place with so many bad memories? Where the worst possible shit that could ever happen to you, happened, and then for some reason you decided to make it home. Yeah, that was pretty screwed, he thought.

But he liked it here, in the empty shell of the asylum. It was quiet, no-one bothered him, no-one came knocking for rent. He didn't care if he didn't have a television or if he didn't have a bath every day; a shower at the community centre every couple of days did the trick. He had a library card, a bus pass and a small pension; and this was where he chose to live. He also had his battery radio for entertainment and he usually 'borrowed' an abandoned paper every day from a café table, or bought one if he couldn't lift one easily enough. He'd read it cover to cover and do the crossword and sudoku; his grade seven teacher had drilled into the class that 'reading was fundamental to functioning in today's society'. He didn't know what that meant then, but now, he thought she might be right – all the smart people seemed to do it, and it kept his mind from wandering; that's why he liked the talkback radio station.

Every now and then people came through his home, like the ghost tours but he hadn't seen them for about a month, and there were those two guys the other night. Who the hell were they? He stayed out of sight but he didn't always. He hadn't performed his bit of theatre for a while but maybe it was time to get back on the horse. He had to try and get some justice for not only himself but all the other poor bastards that had come and gone through the place.

He'd given up on trying to guilt the government into coffing up compensation. Hell, he didn't really want money, he wanted an apology, acceptance that they'd screwed up, and look at him, he was okay despite that. But he wouldn't knock back a payment… he could get a permanent van in a caravan park or something like it. If he hadn't been done over, he'd probably have that already from doing labouring work or a trade. Maybe he'd even have a wife and a kid. Yeah, they owed him.

But there's something he wanted more than all of that. He wanted the truth to come out. He wanted to read all the foul shit in the paper about what they'd done to the patients and how none of it was legal. He wanted it out there and everyone knowing about it. And if any of those sons of bitches who called themselves wardens were still alive, he wanted them locked up too.

The thought fired him up, and he decided then and there,

that it was time to take the campaign up again. He had to hold onto that thought, it would help him get up in the morning. He finished off his cheese roll on the strength of it.

*****

**Then...**

Adam lay back on the tree branch, one leg dangling as he let the sun dry him off after their swim in the river. His T-shirt hung on a lower branch, and his towel one branch higher. He closed his eyes, enjoying the warm air touching his skin.

'Do you think there's sharks in there?' Nate asked, leaning back on a branch nearby.

'Nuh, if I was a shark I wouldn't hang around here, would you?' Adam said.

'No way, I'd be in the ocean speeding around underwater and scaring the shit out of people by sticking my fin up in swimming areas,' Nate said, with a laugh. 'But I'd be too fast to be caught.'

A movement caught his eye and Adam spun around. 'Look,' he said.

They turned and looked towards the River Park Lunatic Asylum; a number of figures in white could be seen in the grounds – a woman was being led by a nurse; an older man in a wheelchair was placed half in the sun, half in the shade of a tree; and Joe was walking towards his usual spot but this time he was with a man in a light coloured suit.

They watched the man, probably the same age as their parents, as he sat beside Joe and began rifling through papers. He looked smart like he could get Joe out.

'Might be his doctor,' Adam said, 'except he's not wearing any white.'

'Could be the boss of the loony bin or Joe's brother, he'd be an older brother,' Nate said. 'Joe seems pretty chilled like he knows him.'

The boys sat up and watched as the man put some documents in Joe's lap and handed him a pen. Joe made a mark on the paper and then he shook the man's hand; he watched as the man put the papers away. They sat for a while talking and then the man in the pale suit stood to leave, shook Joe's hand again and Joe watched him depart. The boys watched as Joe then reached for his note pad and began to write or draw.

'Maybe he's signed up Joe's next painting or his book... he said he did some writing,' Adam suggested.

Joe looked around as though looking for them.

'We should visit soon, maybe when there's not as many people in the grounds,' Nate said.

'Yeah, tomorrow,' Adam agreed. 'He might have done the drawing of us, that'd be cool.'

'If he becomes a famous artist and he puts our drawing in a frame, we could be famous too,' Nate said, his eyes widened at the thought. 'Although you're kind of famous already.'

Adam scoffed. 'Only when I'm out with Mum. Dad loves it when people recognise her. I hate it... takes us twice as long to get anywhere and they always want to get photos.'

'I think it's cool,' Nate said. 'Wish my Mum was famous.'

'Nuh, you don't,' Adam said, and changed the subject. 'I wonder if Joe's married or if he has kids like us? He's pretty old so he might have.'

Nate shrugged. 'You'd think he'd say. But they could be dead or he might have got a divorce. You know Julie Grosvenor in our class... her parents just got divorced. She has to live with her mum for one week, then go to her dad's house for the next week.'

'Yeah? Weird,' Adam said.

'Do you think he killed them? That might be why he's in that place,' Nate said, a hint of excitement in his voice.

'Don't know and we're not going to ask,' Adam warned his best friend.

'He won't mind, he said we could ask anything.'

'Yeah, but you might just trip him off, sort of send him over the edge. What if he cried or tried to grab us through the fence?'

'Yeah,' Nate agreed, 'that'd be freaky. Okay, but if he says something like that, I'm asking.'

**Now...**

'We need to talk about the other night, and Joe's diary,' Adam said, not taking his eyes off the football action that was screening in the living room.

Nate rolled his eyes. 'Psychologists... they always want to talk.'

Adam grinned. His gaze shifted from the television to outside, into Nate's yard. 'How long have you got Matilda for?'

'Just the weekend,' Nate said. They sat with a beer at Nate's dining room table where they could see the football game and Nate's five-year-old daughter, Matilda, jumping on the trampoline with her friend from next door.

Nate rose, grabbed a folder from the kitchen counter and

rejoined Adam. 'Do you ever think about Joe? I know its been twenty years, but before that letter arrived, did you think about him much?'

Adam shook his head. 'I feel bad saying it, but I completely forgot about him – once he stopped coming out into the grounds, it was sort of like out of sight, out of mind.' He was distracted by a row of framed photographs that Nate had displayed along a wall rail. In one frame, a younger version of himself stood with Nate; it was just before their teenage years hit and the acne and awkwardness that came with it. It was about the time of their visits to Joe when they were boyish, tanned and grinning. Nate was holding up a fishing rod with a twig on the end of it and Adam was laughing. Today's catch. Nate turned to see what Adam was looking at and smiled at the memory.

'Yeah, we were at that age when we didn't take on too much… heading into our teens, there was sport, and girls, and school, we had a lot going on,' Nate said.

'Sure,' Adam agreed. 'I can't imagine why a creative soul like Joe was trapped in that hellhole.'

'Maybe we owe it to him to find out what really happened to him, if anything happened to him, that is. He might have signed himself in there for all we know.'

'And why has he remembered us in the letter to his solicitor? We were about a minute in his life nearly two decades ago,' Adam said. 'It can be the first case we work together. Lord help us.'

'Yeah, you're dying to work with me,' Nate ribbed him. 'You can read heads, I'll read the clues.'

Matilda ran in. 'Uncle Adam, come and jump with us,' she said, grabbing his arm.

'He can't right now, Tilly, he's in a meeting with me,' Nate answered.

'I am, but I'd love to come and jump another time,' Adam assured her.

'Then Daddy, come jump with us; you can both jump,' she moved to her father.

'I can't right now because I'm helping our football team,' he said, looking up as a cheer escaped the television as the Broncos kicked a goal.

'*Your* football team,' Adam said. 'The Lions are having a very good season.'

Nate shook his head. 'I don't know when you decided to become Victorian, but I'm not impressed.'

'Daddy,' Matilda refocused Nate's attention. 'Come and jump.'

'We'll leave that to you, Tilly,' he said. 'We can see you both from here; you're very good at it.'

She grinned and ran back to the trampoline, her blonde pigtails reminding Nate of his wife, estranged wife.

Adam read him. 'Are you and Erin getting on any better?'

'Nope.'

Adam nodded.

'And no, I don't want to talk about it... nothing more to say that I didn't dump on you after the last ten beers and emotional trip,' Nate added. 'But if I did want to talk, I'd talk to you,' he said offering him a bone.

'Sure you would,' Adam said, giving him a wary look. He looked back to the ledge of framed photos and at the photos of Nate, Erin and Matilda. No wonder Nate couldn't get a date with those on display, Adam thought studying them. He couldn't imagine having a single photo of Stephanie on display in his home; he didn't need any reminders. He liked Erin though, she was good for Nate, but not many cops'— even former cops'—marriages go the distance. He considered Erin's photo. 'Hard to leave beauty...' he said, absently.

Nate glanced in the direction Adam was looking and viewed the photo. 'Yeah, I put up with a lot 'cause I couldn't bear to think of anyone else touching her… little did I know she was regularly sleeping around,' he spat out the words, shook his head and looked away, reining in his anger.

'Right. Joe, then,' Adam said, taking a deep breath, and with a sympathetic glance to Nate, he changed the subject. Adam flipped open the folder and reached for one of the documents; the solicitor's letter that came in last week's mail.

Nate moved beside him. 'I've checked out this guy,' he said, tapping at the signature on the bottom of the letter that Adam had in front of him. Nate removed a photo and piece of paper from the folder and slipped them over to Adam as well. A large black and white photo and profile filled the page.

'John Liberman of Liberman & Clarke, Estate and Will lawyers,' Nate continued. 'He's bona fide. Look familiar to you?'

Adam studied the photo, his eyes narrowing in concentration. 'Should he?'

Nate nodded. 'I'm going to go out on a limb, a pretty safe limb, and say that we've seen him before, a few times, about twenty years ago.'

'Really?' Adam glanced at Nate and back to the photo. His eyes narrowed as he traced the detail of the man's face, trying to place him. Nate waited impatiently, drumming his fingers on the table.

'So, who do you think he is?' Adam asked handing back the photo and the letter.

Nate paused, distracted by a goal in the Broncos versus Dragons game. He shook his head and pushed away his empty beer bottle. 'If they get any worse, they'll be calling me up.'

'No-one's that desperate,' Adam assured him with a glance to the TV.

Nate held up the photo. 'Remember that visitor Joe had a few times… he usually came with papers that Joe signed; he'd sit with him for a while… I reckon it's him,' he said.

Adam looked at the photo again, really studied it. 'Wow, you've got a great memory for faces, no wonder you made a good cop. I guess it could be.'

'And it is why I will be a sensational P.I,' Nate said. 'Trust me, it's him. He used to wear light coloured suits, and Joe seemed pretty comfortable with him.' he said. 'He would have been our parents' age then or a bit older, mid-sixties now… it's him I'm telling you.'

'So, we've found the diary, what else? Why does he still need to see us?' Adam asked.

'Why would he be representing Joe unless Joe had something to represent… something worth bequeathing maybe?' Nate suggested.

'Maybe Joe has been alive, institutionalised somewhere all this time and he's just died,' Adam said. 'Or Joe's will might have had a date clause and that's why we've just heard from this guy – it's not like we're hard to track down… maybe he wasn't allowed to contact us until this year, maybe it's a significant date to Joe…'

'Maybe he's investigating Joe or some claim against him and we're in his notes somewhere. Maybe we should just go and see this John Liberman,' Nate concluded.

Adam nodded. 'He was right about where we'd find Joe's diary so I guess he's credible. Anyway, we've got nothing to lose; I'll set it up for next week.'

They looked up as Matilda and her friend jumped down from the trampoline and started calling for ice-cream.

'Looks like I'm on the ice-cream run. Want to come?' Nate asked.

Adam shook his head. 'Nuh, but thanks. I've got to get some groceries, there's nothing in the house.'

'Yeah, you've lost weight since Steph moved out… eat something.'

Adam pushed himself out of the chair and with a small sigh said, 'I'll cook a steak and read Joe's diary.'

'Wouldn't it be weird if Joe was famous or filthy rich?' Nate said. 'I'll Google him.'

'An eccentric recluse maybe. It'd be tragic if that's what led him to us… to that place,' Adam agreed.

Nate thought about the gentle man with the soulful eyes. 'Even worse if he never did leave there.'

# Chapter 5

**Extract – Joe's diary:**

*I share a dormitory with eleven other men, the women are across the hall; we see them in the grounds and at meal times. Sometimes they squeeze more men into my ward, sometimes men recover and leave, or they die – they are here then gone, no goodbye, no explanation. It's best not to get attached.*

*Most of my roommates are in here because they have had breakdowns, psychotic episodes, or as my mother would say, are sick in the head. The patient in the bed next to me has several personalities; I like them all. I jest of course.*

*Charlie, the older man across from me, keeps seeing a reflection in the window and requesting to go to that room. When the doctors try to explain that it is a reflection, the man assures them it is heaven and he must go there.*

*No man plans this sort of life for himself, it just happens through circumstances as did mine. At least Charlie has hope that heaven is better.*

The entry finished. Adam looked up and squinted as the morning light reflected off the building opposite and through his office window as if someone had turned on the lights. Poor old Charlie, he thought. A glance to the clock told him Jessica and Nate would soon be arriving; he was enjoying the quiet of the office early that Monday. So different from the hospital where he was last working with its 24-hour traffic and numerous drug and drink-fuelled patients. He turned his attention back to the diary and flicked to the next page. There was an illustration – a pencil sketch of a man standing by the window looking into another room. Reflected in the window was the same man with huge big feathered wings drawn on him to depict an angel. Behind him, sketchy figures were drawn with wings.

'Beautiful,' Adam said to himself, tracing the detailed feathers in the wings and the paradise reflected. He put his feet on his office desk and stared out the window for a moment, thinking of Joe and of Charlie's heaven on the other side of the glass. A few minutes later he returned his attention to Joe's next entry.

*From my ward through a panel of glass, nearly every day I see my fellow residents being strapped down as they're taken away for 'treatment'. I know in many cases that it's shock treatment… I've seen it happen first hand. Today, a young girl fought all the way, I suppose there was nothing to lose. She begged them to help her, cried and pleaded for them not to do it. She begged us to intervene. Who gave them consent I wonder?*

*Her eyes met mine for just a moment and like a defeated man, I looked away. How could I rage against the inhumanity of it all and risk the same treatment? I am a toothless tiger, weak; my pen and my brushes are my only weapons and even the works produced from these tools will be seen as the ramblings of a mad man.*

*I was there when she came out but this time her eyes didn't seek me out, she lay perfectly still... as still as death. I saw her two days later, but her look was not accusatory; she walked around in a daze, her eyes unfocused, searching for a memory to hang onto. Maybe it is her medication, maybe the shock treatment, maybe it is a blessing.*

*Some of the residents here—perhaps we should call them what they are: patients, victims, the forgotten—don't forget the shock treatments. They hide when staff appear, fearing they are going to be sent for treatment again; they stop breathing until the staff member passes. One poor fellow urinates. The staff laugh at him, then he's punished for needing to be cleaned – what did these sick, deserted people do to deserve this? I deserve to be here, but...*

The entry finished abruptly. Why? Adam thought. Why do you deserve to be there, Joe? Drawings filled the next few pages. With another glance to the clock, Adam closed the book and closed his eyes; he could smell the river. Sometimes in the strangest places he would smell the river and be taken back to that time in his life; a very happy, simple time. Now the letter had plunged him there... thinking about those years again when his parents were both alive and his biggest concern was when they'd next have time for him, and if they'd even come home... seemed like a million years ago.

He thought of Joe's face and countenance. Joe seemed like an old man then, but in retrospect, he was probably only in his thirties or forties... hard to say when you've been ill. Adam knew how it could age people; he had seen young patients shrivelled by worry or drugs, and old people buoyed on life. Joe, so gentle, sitting in his loose white garments by the fence in the farthest corner of the grounds

– lucid, educated, a deep-thinker. Hard to tell how old he was or what was wrong with him.

*****

Jessica saw the lights were on when she arrived just after eight o'clock on Monday for day one of her new job. She was excited; it was the first time in a long time that she had woken and been keen to go to work. She was nervous too; the first days were the worst… this time next week would be much better. She checked to make sure her wrap dress was appropriately wrapped and nothing was on display, then pushed open the door and struggled in with her box of supplies that said she had arrived – coffee cup, low fat Cruskits, low-fat cottage cheese, Diet Coke, water jug and glass, diary and a calendar with empowering sayings for women… there was safety in numbers, and she was outnumbered.

She placed the box on her desk at reception and sought out who was in. Adam's door was open slightly and she could see him, sitting back, legs crossed on the edge of his desk, his eyes closed and fingers steepled in front of him. She studied him in his unguarded moment; she could see how he would be swallowed in Nate's shadow – quiet and conservative, prepared to let Nate lead. She cleared her throat.

His eyes flew open and he jumped up on seeing her. 'Christ.' He swung his legs off the desk and stood up.

'Sorry, I didn't mean to startle you,' Jessica said.

'No, all good, I just didn't hear you. You'll work well in Nate's business if you can keep up the stealth,' he said, with a smile. 'Welcome, first day and all.' He rubbed his heart as it pounded; he had a history of strange clients and should know better than to be unguarded.

'Not a great start to give the boss a heart attack,' she said, biting her lip.

'A good heart starter… if you could do that every morning, I'll be ready for the patients.'

'Can do,' she said, with a smile, and moved out to her desk to unpack. She heard footsteps coming up the stairs, the door swung open and Nate arrived bearing flowers.

'For your desk on your first day, won't happen again,' he teased, giving them to her. He tried not to notice how good she looked in her clingy pale blue wrap dress.

'How sweet,' Jessica said, a hint of suspicion in her voice. She inhaled the fragrance of the mixed bunch. 'They're lovely, thank you.'

Adam moved into the doorway of his office watching the scene in reception. 'So thoughtful,' he teased Nate.

'Yeah, they'll make the reception look better,' Nate said, looking around.

'Oh, thanks,' Jessica said, and rolled her eyes.

'But they're for you first and foremost,' he said, assuring her. 'Just didn't want you to think I was hitting on you or anything… not that you're not worth hitting on… I'm going to my office.' He strode off with Jessica and Adam's laughter ringing in his ears.

The door opened and Jessica looked up expecting their first client. An attractive older woman in black pants and a red knitted short-sleeve top entered bearing a cake box. She was the epitome of coordination – her jewellery, shoes and handbag were sensible and matching. She had made an effort.

'Good morning, can I help you?' Jessica said.

'Diane!' Adam exclaimed and moved toward her. He greeted her with a kiss on the cheek.

'Adam, so good to see you. You look as handsome as ever, so like your father, but thin, darling, are you eating?' Without waiting for an answer, she looked to Jessica. 'Hello, you must be Jessica, I'm Natty's mother.'

'Oh,' Jessica said, and brightened. 'Lovely to meet you, Mrs Delaney.'

'Please, it's Diane,' she said, appraising the young woman and sizing her up as a potential future partner for her son. She liked what she saw.

'Diane,' Jessica nodded. 'I'll just get him.' She moved around her desk and stuck her head into his office. '*Natty*, you're mum's here.' She grinned at him as he winced at the nickname. Standing back, she moved out of the way as Nate strode past. She saw the resemblance immediately – fair, green eyes, and a distinct square jaw.

'Mum, and you've come bearing cake,' he said.

'Of course, it's your first official day even if you boys did start unofficially last week. I wanted to wish you and Adam good luck and meet Jessica since you've spoken of her so often,' she said.

'I haven't,' Nate said, turning to Jessica, 'not like that… whatever. Thanks Mum,' he took the box from her and handed it to Jessica.

'Would you like a cup of tea, Diane? We could cut the cake now… it's never too early for cake,' Jessica asked.

'No, Mum's busy, we're busy,' Nate said, 'but a nice thought, thanks, Mum.'

'Of course you're busy,' Diane said with a glance to the empty waiting room, 'but thank you, Jessica,' she said. 'Adam, come around for dinner this week, for a proper meal. You can bring my son with you if you like,' she teased Nate. 'Jessica, you are most welcome too.'

'Thanks Diane, that would be great,' Adam said, enjoying Nate's embarrassment.

'Adam's nearly thirty, Mum, he knows how to feed himself,' Nate said, bustling her out of the office.

'Diane, wait,' Adam said, and he saw Nate roll his eyes. 'Can I ask, do you know a solicitor by the name of John Liberman?'

Diane's eyes darted to Nate, then immediately back to Adam. 'Liberman, yes, I do.' She didn't say anything more. 'Well then, good luck today boys...'

Nate moved in front of his mother to block her exit. 'Hold up. Jess, make that tea and cut the cake. Mum, have a seat,' he pointed his mother to the spare room that housed the boardroom table and chairs.

'Another time maybe,' Diane said, her demeanour changing; she was now in a hurry to get out of there. She glanced at her watch and felt an uneasy weight settling in her chest; if she stayed, she was going to have to come clean on some history that she had managed to avoid until now.

'Mum, you're dodging. Please...' Nate indicated a chair. Diane cast a nervous glance to the exit door, sighed and moved to the chair. She smoothed her top down and sat looking from Adam to Nate as though preparing for an interview. Adam sat down opposite.

Nate began. 'Brace yourself, Mum, but when we were kids, Adam and I had a 'grown-up' acquaintance at the madhouse... Joe... we'd talk to him through the fence.'

'I know,' Diane cut Nate off. 'Well, that's not quite true. Your father and I didn't know until we were contacted by this Mr Liberman.'

Nate and Adam exchanged surprised looks.

'Why?' Nate cut to the chase.

Diane continued. 'When you boys were about ten, Liberman & Co., or whatever their legal name is, sent us a letter requesting a meeting; supposedly they had a client who wanted to set up a trust fund for you both. Mr Liberman wanted to be sure that you boys existed, and to suggest some terms and conditions around the gift, as he kept calling it.'

'From Joe? You never said anything!' Nate exclaimed. 'Did Adam's parents know that too?'

'Oh yes,' Diane confirmed. 'Mr Liberman contacted all of us. Well, you can imagine how we felt about that. We thought you boys were just playing at the creek like all boys did. We never thought for a moment you were befriending insane people from the asylum or were in any danger.'

'We weren't and he wasn't... well I guess he might have been declared insane, but he was anything but that,' Adam assured her. He automatically pictured Joe sitting on the other side of the wire, conversing in his calm manner. 'Even now, looking at it from an adult's perspective, we weren't ever in any danger. He was a gentle soul and we just spoke to him through the fence.'

'A parent's nightmare,' Diane reasserted. 'But, we knew if we insisted you stayed away or banned you, then it would be more interesting and you would be more likely to try and go there. Mr Liberman said the same thing as you, Adam... that the fence was secure and you were never in danger.'

'So, my parents...' Adam started, '... they actually met with the solicitor too?'

Diane nodded. 'We all met with Mr Liberman and he told us...' Diane stopped as Jessica entered with tea and cake. Nate rose to help and invited Jessica to stay. He poured his mother a tea; he knew how she liked it.

'... he told us that, well, you had *'Expectations'* as he

put it,' Diane said. 'It was quaint but somewhat ridiculous. An inmate wanted to create a fund for you boys, with whatever possessions he had – a scholarship, but he called it '*Expectations*'. Clearly, he had read too much Charles Dickens.'

Jessica sighed. 'Poor fellow.'

Adam nodded. 'Poor Joe. He obviously didn't have anyone else if he wanted to make a future for us.'

Diane made a less than sympathetic sound. 'Well as you weren't of legal age and we were still your legal guardians, we asked that you not be informed of the Trust until you were both legal adults or our preference, when you were thirty or when this man passed away,' she said, pausing to sip her tea and try a piece of the sponge cake she had brought to the office.

'Thirty!' Nate bit back his frustration. 'You didn't think to mention this anytime in the past two decades, and don't say you forgot, Mum?'

Diane finished her bite of cake before responding; the men waited, suspended.

'Our reasoning was that by thirty years of age, you would be more settled, know what you want to do, have your education sorted, possibly be married with children, and the funds would be used wisely,' Diane looked from Nate to Adam and back to her son. 'If you had got any money in your teenage years, eventually it would have gone towards a car, travel, parties... Besides, your parents didn't want you to have any part of it, Adam darling, but the solicitor said that would be your decision, not theirs.'

'Who wouldn't want their kid to get an inheritance?' Jessica asked, confused, her cake fork suspended in mid-air.

'I think it was less about the inheritance and more about the donor,' Diane said, lowering her voice as if being discriminatory might catch on, or the discussion was being recorded.

'That'd be right,' Adam agreed. 'Mum wouldn't want that kind of story slipping out… imagine the publicity.'

Jessica frowned and looked to Adam for an explanation. *What publicity?*

'Did Audrey know?' Adam asked, curious.

'Oh yes, your grandmother was all for it,' Diane said. 'She's quite… well out there, isn't she? She thought it was wonderful and wanted to invite this man to her book club.'

Adam laughed; that sounded like Audrey to a 'T'.

Nate continued to press his mother. 'So why now?'

'He's contacted you then, I assume? The solicitor?' Diane asked.

'Yes, just last week we got a letter. We're meeting with him tomorrow,' Adam said.

'Given we haven't just come of age, you don't think Joe's been alive all this time and has now just died?' Nate said.

'Or he's been at another asylum and was just released,' Adam said.

'No,' Diane said, 'I heard he died a long time ago… or did I?' She stopped and looked skyward, searching her thoughts. 'I can't remember now. Anyway, I don't know why the delay in getting in touch with you. Maybe the '*Expectations*' have been squandered.'

Jessica addressed Diane. 'I don't mean to be rude, but when he first made the offer of '*Expectations*', how much was he talking about then?'

Nate and Adam held their breath.

'Well, it's not that clear cut, dearest,' Diane said, addressing her. 'There was some cash, not a great amount, but he had money in trust, and some shares, and some royalties supposedly for something he had painted or drawn,' she waved her hand in the air. 'I have no idea what it is worth today. I suspect you could probably buy a car each... I don't really know. But you'll soon find out.'

Nate sighed. 'So, if he is dead, how did he supposedly die, do you know?'

'I heard he drowned.'

'Drowned...' Adam sputtered. The men exchanged looks again.

*****

## Then...

The two boys lay on their stomachs, hidden from view along the riverbed edge. Nate pushed his baseball cap back from his forehead to get a better look. Adam nudged forward onto the lip of the dirt mound. They watched as two police officers wearing gloves and black gumboots stepped gingerly into the river. Behind them, two paramedics stood on the edge of the river banks waiting.

'Do you think it's a dead person?' Adam whispered.

'Uh huh, sure do,' Nate answered. 'My Dad said people drown here all the time. He said in the old days, they'd throw themselves into the river to escape the loony bin.'

The police officers went only as far as necessary to grab the floating body and pull it onto the mud bank. They dragged the body, gripping at the shoulders. At first, the boys couldn't see anything; just the legs of the body as the policemen blocked their view. Then the policemen flipped the body over and stood back revealing the face and torso.

Adam gasped and looked away. 'Gross!'

Nate stared at the body. 'So bloated, I wonder how long it's been in there. You can't tell if it's a woman or man.'

Adam wiggled his body down from the edge and turning, pulled Nate down by the ankle.

'We've got to go,' Adam said. 'We could get in trouble if they knew we were watching.'

Nate watched fascinated. 'The drowned person... it's someone from the hospital, they're wearing the same clothes that Joe wears,' he said. 'I bet Joe knows him or her. We could ask him.'

Their thoughts remained unspoken; neither boy acknowledged that the body could be that of Joe.

'What's happening?' Adam asked.

'The ambos are just standing there, waiting I guess. The cops are moving around the edge of the river, probably looking for clues or anything that's come off the body. That's what I'd be doing.'

'We'll have to wait now until the police leave or they might see us,' Adam said.

'Okay.' Nate said, pleased to remain where he was; he gave Adam a running commentary. 'They've put the body on a stretcher now... the ambo guy has put a sheet over it... they're lifting it into the ambulance... the cops are walking around the edge again, still looking for something.'

Nate scurried as a voice yelled out. 'Hey you, son...'

'The cops have seen me, come on.' Nate slid down beside Adam, staying as low as he could and started to back away. He hit Adam's arm as he passed; Adam followed in close pursuit. Once clear, they ran faster than they have ever run before, faster than Nate ran when he won the gold ribbon in the school's fifty-metre sprint.

## Chapter 6

**Now...**

Adam had a load of problems, most of them not his. His specialty was working with adolescents and young adults on their issues – anxiety; abandonment; parental divorce; eating disorders and adjustment issues. He had an opinion on social media and social isolation, but with most of the clients his age and younger, it fell on deaf ears; they just wanted an explanation and an easy fix for their lives. He had also clocked up plenty of experience with abandonment; they'd become close over the years and he knew how it rolled out later in life – fear of commitment, insecurity, the need to be the first to leave.

As a boy, he watched as Nate was drowned in love and security by parents who thought the sun shone out of him, while his own parents were barely part of his life; seeing Diane had brought it back. His mother would never think to drop in with a cake on the first day of his new business; the idea was laughable. He was the token child that appeared in publicity photos, the child that almost ruined his mother's figure, as he heard her tell her friends. His parents were away more than they were at home during his childhood.

Adam was closer to his widowed and eccentric grandmother, Audrey, who insisted on being called by her first name, smoked her cigarettes with a long, silver cigarette holder, and wrote letters to the editors of newspapers when she wasn't attending marches and rallies. Her goal was to have 100 letters published. She didn't set a deadline so Adam thought it perfectly achievable. She was the only person who truly ever wanted him around. He last saw her a month ago when he dropped her at the international airport; she was walking the Camino at the moment, finding herself, or another husband. Audrey claimed to have a short attention span when it came to men and it was probably good management on Adam's grandfather's part that he passed away within a decade of their marriage, making himself saintly in her memories.

Adam moved to the window and saw Nate's car turning into the carpark below. Nate's car stopped and his window came down. Adam moved closer to the glass and looked down... he saw Jessica balancing three coffees in a tray, her handbag thrown over her shoulder as she talked to Nate through his car window. He moved back to his desk and sat down. His first appointment wasn't until ten o'clock and he was happy for the late start; he had spent the evening reading Joe's diary and making notes until well after midnight. He often did his best thinking late at night or first thing in the morning when jogging; the two weren't necessarily compatible.

He wondered how they had forgotten Joe; they had just accepted that he was no longer there and not given him a second thought. Now as a trained psychologist, he thought back over the things Joe had said to them, the knowledge he had shared and the way he could speak to them like they weren't just boys, they were friends. He could only imagine how other adults would have perceived the connection and the relationship, if you could call it that.

*What happened to you, Joe?*

He picked up Joe's diary and flipped through to the last page again; past the short stories, illustrations and Haiku—damning illustrations that told of his treatment and of what he was witnessing around him—would Nate interpret them the same way? He stopped at an illustration of a crest; he had seen this before somewhere. It had his and Nate's initials in it and two swords – Joe must have designed it for them. Adam turned the page to read the last entry Joe wrote:

> *I give permission*
> *To myself to be pain-free*
> *Having had my share*

*What decision did you just make Joe? What did you release yourself from? Why were you in there in the first place?*

Adam suddenly needed to get out, to walk and clear his head of Joe, of his mother, of his weariness before his client arrived. He grabbed his keys and wallet and locking the door, bolted down the fire escape stairs to avoid Jessica and Nate on their way up.

He'd walk around the corner to the park and commune with nature for ten minutes; the trees got him – they were the strong silent types too.

*****

## Then...

Joe wasn't the body in the river; he was very much alive, this week. The boys sat in their usual spot on the other side of the wire fence from him. It was a beautiful Brisbane spring day; warm with a breeze carrying the scent of the river. Nate plucked at the grass as Adam leaned against the fence studying the grounds of the hospital. There were a few people placed in chairs in different locations... they sat staring ahead as though watching a screenshot of nature.

'We saw a dead body in the river,' Nate said.

Joe looked up at the two boys. 'That's a terrible sight, young Nathan. I hope you didn't see the body close up.'

Adam shook his head. 'No just from a distance. There were police and ambulance guys pulling him out. Do you know him Joe, was he from the hospital?'

'He could have been, but I don't know of anyone who went missing recently. It's best you head home if you see that again. You don't want to fill your mind with images like that.'

The boys nodded. Joe had a notebook on his lap with poems and scribblings across the page.

'That's a short poem. Did you write one about us?' Nate asked, enthusiastically. 'Will you publish it? We could become famous.'

Joe smiled at the young boy.

'Of course, I wrote a poem about you both; you two are my muses,' Joe said.

'What does that mean?' Adam asked, studying the marks on Joe's wrists.

'Inspiration,' Joe said, 'it means for the poem I wrote, you were my inspiration.'

Adam repeated the word 'muse', locking it away for future use. Joe thumbed through some pages, stopping near the middle of the pad. 'This is Haiku... do you know what that is?'

'Sure, it's those short Japanese poems; we learnt that at school,' Nate said.

'Good, good... yes, ideally three lines long, five syllables in the first line, seven in the next and five in the last line. I have a few here, one is about you lads. Ah, here it is.' Joe stopped and read it. 'Perhaps it isn't good enough yet,' he frowned at the page.

'It will be really good,' Adam assured him.

'Better than we could ever do.' Nate nodded his agreement.

Joe studied the young boys and smiled. 'Well, if you are sure.' He cleared his throat and began to read:

*Great expectations*
*That you will both achieve more*
*Than disappointment*

He finished delivering the three lines and turned to the boys. Adam applauded and Joe laughed.

'Too kind,' Joe said, and nodded at them.

'Thanks Joe,' Nate said. 'Mum says she has big expectations for me.'

'My parents have no expectations for me,' Adam said, with a shrug.

'Oh, I doubt that young Adam. Listen, lads,' Joe cleared his throat and got their attention. 'You may not see me for a few days, but there is no cause for alarm. I'm going to be unavailable.' Joe ran his hand over his chin, stroking a beard that was no longer there.

The boys exchanged looks.

'Are you going on a holiday?' Adam asked.

'So... you can leave here anytime you want?' Nate asked.

'No, that I can't. But I'm going to be absent. There are some things to be done.'

'We'll miss you, Joe,' Adam said and Nate nodded.

The older man looked from one boy to the other. 'Thank you, my young friends, but don't give me a second thought... there's much to do in your young lives, much indeed.'

*****

**Now...**

As one door closed—Adam and his patient disappearing behind it—Nate's office door opened and he saw a middle-aged woman to the stairs, promising her results with a departure wave. The reception was now empty. He closed the external office door, leaned against it and exhaled.

'Another cheating partner client?' Jessica raised an eyebrow from where she sat behind the reception counter. 'I'd be more surprised to find a man who didn't cheat than one who did!'

'What a terrible thing to say about mankind,' Nate said, defensively.

'So you've never cheated?' Jessica put him on the spot.

'Well...' he hesitated just a moment, and she rolled her eyes. 'Don't say another word, please. I need to believe that somewhere out there is a man who can be loyal.'

'You're probably in the wrong job then,' he said.

'Great, thanks. Did you really mean to say that out loud?'

'Okay, back up, this conversation has gone way off track,' Nate said. 'I would love nothing better than to have a committed and loving relationship, and I can be loyal… men can be loyal.' He sighed. 'Anyway, can't complain, the cheaters bring us our bread and butter clients. Better than a missing cat, which seriously, I got a call about last week. But I'd love a good murder. That sounds bad, doesn't it?'

Jessica smiled. 'Yeah, you're on fire today. Well, working with Adam, you might just score one. His second client this morning seemed capable of that – totally wired. Very odd.'

'Still in there with him?' Nate asked looking at Adam's closed door.

'Yeah, Adam hasn't hit the panic button and I can hear low voices.'

Nate glanced at Adam's door again. 'A few years ago he had a stalker.'

'Adam was stalked!' Jessica's eyes widened.

'Shh,' Nate said, and nodded, loving holding the floor. 'He gets lots of patients who fall in love with him…'

'I can understand that,' Jessica interrupted.

Nate raised his eyebrows. 'Hmm, that so? Anyway, I believe it's called transference… when a patient falls in love with his or her psychiatrist. But this chick had covered her wall with images of him. She must have been hiding out in the shrubbery where he used to work snapping away all day. She'd even dummied up wedding shots of them together.'

'Wow, that's weird,' Jessica grimaced. 'So, what happened?'

'He committed her.'

'What?' Jessica exclaimed, again too loudly.

Nate indicated with his hands to keep the noise down. They both waited, heard the drone of voices from Adam's office and continued.

'That's a bit extreme, isn't it?' Jessica asked.

'He didn't put her away just for that,' Nate assured her. 'There were a number of incidents that led up to it. He came home one night and she was in his bed waiting for him.'

'Holy crap! No wonder he jumped when he saw me standing silently in the doorway this morning.'

'Probably thought she'd broken out. But that wasn't the final straw,' Nate said, crossing his arms across his chest.

'There's more?' Jessica asked.

'Yep,' he said, looking smug that he held the trump card. 'She came into his clinic at the hospital and cut herself, and then tried to cut him so they could mingle their blood together, forever. Aren't my clients looking a lot better?' Nate asked.

'Hell yeah,' Jessica said, and shivered. 'Mm, maybe we do need better security. By the way, I like your mum. So, what's the story with Adam's mum and what did he mean by her not wanting the publicity? Is she a politician or a doctor too? Should I be expecting her with a cake?'

Nate laughed. 'Not likely, although she does love a good publicity angle... but an alleged loony in a mental asylum giving her son money wouldn't cut it.'

Jessica looked confused. Nate lowered his voice, again.

'His mother's a model, socialite, celebrity... whatever you call those types these days.'

'Really?' Jessica narrowed her eyes as she thought, 'Adam Murphy... Murphy... hmm, would I know her?'

'She goes by her maiden name... Keeley.'

'Keeley,' Jessica rolled the name around, then her eyes grew huge. 'Oh my God, his mum is Winsome Keeley, the *IT* girl?'

Nate nodded. 'Best not to mention her to him unless he brings it up.'

'But didn't she...'

'Yes, she did,' Nate said, and turned to enter his office. 'Speaking of talent, Dan will be here in a minute,' he said. 'Not in the diary, sorry, but Dan does all our surveillance on cheating partners, I've got a few to hand over.' Nate disappeared into his office, leaving the door slightly ajar. 'You know a coffee and some more of Mum's cake would be great, wouldn't it?' he called out.

'Sure would, thanks,' Jessica said, and rolled her eyes. Not even twenty-four hours and he'd forgotten the rules. She went to the kitchen to make coffee, only because she wanted one as well; she wanted a slice of the cake more.

'Winsome Keeley' she said, to herself. Jessica recalled the image of the beautiful, petite, blonde woman who was winsome in every sense of the word and thought of Adam – he had some of her features. Wow, Winsome Keeley, the most sought-after woman of her era, Jessica thought. Everyone wanted to be Winsome; babies were named after her, songs were written about her, and then there was that affair that the whole country got swept up in.

Her thoughts were distracted by the bell above the door and she returned to reception. A sassy, attractive black woman was about to enter Nate's office. She was dressed in a fitted black top and had the tightest jeans on that Jessica had ever seen. *Must have painted them on,* Jessica recalled her grandmother's old saying. High-heeled black ankle boots gave a couple of inches to her slight frame. Her eyes were dark chocolate brown, and her long, brown hair was streaked with red and pulled back in a high ponytail. Jessica guessed she was about thirty. *Is this the ex-wife?* She wondered.

'Can I help you?' Jessica intercepted her before she entered Nate's office.

'Oh yeah, hi, I'm Danielle Walters, here to see—'

'Dan! Come in,' Nate called from his desk before she finished her sentence.

'Oh, you're Dan. I was expecting...' Jessica paused, sizing her up.

'An overweight white guy who spends his days sitting in a car eating junk food and watching people for money?' Danielle said, with a smile.

'Yeah, something like that. I'm Jess, the new office manager.'

Danielle grinned. 'Welcome, and good luck with that,' she glanced to Nate's door, 'you'll need it.' She slipped into his office.

# Chapter 7

**Then...**

'I'm going to ask Joe why he's in the loony bin,' Nate said, handing Adam a sandwich. 'Mum made you one too.'

'No way!'

Nate shrugged. 'It's no big deal, she likes you.'

Adam look confused and took the sandwich. 'Not the sandwich, thanks. But you can't ask Joe. He has to tell us if he wants to.'

'Why?' Nate leaned back against the tree, jigging his fishing line a little.

'Because that's what you're supposed to do,' Adam said.

'Dad says there are bull sharks in the river. Shark soup for dinner!'

'The Japanese eat shark... I think,' Adam added. 'When are you going to ask Joe?'

'Next time we see him.'

The two boys looked across to the fence; several people were in the grounds, Joe wasn't one of them.

Adam spoke with a full mouth. 'What are you going to do if he says he's in because he killed someone?'

Nate shrugged again. 'Nothin. But he'd be in prison if he did that.'

'Not if he went mad and killed them and then the judge said he was insane and should be locked up instead,' Adam said. 'I saw a show like that on TV.'

'What if he breaks out and kills us?' Nate said, wide-eyed.

'Then we'll be dead.'

'Yeah.' Nate grinned. He spotted a figure in white heading to the fence. 'He's here, Joe's in the yard!'

Adam turned and watched Joe wandering across the grounds to take up residence in his usual place. He had been absent for nearly four days. They ate as they watched him sit and a man who looked like a doctor walked by and spoke with him briefly before moving on.

'I don't reckon you should ask him,' Adam said.

'Chicken?' Nate asked.

'As if,' Adam said, full of bravado. 'Let's go then.' He polished off the rest of the sandwich, pushed himself to his feet, and started towards the fence. Nate put a rock on his fishing line to hold it in place and caught up.

'I'll do the asking,' he said.

'You got that right,' Adam said.

'I'm just going to say, hey did you murder someone and see what happens,' Nate said, as they kept low and made their way towards the fence.

Adam hit Nate's arm. 'If you do that I'm leaving straight away and you'll be on your own with Joe,' he threatened.

Nate laughed. 'I wouldn't, just reeling you in. You can ask.'

'I'm not asking.'

'Maybe he wants to talk about it,' Nate said.

'Maybe he'll tell us if he does.'

Nate grabbed Adam by his T-shirt and pulled him down.

'Stop, there's someone coming across the grounds towards him.'

Both boys lay flat on the grass, their heads barely visible on the slope. They watched as a staff member in uniform brought an old man in a suit towards Joe. The man stopped in front of Joe and eventually Joe looked up, squinting into the sun. Nothing was said, but Joe studied the man, before inviting him to sit. The staff member left them alone.

'They're not saying anything,' Nate, who couldn't stand silence, said.

'Maybe they know each other and have nothing to say,' Adam suggested.

'You think it could be his dad?'

Adam nodded. 'Could be.'

The older man began to talk and Joe nodded occasionally; then, the man touched Joe's shoulder.

'Joe doesn't look happy. Might not be a good time to ask him why he's in the loony bin,' Nate agreed.

Eventually, the old man leaned forward, webbed his fingers on his knees and turned to Joe. He said something else, offered his hand for shaking, and after the two men shook, he rose and left. Joe didn't watch him go, he didn't move his body at all.

'Maybe we can cheer him up,' Adam said.

But then they watched as Joe lowered his head between his hands and shook with big sobs.

'Yeah, we're out of here,' Nate said, sinking backwards.

Adam rose and moved silently towards the fence, and Joe. He stopped short, but Joe's head shot up with alarm.

'Don't cry, Joe,' Adam said, and then he didn't know what else to say. Nate came and stood by his side.

'Can we do anything?' Nate asked.

Joe smiled at the boys and wiped his sleeve across his face.

'Thank you, my young friends, but there's no cause for alarm. I'm just being silly.'

'Was that your dad?' Nate asked.

'My dad... oh, no, my father is gone now. I wouldn't be here if he wasn't...' Joe said, looking skyward. 'But you young boys are free on a beautiful day, you mustn't spend it here near this place of misery,' Joe said, his voice trailing off as he looked behind him, forgetting he was talking to two young boys. 'No, no-one wants to be here.'

A nurse started walking towards Joe.

'We'll be back Joe, soon,' Adam said, 'don't be sad.' And hitting Nate on the back, they moved away quickly.

# Chapter 8

**Now...**

Jessica made another appointment for Adam's last patient of the day – no prize for guessing what she needed help with... Jessica could almost see her skeleton she was so thin. The waif-like woman gingerly accepted the appointment card from Jessica as if touching a shared item might transfer kilojoules. Jessica watched her hurry to the door and exit. She whispered to Adam as he surfaced from his office, 'She's an odd one.'

'You have no idea,' Adam agreed.

'Aren't you ever nervous, you know, about the weirder clients?'

'Sometimes. I've only ever had one that totally tripped out on me,' he said, leaning on the reception counter.

'Is that the blood one, the one who wanted to swap fluids with you and created the marriage pics?' Jessica asked.

Adam looked surprised. 'Wow, have you read through all the history files already?'

'No, Nate told me,' she said.

Adam rolled his eyes. 'Of course he did. Yeah, she was something else...'

Danielle and Nate burst out of Nate's office, laughing.

'Adam!' Danielle squealed with delight on seeing him and swallowed him in a hug. They looked good together, Jessica thought, and Adam clearly didn't mind being accosted by the surveillance operator.

Jessica cleared her throat. 'So, no need to introduce you two then.'

'God, no, we've been friends with benefits for years,' Danielle said, and hit his arm.

Adam looked embarrassed which only made Danielle laugh again, and louder.

'You've got to watch the dark, silent types,' Danielle directed her comment to Jessica.

'Yep, well better get back to it… work to do,' Adam backed towards his office, uncomfortable with being the centre of attention.

'Me too now, thanks Nate,' Danielle waved a file. 'See you soon Adam? And you guys be good to Jessica,' she ordered as she took to the stairs, slamming the door on her exit. A stillness returned to the reception area.

Nate breathed out, shook his head, and followed Adam to his office. He stepped inside and took a seat.

Adam sat opposite and sighed. He ran his hand over his eyes.

'You alright? Skinny girl not getting better?'

Adam looked to Nate and grinned. 'So sensitive. No, she's alright. I've been reading Joe's notes,' he nodded towards the book on his desk, 'and trying to remember what I could about him.'

'He always liked you best,' Nate said, drumming a tune on his leg.

Adam scoffed. 'How'd you come up with that?'

Nate smiled. 'He thought you were quieter, a deeper thinker, more pensive,' Nate waved his hand around.

'Yeah, well that's me,' Adam teased.

'Sure it is. So, what did you come up with?' Nate asked.

'Do you remember when you wanted to ask him what he was in for?' Adam asked.

'Yeah. But we never did. There was that time that he implied he had killed someone, remember? But then he drifted off in thought… he did that, a lot. Probably the drugs now that I think about it,' Nate said.

Adam drew a deep breath. 'I believe something happened but I always thought he was wrongly accused… like everyone is in prison or hell.'

Nate nodded. 'I can't believe he was capable of anything violent… and yeah before you start giving me examples of '*When good people go bad*', I know it happens; I just can't believe it would be in Joe's nature.'

'I know,' Adam agreed. 'I wonder what Joe would make of us now… both single again, you with a daughter, and the pair of us branching out in a new joint business.'

'I reckon he'd say, "It's good to dream young fellows – go find your passion" or something like that,' Nate said imitating Joe's mannerisms.

Adam smiled at the memory. 'Yeah, that sounds like Joe. Do you think he's still alive?'

Nate thought for a moment. 'Before I was a cop, I would have said no way, but now… you wouldn't believe how many people go missing every year in Australia.'

'How many?' Adam interrupted.

'About forty thousand.'

'Wow, seriously?'

Nate nodded. 'It wouldn't be hard for Joe to be one of them, especially if he was financially independent. He could be out there somewhere, right now.'

\*\*\*\*\*

The solicitor was either doing very well or wanted to give that impression. John Liberman's office sat on the river's edge in the city. Floor to ceiling windows ensured you didn't miss the view of the Story Bridge and river ferries cruising up and down the river. You could fully appreciate what the lease would cost and anticipate your bill to reflect it.

'If Joe's left us anything, by the time this guy takes his cut we'll get a dollar each,' Nate muttered as he stood in the waiting room looking out over the water. He dug his hands into the pockets of his grey suit pants and rocked back and forth.

'We'll probably have to pay him,' Adam agreed, sitting back on a soft, dark green leather couch.

'You're probably sitting on a thousand bucks,' Nate glanced at Adam, as he continued to complain.

'Mm, Chesterfield, beautiful,' Adam said and extended his arms along the top. 'Closer to about four grand for this three-seater.'

'How do you even know that?'

'Mum,' Adam said. 'She had this thing for Chesterfield… Dad wanted a library and Mum wanted a piano and a Chesterfield lounge in it – our lounge was a dark red. They never used it, and I wasn't allowed in there. Just show and tell.'

'We had a couch from Freedom,' Nate said.

Adam laughed. 'Show off.'

Nate grinned and resumed rocking. They were the only clients in the waiting room, although voices drifted from other closed-door rooms.

'Jess seems to be happy enough,' Adam said, after a while.

'Yeah, she'll be fine. She doesn't play well with others, so she likes being in charge of her own area and having no-one to deal with, except us. She's single if you were…' Nate let his voice trail off as he raised an eyebrow in Adam's direction.

'Come on, she's mad about you,' Adam said.

'She's mad *at* me, more like it.'

They were interrupted.

'Gentlemen, Mr Liberman's free now,' his mature-aged assistant said, returning to collect them. Adam pushed himself off the couch and followed the slim woman and Nate down the hallway. As they entered, a tall man with greying hair, rose to greet them. His light-coloured suit matched Nate's for anaemic, and he was groomed to within an inch of his life. Adam put him in his early sixties. He shook both their hands and directed them to a group of single lounge chairs. They declined the offer of tea and coffee, and the assistant departed, closing the door behind her.

John Liberman ran his eyes over the two men. His face was kind, his eyes weary.

'So, you are Nathan and Adam,' he said, and smiled.

'And you were a visitor to the asylum; I saw you several times,' Nate said.

John Liberman looked surprised. He glanced at Adam. 'You remember that too?'

'I remember Joe having guests but I couldn't swear it was you,' Adam said.

John returned to study Nate. 'Impressive. It was me, but I don't think Joe received many guests during his internment. I imagine it seems strange being invited here today to remember a man that you had an encounter with almost two decades ago, but there are two reasons for the requested meeting.' John Liberman leaned forward. 'Just out of curiosity, when was the last time you saw him?'

Nate exhaled and looked at Adam. 'Just before Christmas… that summer before we went into grade six or seven at primary school.'

'That's when high school used to start at year eight,' Adam said. 'That'd be right, though… we were going on eleven. He gave us both an early Christmas present because he said he would be going away for Christmas.'

'A treasure map,' Nate said, and laughed.

*****

**Then…**

'We're going away too,' Adam told the man in white on the other side of the fence. 'Mum has a booking in Sydney so we're going there for Christmas.'

'Adam's mum is a model,' Nate explained to Joe. 'She's famous. So, are you going home for Christmas, Joe?'

Joe smiled and nodded. 'You might say that boys, yes indeed… going home.' He slipped his hand under his shirt, looked around and when he was content that the coast was clear, pulled out a piece of paper.

'I have an early Christmas gift for you both,' he said, rolling it up into the size of a cigarette and passing it through the wire fence.

'What is it?' Adam asked.

'A treasure map,' Joe said.

'Cool,' Nate grinned and took the offered gift. 'Thanks, Joe.'

'Yeah, thanks, Joe,' Adam said.

The boys unscrolled the map and their eyes widened. It was covered in small drawings of dragons, castles, rivers, trees and footsteps. A compass and crest were in the corner; the crest featured their initials and swords.

'Wow, this is amazing,' Nate said, his eyes following all the detail. He looked at the drawing of the tree with

62

a door in it and turned to find it in the park behind him.

'It's special code, but I'm sure you'll work it out,' Joe said. 'There are two treasures... one for you boys for Christmas... it's marked by the dragon, and the other treasure is a time capsule, to remain there until you are grown up.'

'We did a time capsule at school, but it was lame,' Adam said. 'This is cool, I can't wait to solve it.' The young boy looked up at Joe. 'But we don't have anything for you because we didn't know you were going away.'

'Well that's how it should be,' Joe assured them. 'What would I possibly need or want more than your company?'

'I want a Nintendo Game Boy but Mum said I had to have something that gets me outdoors,' Nate rolled his eyes.

'She's very wise your mother,' Joe said. 'My gift will keep you outdoors...'

Joe's words were interrupted by a loud siren.

'Does that mean there's a fire?' Adam asked, wincing at the noise.

'Ah, it means I have to go inside quickly,' Joe said, pushing himself up from his seat. 'Goodbye my young friends,' he said, his gaze lingering on them for just a moment before he turned and quickened his pace to get inside. Two staff members appeared in the doorway and began to head down the path towards Joe and several other residents, calling and summoning them inside, pushing those in chairs towards the asylum entrance.

'C'mon,' Nate said, hurrying away. 'We don't want to get him in trouble. That woman always looks cranky.'

'If I was in the hospital I wouldn't want her for my nurse,' Adam agreed. He glanced back at the same time as Joe turned in the doorway, and raised his hand in a wave to the young boy.

**Now ...**

'So, did you find the treasure?' John Liberman asked.

Adam rolled his eyes and looked to Nate to explain.

'I might have left it in my jeans and it went through Mum's next wash,' he shrugged.

'Treasure gone, and it was a beautiful hand-drawn map,' Adam said, with a sigh. 'So, down to business, what are we doing here? Where's Joe? We know that Joe might have left us something when we were kids and our parents railroaded it. Can we see him?'

'My mother just decided to come clean,' Nate explained.

'Ah, yes, that,' John said, and straightened his tie, again, an action he did regularly; Adam noticed. He leant forward and opened a thick, cream-coloured folder in front of him. The top pages were crisp, but yellow pages in the mix gave away its age.

'Not railroaded exactly. You can imagine not many parents would be excited about their children hanging around a mental facility,' John said. 'But yes, there's a gift from Joe, and I want to hire you as well,' he said, looking at Nate. 'Or maybe it's a case for both of you.'

'What exactly did you have in mind?' Nate asked, his general distaste for solicitors evident in his tone.

'Well, something happened almost two decades ago,' John said, 'but that doesn't mean it should remain a mystery. I want to find Joe.'

# Chapter 9

It was 4:30pm, thirty minutes before Jessica could close shop for the day. Nate and Adam were with the solicitor and she had the office to herself. Making a cup of tea, she decided to do some research of a not-quite-work-related nature. Winsome Keeley. With a glance to the door to confirm the all clear, Jessica typed the name into Google – 13,500,000 results and a bio that read: 'The generation's *IT* girl, model, actress, activist, agitator and animal rights campaigner'. The pixie face with the enormous brown eyes stared at Jessica. She was beautiful, vulnerable, cute... Jessica could see a little of Adam in Winsome's features.

Jessica knew some of the stories – everyone remembered the infamous Winsome Keeley, the woman who brought down a government. The shot was there that caused such a scandal; Winsome and the then married, Prime Minister, Andrew Barker, caught in a kiss, thinking they were alone. He was handsome, tall, powerful and she was young and beautiful. Andrew also had a wife and three kids and was running for his second term as Prime Minister; until the images of their affair emerged and the government went into damage control. With his deception revealed and his party collapsing around him, Labor lost to the Liberals but not before he came out with all the appropriate statements – he loved his family, slip in judgement, etc., etc.

Despite Winsome being the 'other woman', she didn't suffer too much… one glance at that young pixie face and the public forgave, and more importantly, protected her as an innocent and misled woman seduced by an older man who should have had a moral compass.

Jessica scrolled through the images of Winsome before the affair with the Prime Minister; she was seen in all the right places on the arm of many a man—artists, a TV soap star, a model, a British rock star, another lover who committed suicide when she broke up with him—until the affair with the Prime Minister changed her. Then, as if she realised she had to play it straight—or was advised by her manager to do so—she settled immediately on the conservative, powerful and extremely debonair James Murphy – Adam's father. Ten years older than Winsome, a successful financier, a close friend of the country's leading media moguls, and, after what the media termed a whirlwind romance of two months, they eloped to Paris and he returned as her agent and husband. Adam was born 'prematurely' – less than nine months after they met… no wonder there's plenty of stories around and suspicion about his paternal gene pool.

Jessica read some of the comments about James Murphy: commanding, brilliant, cool and cunning… whatever he was, he succeeded at making Winsome an even bigger commodity with his controlling management and soon, she was exclusively signed to a number of elegant brands and worth a cool fortune. Her image not only intact but glossy.

'Yep, gorgeous too,' Jessica said, aloud as she admired Adam's father. 'Can see you in him as well, Adam.' She found the publicity photos of Adam's birth – the nude photo of

Winsome with baby Adam lying across her chest, not that you could see anything as the most important parts were covered by her hands or Adam. I bet he hates that photo, Jessica thought.

More shots of him over the years with his parents; always looking like a young model, always dressed in the latest kids' fashion labels, and always avoiding looking at the cameras. The model kid with beautiful parents. If they had Facebook then, Jessica had no doubt Adam would have been managed and had a huge following. They couldn't have bestowed the attention on an unhappier recipient, she thought. Nate, on the other hand, would have lapped it up... the big ham. She smiled thinking about her brash boss.

Why didn't they live in Sydney or Melbourne where most of Winsome's work would have been? Jessica thought. She flicked through the online pages and came across the funeral shots: Adam about sixteen years old—tall, dark, beautiful in his suit—with his petite mother clinging to his arm, widowed at thirty-six; glamorous in black at the funeral of her husband and Adam's father. Jessica increased the size of the screen to make out the people in the background; plenty of celebrity faces, plenty of media and not many 'real' people. No sign of Nate or his family, no sign of school friends or anyone who looked Adam's age.

She scrolled through; Adam's life and that of his mother, was played out online—so many highlights and controversial moments—and there it was, the National Art Award. Winsome's portrait that was entered by an artist when she was thirty-seven, and it won. More controversy as the subject was supposed to be someone distinguished in the prestigious fields of science, or art, or literature, or politics... but those boundaries had softened over the years and a portrait of a celebrity won. She clicked the story open.

Winsome was portraited in gold; her blonde hair falling around her elfin face and the light almost translucent. 'The innocent', Jessica thought, no matter what damage she left behind her. It was clear the artist was in love with her. I wonder how many sittings they had together, she mused.

*****

John Liberman fished a few pieces of paper from the file and sitting back in his chair, addressed the two men.

'The gift first, then the case,' he said. 'Joe wanted to provide for you both to go on to university – pay for your degree, books, a car, whatever you needed to get ahead at whatever you wanted to study. He was quite a wealthy man...'

'Really?' Nate asked, surprised.

'You'd think our parents would be okay with that,' Adam said, shaking his head.

'Hmm. He wanted to do a 'Magwitch' from Dickens' *Great Expectations* and give you 'expectations' – he loved his literature,' John said, with a smile. He held up his hand as Nate began to interrupt. 'I think I can explain what happened... in your parent's case Nate, it wasn't pride as much as fear. What obligation might you have if you accepted money from this stranger? Was it safe money? You know, not money that was gained illegally or it would be contested by Joe's family members who would come out of the woodwork after you had received it. In your case Adam, your parents were fairly indignant of the situation... they certainly didn't need or want Joe's money and they didn't want the stigma of a story coming out later that their son was educated by a... well as your mother said at the time a "*psychopath*", if I remember correctly.'

Adam rolled his eyes. 'Yep, that sounds like Mum.'

'I didn't want to return to Joe and tell him that his generous gesture had been thrown back in his face; it might have pushed him over the edge. So, I persuaded them to accept the gift on the basis it was bequeathed after you came of age – that's 21 not 18 years of age. That way, it would be your choice if you wanted to accept it or not,' John explained.

'Well that didn't happen given we're just hearing about it now,' Adam said.

'Mm, that's right,' John agreed. 'Your parents had a few conditions and an agreement was reached. I told Joe they were grateful but decided that providing the gift later in life would allow you to make more mature choices.'

'How did he take that?' Adam asked.

'It wasn't what he wanted to achieve, but he understood.'

Nate pushed himself up out of his chair and moved to the window. He looked out, crossing his arms across his chest. 'So why now? What was the final condition?'

'Joe just died,' John said.

Nate turned quickly to look at John.

'What? How?' Adam asked.

'Legally died,' John explained. He glanced at his watch, then to the two men. 'Perhaps I should explain over a drink?' he offered.

Nate looked down on the street below and the boutique bar scene. 'Is there somewhere we can grab a beer that's not too try-hard?'

Adam grinned and rose from his chair. 'Yeah, we don't want to be seen in all the right places.'

'Mm, tricky around here,' John said, 'but come on, there's an Irish pub on the corner; it has some soul. I'll tell you what I know and what I don't know about Joe.'

# Chapter 10

The good thing about not having daylight saving in Queensland was that dusk arrived earlier and Harry Bond could get the ghost tour underway by seven o'clock. He did one final check before his victims arrived; he always called the tour guests victims, but in reality, if anything happened to the guests booked on his tours, he'd be up shit creek and he knew it. Sure, he had insurance but there was always a loophole that ensured your butt was exposed and the insurance company was covered.

Harry had fifteen people booked for tonight's tour of the asylum; twelve was supposed to be his limit but he hated turning anyone and their money away. It had taken him close to a year to get approval to take tours in the abandoned asylum and now it looked like he was about to lose that again due to safety concerns.

While the Council thought about it, he'd been told to standby; that lasted a month and it was only because his landlord—who had his own vested interest in Harry's business continuing—knew the local councillor, who knew someone on the planning committee, whose distant relative was a twice removed cousin of the person who made the decision, that Harry was allowed to resume business until further notice. Okay, it might not have been that convoluted but it felt like it to Harry. Now, his mission was to get as many people through the door as possible on weekends.

He wore his traditional all black outfit, and he knew the script like the back of his hand... which areas would give the greatest chills and thrills... where the most dangerous patients were kept, the rooms where surgery and solitary confinement were contained, and the women's madhouse – these always got the best reactions. He glanced to the top floor of the asylum.

'Make as much noise as you like,' he said, encouragingly to the ceiling above him. It was an added bonus every time the tour group heard the footsteps or boards creak above them... you couldn't pay for that kind of authenticity.

He glanced at his watch as the first set of headlights pulled into the carpark with another car close behind. Twenty minutes to the hour – it was almost showtime.

*****

The three men made their way to street level, got a table inside the Irish pub and Nate bought the first round. They made small talk until their drinks arrived. Nate claimed the beer, Adam the vodka and lime, and John the red wine.

'So do you want to know what you have inherited or hear about Joe's history first?' John asked and took a sip from his glass.

'History,' both men said in unison.

John looked surprised. It rarely happened that his clients didn't want to cut to the chase. 'Right,' he started. 'I don't know how much he told you about his life—'

'Nothing,' Adam cut in. 'He showed us his poems and

drawings, looked skyward once to imply his father was dead, but I can't remember him saying anything about his family or why he was there.' Nate nodded his agreement.

'Okay, well in a nutshell… Joe grew up in a pretty tough home environment. He was an artist; gentle like his mother, Larissa, who was a bird-like creature. He had an older brother, Stephen, who was rough and tumble, like their father. The boys were chalk and cheese, but fortunately, Stephen adored his young brother, Joe, and his mother – I guess there was something protective and good in his rough nature. Joe's father, Gordon, didn't like 'pansy types'… his name for artistic types, and he would force Joe to play football, learn boxing… all the things a 'man' should be able to do,' John said, and shook his head.

He continued. 'His mother overcompensated, protecting and supporting Joe. But his father was pretty quick with his fists and his belt strap… for years the two boys and their mother were beaten by Gordon for the smallest provocation. When Stephen was old enough and big enough, he got apprenticed as a builder and got a bit of courage under his own belt. He was a big lad, like his father. One night, he came home from work to find Joe and his mother in a bad way after a thrashing by a drunken Gordon and he snapped, *allegedly* killing his father,' John said, emphasising the fact the murder had not been proven.

'Holy crap,' Nate mumbled.

'Saw that coming,' Adam sighed.

John nodded his agreement. 'But this is where it gets tricky and where you both step in. According to Joe, he and his mother made Stephen leave immediately and they told police that Gordon came home from work drunk, and looked like he'd already been in a fight. After getting stuck into them, he collapsed and died. Larissa told the police that Stephen only stayed with them occasionally now that he was apprenticed and they hadn't seen him for a while.'

'What about witness statements from the neighbours, or Gordon and Stephen's work buddies?' Nate asked.

'No-one saw anything,' John said. He finished the last mouthful of his wine. 'Let's not kid ourselves, Gordon wasn't Mr Popular and everyone stepped up to protect the family. Larissa got a bit of life insurance—it was a policy set up by Gordon's employer—and the family was better off without him. Joe was fifteen when all this happened, and within a few months, had his first breakdown.'

'Many would after seeing your father killed and having to maintain the lie,' Adam said, swirling the ice around in his glass.

'Another round?' John asked, and after a few failed attempts caught a passing waiter's attention to place an order.

Adam thought about Larissa, and when the waiter left asked: 'Did Larissa remarry the same type?' he asked.

'No, she never remarried,' John said.

'Surprising,' Adam said. 'Sadly, abuse victims often do get hitched to the same types.'

John nodded. 'I think being financially independent allowed her to avoid repeating her past life, and I suspect having Joe at home staved off loneliness. But when Joe had his first breakdown he wasn't hospitalised, Larissa looked after him, and with the payout from Gordon's insurance, they could afford for him to see someone privately. They had a roof over their head and were comfortable… except Stephen wouldn't come home. He went outback, as Joe called it, finishing his apprenticeship out there.'

'Probably didn't have a lot of happy memories in that home,' Nate said. 'So, what happened to him?'

'Joe said for a while Stephen would send the occasional postcard or call, until that stopped after about five years and they never heard from him again.'

'And Joe couldn't handle that?' Adam asked.

'He was always nervy and on edge. He'd spent his childhood waiting for a beating, repressing his artistic skills because they weren't manly enough for his father, and now he was waiting for the police to come back and arrest them all, or to hear bad news about Stephen. He never had security in his life, his nerves were shot, and it lead to him being fairly unstable,' John said.

Their drinks arrived; John pressed his credit card against the mobile card reader and thanked the waiter.

Nate did the maths. 'So how old was Joe when we knew him? He seemed pretty old to us back then,' Nate said.

John nodded. 'Late thirties.'

Nate shook his head. 'In his thirties! Bizarre to think we're about to hit that decade ourselves now.'

'So, he was about the same age as our parents then,' Adam added, raising his voice above the growing din, 'and he'd be late-fifties now...'

'Correct,' John said. He leaned in closer to the men to be heard. 'His brother, Stephen, would be closer to sixty.'

'There's a table outside, let's clear out of here,' Nate said, grabbing his drink and rising; John and Adam followed. They took a table furthest from the entrance where a group gathered.

'Better,' John agreed. 'So, Joe had been in treatment on-and-off since he was fifteen. But he was bright and had talent; he had years where he got himself together. He left home for a while – went and worked for a sign writing company, packed shelves at night, that sort of thing. Things changed when Larissa encouraged him to go for an art college scholarship and he got it; he did some amazing stuff... but most of it was violent and dark. After that he got signed by an agent and his work was shown in galleries. By the time he hit his early thirties, he had abandoned the painting for a while and hit the road. He worked in a hospital for a bit and just travelled living off his art earnings – he was a wealthy young man. But Larissa got cancer, so he came back home to care for her until she died, she went quickly. He couldn't find Stephen so he had a small ceremony for her. He hired a private detective who eventually reported that Stephen died in a building accident but couldn't produce a death certificate or any evidence.'

'Do you think Stephen paid the P.I. to say that?' Nate asked. He took his tie off and rolling it up, put it in his coat pocket.

'Don't know, but possibly,' John said. 'Stephen might have stayed away to protect his brother from the memories, or because of his own guilt, or to prevent the police coming back to question him... or maybe he couldn't face the scene himself. Maybe he knew Joe was fairly successful and thought his brother wouldn't want to see him. Anyway, as his success increased and he felt the pressure of that, Joe didn't cope, and he rang the police and confessed to his father's killing.

*****

'This room is where the shock treatment was done... move in, everyone, move right in,' Harry said enjoying his tour group's discomfort. The groups were usually predictable: there were always one or two members who were cynical; several guys full of bravado with their girls clinging to them; ordinary folk after a fright night; and scaredy cats who watched movies through webbed fingers, read Stephen King novels in the daytime and loved to be scared but safe... they were the best.

The group shuffled into the room where hooks jutted out from the walls, windows were barred and ominous stains could be interpreted as needed. Harry pointed to the old frame of a bed leaning against the wall, its straps dangling from it. It was highly unlikely the bed on display was involved, but Harry never let the truth stand in the way of a good story.

He continued. 'Shock treatment happened regularly in this asylum, but what's worse is that many of the people in here were just like you and me. Wrongly committed, placed in here for depression or minor illnesses, or by revenging partners, or because they didn't fit into the jail system.' He paused for effect.

'Imagine if it was you,' Harry said, with a touch of theatrics.

'You can see the wardens coming... you don't know if they're coming for you, and you try not to look at them, but you have to keep glancing up.

'They fix their eyes on you and then you're dragged past everyone, down the hallway to this room.

'You ask for help, you ask everyone... but there's no point... it's your time.'

A young woman in front of Harry shuddered.

'Men and women were subject to it,' he said, with a glance to the males in his group. 'Now they have you in here, they push you down onto the bed, and strap you down... spread eagle, you can't move.'

A loud thump echoed above their head and one of the girls stifled a scream as everyone looked up.

Brilliant, Harry thought. 'Happens all the time in here,' he said. 'Lots of tragic stories, some people's souls never left the place. Especially those who were treated in this room...' he said, dramatically. He drew a deep breath, letting the silence fill the room and then began again. 'You lie defenceless, unable to move as they stand over you, looking down on you knowing what is to come. They put a wedge in your mouth and an electrode on both sides of your head. But the scariest part is...'

One of the women screamed a blood-curdling scream and Harry stepped back in fright; he hadn't even got to the dramatic part. She pointed to the doorway and everyone began to scream and push towards the door to get out. Down the hallway, they could see a figure... a person hanging from the neck.

A sign was pinned to the hanging figure's chest, with one word evident: 'TRUTH'.

# Chapter 11

The passing traffic had eased a little now with rush hour almost done and night had encroached. Adam shouted the final round, as he and Nate took in the news that Joe had admitted to his father's killing.

'You don't believe he did it, do you?' Nate asked John.

'No, not for a minute could I believe that. But, he was put on trial.'

'Crap, this just gets worse,' Adam said, rubbing his hand over his face. 'I'm guessing they found him not capable, and that's how he ended up in the asylum? Around the time that we met him?'

'You guessed right,' John said, sitting back and sipping his wine. 'You wouldn't remember it of course but it was a big deal in the art world... the mad genius.'

'Vincent Van Gogh,' Adam said, swirling the vodka in his glass.

'His paintings soared in value, ironic really,' John said, 'and of course it brought his father's death back into the spotlight along with the mystery of the missing brother. I remember even the private detective being interviewed... the one who declared Stephen dead. Nothing was solved but it was the hottest story around for a few weeks.'

'Did Stephen come out of the woodwork then to save his brother from the asylum?' Nate asked.

'No, and I honestly believe if he was alive, he would have. Unless he was living under a rock, he would have heard about it.' John sighed.

'So… how did Joe die then?' Adam asked.

'Probably around the time you last saw him. That Christmas when he had the treasure map for you, I received a call to come to the asylum immediately. When I did, they told me that Joe had jumped the fence, and drowned in the river. They gave me some ashes in an urn.'

'Jesus, so they declared him dead, had him cremated and then contacted you? They can't do that!' Nate exclaimed.

'Oh, they've done a lot worse than that, and they've got away with it. I tried to take it higher but got nowhere,' John said. 'In the end, as Joe had no living relatives I knew of, I kept his urn; it's in my office, still. So, that's the history… that's all I have. Now to the inheritance. Joe kindly left me just short of one hundred grand for loyalty…' he nodded, acknowledging the shocked looks on both men's faces.

'I didn't know, I didn't draw up his final will,' John said. 'I was away when he wanted to finalise it and I had sent one of my colleagues to record his wishes. The rest of his fortune he left to both of you. So, your '*Expectations*' include a little house that he lived in, which was in a fairly ramshackle area when Joe was a kid… it's not so rundown now. I think you'll find the workers' cottage in Red Hill is worth a tidy sum.'

'Red Hill?' Nate's eyes widened. 'Wow.'

'And he has a collection of art, his own, that will be worth a packet if you want to keep a few and sell a few; and there's a cash amount of close to $400,000 for each of you,' John said, and waited for their reactions.

'Bloody hell,' Adam said, and exhaled. 'Who would have thought that scruffy little guy was worth something. Thank you, Joe, mortgaged paid off.'

'Really?' John said, surprised. 'Sorry, I thought with your connections… sorry, presumptuous of me.'

'I don't live off my mother,' Adam said.

'His mum would make him pay it off in publicity appearances and interviews,' Nate said with a sly grin to Adam.

Adam smirked, but nodded his agreement. He turned back to John. 'Sorry, just stepping back, so you said earlier in your office that Joe was now declared legally dead? It has to be a lot longer than the standard seven years for the presumption of death.'

'It is, but no-one declared it… until now.' John held up his hand as both men started to ask questions. 'I'll explain in a minute… but first, with the money Joe left me, I want to hire you to find out what happened at the asylum. If Joe drowned, if he was murdered, if he even died when they told me he did; it won't be easy. I want to give him a burial. And I want to find his brother, Stephen, or at least get to the bottom of what happened to him. If you find anything at all that requires legal representation, my services are free where it involves anything to do with Joe… no limit.'

Adam and Nate exchanged a look and understood each other.

'Keep your money John, you don't need to pay us to investigate,' Nate said. 'We want to do this for Joe, but we'll take you up on the free legal if we need it.'

Adam nodded his agreement.

'Thanks,' John said, sincerely. 'There are two things you need to know: firstly, Joe set up a trust fund with a sizeable amount in it that earns enough interest to provide a good annual salary for someone. From this, a monthly amount is paid – a stipend is the best way to explain it. It's generous enough to cover rent and weekly living expenses. I've been paying it for over a decade—CPI adjusted—to a numbered bank account with no name. I don't know who owns the account... I don't know if the money is being used.'

'Why didn't you petition the bank and find out?' Adam asked the obvious.

'Because part of our agreement with Joe included a confidentiality clause around this. I can't do it, but you can. The second thing...' John drew a breath.

'This is something to do with declaring him legally dead?' Adam asked, suspicious.

'Yes, it is. I've been directed to make it happen... by Joe's ex-wife,' John replied.

# Chapter 12

It was Friday… the new 'tradition' for the business was to hold a weekly meeting at 8.15am before client appointments started at 9.30am. It was 8.25am and everyone was present, except Nate.

Jessica shook her head. 'So not surprised, he was like this when he was a cop too… always late, with *everything*. He'll be late for his own funeral, as my grandmother would say.'

Danielle laughed. 'Bet that's true. We'll all be waiting when the hearse arrives with him in it!'

As she finished her sentence, Nate rushed in and closed the door behind him. He pocketed his keys and put his jacket on the vacant chair that called his name. A coffee rested in front of him, and a plate of croissants and muffins sat in the middle of the table. Nate sat and looked at the faces of Adam, Jessica and Danielle around the table.

'Sorry I'm late,' he said, reaching for the coffee. 'Ah, thanks for this.'

'No excuse?' Jessica asked.

Nate looked at her. 'Gee, you've heard all my best ones… but I could come up with some new material I guess. There was this thing…'

Jessica rolled her eyes.

'Seriously though,' Nate continued, 'I had to drop Tilly to school and a flock of mothers wanted to chat.' He shrugged. 'I'm irresistible.'

'Of course you are,' Adam said. 'See this?' he pushed a small article in the newspaper towards Nate and Danielle on the opposite side of the table.

'Wow,' Danielle said, and began to read it aloud.

## GHOST TOUR GUESTS RUN SCREAMING FROM ASYLUM

Fifteen guests on a ghost tour through the former River Park Lunatic Asylum got more than they bargained for when they encountered the figure of a hanging man during the tour.

The hanging figure turned out to be an effigy of a patient in a straitjacket tied to the beam of the ceiling, with a sign attached reading 'Truth'.

Owner and tour leader, Harry Bond, 24, said the group had heard footsteps earlier but thought it was an animal or a ghost.

'I was nearly halfway through the tour when one of the ladies screamed and we all looked towards where she was pointing,' Mr Bond said. 'A man was hanging from the ceiling, and we didn't know at first that it was a dummy.'

Mr Bond said he ran towards the figure in case the person could be cut down and saved.

'Fortunately, it was a fake, but I still got the tour guests out of the building immediately and called the police,' he said. When he re-entered with the police, the hanging man dummy was gone.

'I don't know what the message meant, but it's not hard to guess,' Mr Bond said. 'There was a lot of stuff that went on at the asylum; it's rumoured the inmates were tortured, truth serum was injected into them, and they had shock treatment. Maybe someone's trying to bring attention to its past.'

Carly Mannet, 32, said she was on the tour with her sister and it was the first time they had been inside the asylum.

'It was a really freaky place, but we didn't expect anything to happen,' Ms Mannet said. 'We just expected some bumps and creaks. Then I looked up and there was a man hanging there; it looked so real, it was really terrifying. I didn't even get a chance to take a photo.'

Sergeant Matt Burns said the police were investigating and—'

Nate cut in. 'Ha, Burnsey's on the case. We went to the academy together and were stationed together for a few years. Remember him?' Nate asked Jessica.

'Matt Burns… mm, not by his name. Might remember him by sight,' she said, rolling his name through her memory banks.

Danielle looked from Nate to Adam. 'What's going on? Why are you interested in this?'

'This is our new case,' Nate said to Danielle.

'Really? I'm on a case? Fantastic,' Danielle smiled. 'I'm sick of cheating partners; ghosts will be great.' She was the only person at the table who looked truly excited about the case.

'Are you both working it?' Jessica asked, looking from Nate to Adam, 'your first case together?'

'It will be our first case together,' Adam said, with a smile, and put his hand on his heart. 'A historic moment. Right, over that,' he said, moving on.

'Well that was sentimental,' Nate smirked. He looked at Jessica to explain. 'We're looking for an old friend of ours who spent some time at the asylum… and before you say anything, no he wasn't mad, well not that we know about.'

'We need to know why he was in there and why or how he left, if he did leave,' Adam said. 'This truth stunt by whoever is making it might be close to home for us… it might flush out what happened to Joe,' Adam said. He looked to Nate. 'I want to go back to the asylum.'

Nate's eyes widened. 'What the hell for?'

'I want to take a look around; get a feel for it, and what it might have been like for Joe.'

'It was pretty bloody miserable, will that cut it for you?' Nate asked, unenthusiastic about the idea, but knowing he'd be dragged along.

'There must be other stuff there… not just Joe's diary. We heard movement upstairs… we might find this truth guy, he could try the same stunt with us if we're lucky.'

'Lucky? He's probably just a squatter or a relative trying to get compo for something,' Nate cut him off.

'But what if it was someone who knew something?' Danielle said.

'What if there are records stored somewhere there that haven't been cleared away?' Jessica continued.

'I'm thinking maybe you all need to be committed,' Nate shook his head. 'Joe's diary was only preserved because it was well hidden. We can't pry up every floorboard or knock down every wall.'

Adam frowned. 'I'm just trying to get a mindset on Joe… like returning to the scene of the crime, and if we encounter *truth guy*, all the better.'

Nate sighed. 'I guess we can go back and have another look around. I'll talk to my contact about getting clearance again.'

'Knew you'd come around,' Adam said, and smiled.

'I'm a bloody idiot,' Nate said.

Adam continued. 'Between clients, I'm going to chat to my banker friend about what we need to be able to access those bank account details; then see if I can get access to any of the original asylum psychological reports; and try and find any doctors or psyches who worked there and will talk.'

'That'll be challenging given you've only got about two free hours between clients,' Jessica cut in. 'But I've left you an hour for a lunch break.'

'Can't believe so many people need help,' Danielle shook her head. 'Or maybe you're really, really good… maybe I should make an appointment.' She joked.

'You'll need more than one,' Nate said, and ignored the punch she gave his arm. 'I'll check with John to see if Joe's ex-wife has agreed to meet us, but right this minute, Dan and I are going to go visit this guy,' Nate said, tapping the paper, 'the ghost tour guy. Might give Sergeant Matt a call too and reacquaint, can't hurt. How long we got?' He asked Jessica.

'About ninety minutes before your first appointment,' she said, with a glance to the clock.

'Let's go,' Nate rose, declaring the meeting over. 'Jess, Adam will fill you in on the rest, and I'll get Dan up to speed in the car.'

'Um, I'd leave your suit coat here, you'll be overdressed

for the Valley,' Danielle said, as Nate reached for the coat. He grabbed his keys, wallet and phone out of it, and followed Danielle out the door.

Adam stayed seated, so Jessica sat down again. He pushed some paperwork towards her.

'We need to start a file for Joseph O'Connell,' he said.

'Sure. Is this your asylum friend?' she asked.

Adam nodded. With a glance to the clock, he said: 'In a nutshell, it begins with a guy in his thirties who was locked up in a mental asylum...'

*****

'Dodgy area,' Nate said, as they walked along a laneway in a derelict part of Fortitude Valley. The city's laneway rejuvenation project hadn't arrived there yet, and several doorways displayed the leftovers from last night's club scene. Windows were patterned with faded leaflets and the occasional whiff of Chinese cooking drifted out to greet them.

Nate looked at his watch; he was hungry. 'I spent half of my cop working life in the Valley. Nice to be back... not.'

'It's got character,' Danielle said. 'Don't know why it's never really taken off... you know, it's close to the city and all that.' She stopped to consult the address again on her phone. 'The red dot says it's down the end of this lane.'

'That's it,' Nate said pointing to the sign above one of the small holes in the wall masquerading for stores. It read 'Ghost tours' and in small print, 'scare your pants off'.

'Let's go do just that,' Danielle said, and ducked under Nate's arm as he pushed open the door for her to enter. They eyed the tired premises and the ghoulish posters covering every inch of the store. A counter took up the entire length of one wall and the opposite wall displayed racks full of brochures featuring all of their tour options; it was deceptively larger than it looked from the outside.

'Oh look, Nate,' Danielle waved a brochure at him, 'hen's and buck's night ghost tours. Good to know.'

Nate smiled. 'Something you're not telling me?'

'Not likely,' Danielle sighed. She rang the bell and waited. Through a plastic fringe hanging over a doorway, she saw a man walking around in the next room talking on the phone. He stuck his head out, held up his hand to tell them he'd be there in five, and disappeared again.

Danielle continued, warily. 'I thought when Adam got divorced he might have asked me out,' she said, replacing the hen's night brochure and fishing for information from Nate. She trailed her fingers along the brochure rack trying to appear nonchalant as she stammered on. 'But nope, barely knows I'm alive. I mean, getting your attention is easy... I just have to lay down and draw a white chalk outline around my body.'

Nate smirked at her. 'Ha, ha. Yeah, I guess you can't appeal to Adam through his work... he can't date patients. I didn't know you were that into him, besides you're a bit too over the top for him.'

'I am not,' she said, defensively.

'How many times have you gone out this week? Every night?' he asked.

'No... okay almost every night,' she conceded. 'But I was home early... it was just dinner, and the movies, and a couple of nights catching a local band... I like live music.'

'Adam needs a nice quiet girl who likes to stay home and is happy with her own company and his. Maybe cook a meal together, watch some television, drink some wine...

you'd wear him out. His idea of a big night is a few beers, the remote, and Foxtel Sports channel... not that there's anything wrong with that,' he thought as the prospect appealed to him.

She shrugged and brushed off the subject. The plastic flaps behind the counter parted and the store owner appeared. He was tall, in his early to mid twenties with what appeared to be a shaving rash. He was dressed top-to-toe in black and wore his hair shaved close to his head.

'Sir and Madame,' he said with a look of delight, and theatrics. 'Harry Bond at your service – Harry like the Prince, Bond like 007,' he said trying to be suave.

Nate introduced himself and Danielle, and passed over his business card.

'Is that your real name?' Nate asked.

'It is now,' Harry said. He looked at their business cards. 'So, you're looking for a ghost? You probably just scared them off with that Private Investigator logo,' Harry said, and laughed, amused by his own wit.

Danielle laughed along. Whatever it took, she knew the game. She noticed Harry had already checked out her form in the tight jeans and boots she was wearing.

'We'd like to ask you a few questions about the ghost tours you run at the former River Park Lunatic Asylum and the incident last night,' Danielle said, 'we thought you might be able to help us given your experience and insider knowledge of the place,' she flattered him.

'Sure, have you got a client interested?' he asked, then frowned. 'You're not with those developers are you?' His friendliness chilled.

'We're sure as hell not with them,' Danielle said. 'I hate how everything's being pulled down and replaced by units.'

He warmed up again. 'Yeah, right, me too. Want to come in and sit down.' He opened the curtain to a room with a couch, TV and coffee table.

'No, we're good out here, but thanks,' Nate said, not planning on being there for too long.

'Okay, questions… go ahead then, shoot. Not literally,' he warned Nate and laughed again.

Nate did his best to smile and not look pained. 'So, can you tell us what happened last night, other than what we read in the paper.'

'Sure,' Harry said, and proceeded to give the same version as written in the paper but with the added theatrics of eye rolling and hand movements.

Nate cut him off. 'Have you ever seen this hanging man before?'

Harry shuddered. 'Holy crap, no! You wouldn't forget that. Besides, that's brilliant for publicity; I'm booked out for the next few months now. But, I've had other things happen that were pretty scary, and I think I've heard hanging guy before. I'm pretty sure someone's been upstairs for quite a few of my tours.'

'Couldn't it be a ghost?' Danielle asked, almost disappointed.

'Nah, don't be crazy.' He stopped and bit his tongue. 'I didn't mean to say that out loud and I'll deny it if you repeat it! Yeah, it could have been a ghost…'

'So, what else happened that was scary?' Nate prodded him along.

'Yeah right, besides the hanging guy, I've had a running guy…' His face lit up, loving being important and the centre of attention. 'We take a tour group through every Friday and Saturday night; we've got a set route we're allowed to use that's deemed safe… and we use a bit of theatrics,' he shrugged, 'you know the occasional noise and lights but one night we all nearly had a heart attack.'

'Go on,' Danielle encouraged him.

'About a month ago on a Saturday night, I almost get to the end of the tour when one of the girls on the tour starts screaming hysterically. Well, I was rapt … bring it on, that shit is great for bookings!'

Nate restrained a yawn… the guy could rant on.

'Yeah well, when I caught up with the front of the group, there was this man running down the hall and he looked like he was in a straitjacket… the arms were flapping by his side. He turned back and he had a sign pinned to him that said, *Truth*. He looked real enough but I'm not saying he was real.'

'So, was he or wasn't he?' Danielle asked.

'I don't know. By the time I got my group out and came back, he was gone. It happened, in the same way, one more time. I think it was just someone grandstanding,' Harry said, and folded his arms across his chest. 'But it got me a lot of social media talk and bookings almost doubled. Then the State Government stepped in and closed us down because they decided the area was unsafe,' he said, with a scoffing sound. 'We've only just been allowed back in.'

'And you think the government has a different motive?' Nate asked.

'Hell yeah. I think they don't want the truth to come out!'

'What truth? What is the truth?' Danielle asked, exasperation lacing her voice.

'How do I know,' Harry shrugged. 'I'm just taking people through to show them what it used to be like for some people who were either really nutso, or had nothing more than depression or anxiety... you know all that stuff that we're supposed to be so 'PC' about now. If you want to know what's going on, ask the hanging straitjacket guy.'

# Chapter 13

**Then...**

'I bet she's sixteen,' Nate said, watching a young red-haired girl wander around the grounds. She was thin, lanky, but striking... her long wavy hair surrounded a petite face. She ran her hand over everything... touching the top of the timber bench, the trim of the shrubs, the roughness of the wire fence.

She stopped when she saw them laying on the crest of the rise, a stone's throw from the fence. She tilted her head to the side.

Adam raised his hand in a wave, and hesitantly she approached the fence, wrapping her fingers through the wire.

'Who are you?' she asked.

The two boys checked out the area and deeming it safe, pushed themselves up and moved closer.

'We live around here,' Nate said, with a nod to the houses down the street. 'Who are you?'

'Kelsey,' she said, as though that would explain everything. 'I live here... I guess.' She turned back to look at the building behind her, before returning her gaze to the two boys.

'You don't look...' Adam stopped himself from saying the word sick... 'very old', he finished.

'I'm thirteen. How old are you?' she looked from one to the other.

'Ten, nearly eleven,' Nate answered. 'Why do you live here?'

'I couldn't live with my stepfather, so I played up, and when that didn't work I ran away... a few times. When they found me, I locked myself in my room and wouldn't come out, so they put me here,' she said, and shrugged.

'Is it better living here?' Adam asked. 'Wouldn't you rather go home?'

She sighed and looked over their heads. She didn't answer for a long time, and both boys turned to see what had got her attention; nothing.

'Do you know our friend, Joe? We're looking for him,' Adam asked.

'He's an artist, got short hair and a beard,' Nate finished. 'He usually sits over there in the corner on that white chair and draws, or sometimes he writes poetry.'

'I think I know who you mean. He's in the hole this week,' she said, and shrugged. She ran her hand over her head. 'They wanted to cut my hair but one of the nurses stopped them.'

The boys didn't know what to say.

'What's the hole?' Adam asked.

'It's time out, you know, like a room away from everyone else... I think he's there. Might not be him. I dunno.' She looked from one to the other. 'Can you help me escape?'

'Um...' Adam looked to Nate.

'Where would you go?' Nate asked.

'Somewhere... anywhere... I can swim,' she said, with a look to the river. 'I could hide at your place and you could bring me food, and stuff.'

'We have to talk about it, Nate and me, but yeah, we could do it,' Adam said, starring at Kelsey with the stirrings of adolescent curiosity and attraction.

'Okay,' she said, and smiled at Adam. 'I'll be here tomorrow. You can let me know and we could make a plan. If you can't hide me, that's okay... you'd never see me again if you got me out, promise... you wouldn't get in trouble, I'm excellent at hiding.'

'Then why haven't you run away before now?' Nate asked.

'It's hard to get out but once I'm out, I'll be fine. You'll talk about it?'

The boys nodded, and she smiled at them and turned to leave. She looked back at them. 'I won't tell anyone I saw you.'

'Right,' Nate said, 'thanks.'

'Yeah, thanks,' Adam repeated, his mouth slightly open.

They watched her walk off. Nate nudged Adam.

'You in love or something?' he teased.

'No, get real,' Adam scoffed. 'What do you think she meant by not telling anyone she saw *us*?' Adam asked.

Nate shrugged, then stopped. 'You don't think Joe's in trouble because he's been seen talking with us?'

Adam looked worried. 'Maybe. Do you think the hole is really a hole?'

'Yeah,' Nate said. 'I bet it's a hole in the ground. Maybe we need to rescue Joe instead of her. Maybe she can help us do it.'

'Yeah,' Adam agreed. He looked back to see if he could spot her again but she was nowhere to be seen.

**Now…**

Adam paced, hands in his pockets, as they waited outside the asylum gates for Danielle to arrive. Every time he turned, he could sense its presence, looming in his peripheral vision, waiting to share a secret. He turned away and saw Nate watching him.

'What's got into you? This place make you nervous?' Nate asked.

'I feel like I'm always waiting for someone…' he said.

'That's because you are,' Nate agreed. 'The question is, are they worth waiting for? Analyse that!'

Adam gave him a wry look.

'Come on, Dan,' Nate muttered with impatience.

'Yeah, late people are so annoying,' Adam agreed, with a dig to Nate. 'Hey, do you remember that girl we met here that time we were waiting for Joe?'

'Yes! But you know what's weird, I had completely forgotten about her until now. We only met her once and she wanted us to break her out.' Nate leaned against his car's bonnet.

'Yeah. Skinny, tall, with long red hair; she said they were going to cut it but a nurse stopped them… someone was on her side. She wasn't there when we went back to help her, or we missed her.'

'She was thirteen, wasn't she?' Nate asked. 'You liked her, I remember now. How many times have you thought about her?'

Adam stopped pacing, thought about it and shrugged. 'A few times. She was a runaway. Why would they put her in here?' He said, with a glance back to the building. 'Wonder what happened to her.'

'What was her name again?' Nate asked, but the question hung in the air as they were lit by headlights;

Danielle drove her VW into the carpark. She stopped, cut the ignition, and jumped out.

'Sorry guys, traffic's shit.'

'But yet we're here,' Nate said.

'Yeah but you're brilliant; a born rally driver, and oh yeah, coming here is against the traffic for you,' she said.

'Right on two counts,' Nate shot back.

Adam grinned. 'Let's go,' he said, and began to walk towards the entrance.

'Woah,' Danielle said, and both men stopped to look at her. 'It's scary imposing isn't it?'

'Sure is,' Adam said, 'then and now. Still, want to come in?'

'Hell yeah,' she said, full of bravado. She followed the men towards the entrance. Nate fished out the key he was given, put it in the lock and with a grunt, he turned it, giving them access.

'My contact said to not draw attention to ourselves...' Nate said. 'Just get in and get out quickly. So, don't put the overhead lights on,' he joked. It had been years since any electricity had run through the asylum.

Adam pulled the torch out of his jacket and its rays lit up the entrance hallway. He flicked it to the ceiling; nothing was hanging there. He breathed out, relieved.

They stood for a moment, getting their bearings, getting a feel for the place; the silence was unnerving.

'I bet this hanging guy's not going to show himself,' Adam mumbled.

'We're here. Where are you?' Danielle yelled out, making both men jump. They turned on her in surprise.

'Holy crap,' Nate said, patting his heart.

'What?' she shrugged. 'There's only us here... and him... we're not waking anyone.'

Nate sighed. 'C'mon. Let's look around. He might be the nervy type and Dan's just sent him packing.'

'Sorry,' she whispered.

'I'll check the carpark at the back, see if anyone is running for their life now,' Nate joked. 'Dan, you cover Adam's back and vice versa.'

Adam, with Danielle close behind him, began to walk down the corridor trying to minimise the tap of his own shoes on the hard surface. He didn't trust the situation; didn't trust that this person wasn't volatile. He stayed close to the wall, listening and looking as far ahead as he could see by torchlight, his arm pushing Danielle behind him every time she strayed in front. He entered the first room to his left; nothing had changed since their last visit – the rusty old iron beds were still piled by the window; the dank and stale smell was overbearing.

'God almighty, that smell. This place is miserable,' Danielle said, taking in the room.

'You can say that again,' Adam agreed.

'Can you hear that tapping noise? Was it here last time?' she asked.

'Yeah, it's coming from up there,' he indicated the next level with his torch. He looked back at the exit. He knew coming here was his idea, but now he was thinking it wasn't his best one. Having started, he continued forward.

A door slammed behind them and they wheeled around. Adam shone the torch into Nate's face.

'For chrissake,' he swore and breathed in deeply.

'Sorry, the wind caught it,' Nate said, holding up his hands in a surrender motion. 'Scare you?'

'No, this is usually how I spend my nights,' Adam grimaced and turned his torch away.

'No vehicles outside, but he's probably on foot,' Nate wrinkled his nose at the smell. 'He might live here.'

Adam moved back into the hallway and glanced into

the room opposite. Nate and Danielle followed close by, breathing down his neck. Adam turned.

'Do you have to walk so close? Can't you two take that room to the left?' he gave a nod of his head towards the other room. 'I want to find the treatment room and the solitary confinement area that Joe mentions in his diary.'

Nate looked over at the dark room and back at Adam. 'Fine.' He grabbed the torch from his jacket pocket. 'Dan, stay nearby.'

'Yeah, Dan, better go with Nate, he'll be having nightmares about this tonight,' Adam said.

Nate rolled his eyes. 'That was a scary movie, you've never let me live it down… we were ten,' he said to Danielle.

Adam chuckled. 'C'mon on, let's get moving.'

Nate moved away with Danielle behind him. Adam continued into another room. It was a long dormitory with an exit at the far end. A hint of light from the hallway filtered through the far door and Adam noted up to a dozen rusted iron single beds left randomly in the room. Marks on the floor and walls shadowed where additional beds were once placed – as many as twenty packed in. He imagined what it must have been like: patients all in white, shuffling around, some silent and staring, others loud and rowdy; the smell of fear and humanity mingled with disinfectant; staff always watching them; and the promise of another life outside the window.

He stopped to glance at his watch… it was ten past the hour. *Where is this clown?* He moved towards the exit; his torch flickered out and he stood in complete darkness.

'Crap,' he muttered trying to get it to work and tapping it in his hand. He waited for his eyes to adjust to the dark and controlled his thoughts and breathing, trying not to let the irrational fear of being in a former insane asylum at night overtake him. He kept expecting to feel a hand on his shoulder, or something brushing past him.

Adam unscrewed the torch, pushed on the battery and the light sprung on again. He screwed the torch back together and gave a silent prayer of thanks to the God he believed in when convenient.

He moved quickly through the room, casting the light into the crevices and shadows. He flicked the torch towards the window where he thought he saw a movement; nothing, maybe his own shadow.

Moving out into the hallway from the far exit, he saw Nate and Danielle coming out of the room on the left. Nate indicated he would continue to the next room and Adam nodded. He realised that most of the rooms and storage areas had been stripped or filled in and looked like every other room now... some of the detail that Joe had mentioned in his diary—iron doors, shelving, holes in the walls and floor, security bars—was now long gone and it would be harder to identify where he was.

Adam walked into the next room on the right of the corridor—a larger room than the other dorms—and flashed his torch around. He stumbled back in shock.

'Nate!' he yelled. He steadied himself against the door frame, hearing Nate and Danielle running up the hall towards him. Nate arrived at his side.

Adam held the torch high to the ceiling. At the far end, above them, a man in a white straight jacket hung from the ceiling by the neck. Attached to his chest was a piece of paper with one word scrawled on it in black. *Truth.*

A door slammed in another room of the empty wing. Adam turned and ran towards the noise, his torchlight bouncing around the walls. Nate and Danielle followed close behind. At the end, he came to a dead end.

'Where was that door we just heard?' Adam looked around. They heard it slam again, this time right back where they first entered.

'This way,' Danielle called. Adam ran down the hallway retracing their steps. He skidded to a halt outside the room where the man was hanging.

'What the hell?'Adam raced into the room and looked around. He glanced out into the hallway to check he had the right room.

'Tell me I didn't imagine it?' he said, as Nate and Danielle piled in behind him.

'He was there a minute ago... hanging, dead as...' Danielle groped for words. She began to yell: 'Hey, hanging guy, if you don't want to show yourself, write to us… Delaney and Murphy.' She repeated the name again, and shrugged at the two men. 'He might be afraid of us but want to tell us what truth means, and we don't want to leave a card since we're sort of not meant to be here...'

They heard another door slam above them and then the strangest long moan. The wind flapped the plastic at the window next to them and made them all jump.

'Want to go up there and follow that noise?' Adam asked.

'Nuh. Let's talk about this outside,' Nate said.

'Yeah, good idea,' Adam said, pushing Danielle in front, as they hurried for the exit.

# Chapter 14

Adam yelled out. The voice jolted him awake—his own—and he sat up, drawing short, shallow breaths. He was home, in his own room, in the safe environment he had created.

He swore under his breath, pulled his T-shirt off, wiped it over his face and threw it on the floor. Adam lowered himself back onto the bed; he had the whole bed to himself now, not by choice. It wasn't the first time he had woken in a cold sweat, it wasn't even the hundredth time, but it had been a while since *that* dream had woken him. It was always the same; a recurring version of the same dream – people leaving. First his wife, then back to his childhood and his deserting parents. He stood, a kid at the gate, not able to find home or knowing where to go. He kept turning, back, front, no-one was around. When he found his home, it was empty; the yard was empty, the grass was long, the street was empty... *what do I do, what do I do, what do I do...*

Once, he overheard his grandmother saying, 'Why did they bother having a child? Neither of them has the time for the poor little bugger.' That's what he wanted to know too.

Adam glanced at the clock; nearly 5am. He'd get up and go for a run soon. His mind drifted to Joe; he never realised how much the non-judgemental friendship of two young boys had meant to Joe – how he might have needed that. He pulled open the curtain; it was light already. He reached for Joe's diary, finding his bookmark and resumed where he left off:

*A note to my two young friends:*

*Lads, have you yet read 'Great Expectations'? I know boys your age find many things to do besides reading, but a book can offer you escape and solace. One day, I hope you will understand what that means. You will enjoy this book, I promise you; it's about a young man like both of you, a young man named Pip who has options – he's given an opportunity and turns his back on his home. I never understood why he did so... all I ever wanted was a loving home, but Pip thought he saw a better life... love, respect, wealth.*

*Every time you visit, I see all your potential... you have the whole world ahead of you. I wonder what decisions you will make, what sort of men you will be. Will anything stop you reaching your best? Family, wealth, support, encouragement... I don't know your stories but you are such different boys, I am buoyed by your energy and promise.*

*So, I have made a decision, and one day you will hear of it and I hope you will think of me fondly then and not as presumptuous or condescending. The moments of happiness you gave me are immeasurable in this white-walled home. You can't know how it is not to be judged, or watched, to be liked just for who you are. Thank you.*

*When you receive this notebook, you will be young men and you can choose to read it or throw it away – you may have forgotten your friend, Joe, by then. But let me share some stories with you—if you choose to read this diary—of what my life is like and why.*

*Perhaps it is best not to look back. They say we learn from history, but I think sometimes we should file it all away in our minds and not let it hold us back. That's what many returned soldiers had to do, to get on with their lives after what they had seen and had to do for their country.*

*That said, I am not shirking my part in what has become of me; I have been weak and I need to take responsibility for my journey. I cannot help, however, but to blame my situation on my father. I've had enough contemplative time to be able to stand outside of myself and reflect on all that took place.*

*There is no doubt in my mind that my father contributed to his own death and ruined my brother's life. I did confess to killing my father to encourage my brother to come home, to free him from being on the run. They put me here, unsure of my guilt, unsure of my sanity. I'm not sure if it is better or worse than a prison cell.*

*But my lads, I promise all my writings are not this morbid. After all, life is full of good and bad times as you will discover. My art gives me great comfort, as does your friendship and your potential. You have each other and I hope that will be an enduring friendship for you both. The friends we make as young people are the best... they like us for ourselves, not for what we might have become. I hope you will be friends forever.*

*****

Adam knew something wasn't right; his phone was buzzing with messages as he entered the house after his run. He had a separate mobile phone for patients, and it wasn't that phone. Something must have happened to a friend or family member. His first thought went to his grandmother walking the Camino… his stomach clenched as he reached for his phone. He scrolled through the messages from a cousin and friends, his eyes narrowed and he hit on a link.

'For Christ's sake, Mum,' he muttered. She was all over the media, again; it was the thirtieth anniversary of the day she brought down a government. He sent quick notes back to thank everyone for the heads-up and opened his iPad – plenty of photos of his beautiful, vulnerable mother—as she played the role then—with the former Prime Minister, and shots of her now dodging media… and loving every minute of it, Adam thought. He took a deep breath and headed to the shower knowing what the day ahead would be like. He would call her when he came out, allowing himself time to cool down… he was always telling his patients to do that. It wasn't really her fault after all, unless she fed the story to the media.

Bet she has, he thought, some things never change.

Twenty minutes later, clean and dressed for the office, he didn't feel any calmer. He would leave it a while longer and call her when he got to the office.

## Chapter 15

Adam liked Stones Corner in the early hours of the morning; it felt like a village – café staff carried furniture to the footpath in readiness for the breakfast crowd; baristas were already selling coffee hits through holes in the walls of cafes; milk and bread sat outside the doors of unopened venues; a few dog walkers, joggers, and some elderly folk on scooters traversed the street with a nod or a wave; and shift workers had a beer or a coffee at the pub on the corner as their day ended where it began for others.

Adam saw it before he was even close... the media scrum – half a dozen reporters and photographers outside his building, waiting.

'Great,' he mumbled. He slowed down and drove forward. He could see the entrance to his carpark and the waiting pack clearer now. As he approached the scrum became alert, cameras flashed and he drove through, lowering his window shade in the hope of avoiding shots. Several photographers knocked on the windows of his car, and he hastened into the carpark, the iron gate closing behind him.

He took a deep breath and got out of the car. Three photographers and a journalist had followed him into the carpark. He would have to let them out and then face the others at the same time.

'Where's Winsome?'

'What's it like to be the son of the woman who brought down a government?'

'Does she have any regrets?'

'Is there any truth to the rumour that you could be the former Prime Minister's son?'

Once these questions would have riled him, but there was nothing new amongst this lot. Okay, the last one still pissed him off. He held up his hand.

'Winsome is not here and she won't be here today. She's in Sydney, and I know who my father is, thanks. If you could get off the premises that would be really appreciated.'

He flicked the garage door switch to let them out and unlocked the internal door to the building as more media came through the garage. Adam closed the office door quickly, forcing them to rush to get back out of the garage or wait for the next car to enter.

As he took to the stairs, he dialled Jessica, and she answered on the second ring.

'Hey there, what's wrong?' she asked. 'Is this an early coffee order?'

'I wish,' Adam said. 'Nothing's wrong, just a warning that the media is here... just something to do with my family. Be careful driving in, I'll warn Nate now.'

'Winsome?' she said.

Adam frowned. She had obviously done her research. 'Yeah, Winsome.'

'Oh! I'm just scrolling through my feed now... it's thirty years since... wow,' she said, her voice trailing off.

'Apparently. Can you ring my clients when you get in... just warn them to come in the back entrance? If anyone wants to cancel, that's no problem, don't charge them of course. Or if they are really struggling and must have an appointment today, but don't want to risk coming here, I can go to them.'

'Will do,' Jessica said. 'You sound pissed off, are you okay?'

'I'm fine, nothing I haven't been through before,' he said. 'Also, we may have to turn down any new clients for a few days too... until it dies down. We'll see how quickly the media leave and if any of them bother running it.'

'Running what?' Jessica tried to catch up.

'The story – me saying piss off basically.' He heard Jessica laugh and lightened up a bit. He unlocked the office door, entered and relocked it.

'Nate will love the publicity for his business,' Jessica said. 'Let him know, he can go down and turn them away, preferably in front of his P.I. sign at the front of the building.'

'Yeah, that's a good idea,' Adam brightened.

'So why are we not accepting new clients?' Jessica asked.

'Because last time the media came to my work looking for Mum, I got a rash of new clients who didn't really have anything wrong, they just wanted to talk about her. You also get some fruit loops who think they are getting celebrity counselling by seeing someone once removed from fame! People are strange.'

'Occupational hazard I'd say,' Jessica agreed.

'True. So, just knock back any clients for the next week until we see what pans out,' Adam instructed her.

'I'll call Nate and Dan,' she said, 'give them the heads-up.'

'Yeah thanks, I've got to call Mum and find out where she is,' he said. 'See you soon, and hey, thanks Jess.'

Adam hung up and turned as he heard a knock on the door. A photographer snapped his photo. He moved to the two large office window panels and closed the thin, white venetian blinds. The photographer was knocking on the glass window asking to come in for a shot. Adam walked into his office, closed the door, and dialled his mother.

'Hello Adam,' she answered on the second ring, her voice soft and willowy. She never abbreviated his name, never called him sweetheart or darling or any of the terms of endearment that Nate's mother used. Occasionally she would call him 'Son', but that was more for effect than endearment.

'Mum, where are you?' he asked, exasperation lapping on the fringe of his voice.

'I'm in Sydney; I would have called you but we're an hour ahead down here and I wasn't sure if you would be up yet.'

'I'm at work and…'

'Before you start,' she cut him off, 'it was your wife's idea! There's a few irons in the fire and Stephanie thought this might just raise the offers.'

'Ex-wife,' Adam reminded her, 'and still your publicist?'

'She's the best, and it's tiresome breaking in new staff. Anyway, I'm about to re-negotiate my fragrance contract and there's a potential book deal in the wings, so we're showing them just how much column space I can still get.'

'Of course, good business,' Adam rolled his eyes.

'Absolutely,' Winsome said, oblivious to his displeasure. 'So, Steph has me in hiding today to increase the hype. Do you want to speak to her?'

'No, thanks. What hype is she hoping for?'

'Publicity, Adam, about the dismissal… it's thirty years today,' Winsome said it as if surprised it wasn't the focus of Adam's day. She continued, 'I can't believe I was 20, thirty years ago,' she sighed. 'Your father's been gone for so long, Adam. I still miss him… I can't believe I have a son who is almost 30… but Jack says I look half my age,' she said, referring to her boyfriend.

'Of course he does, and you look wonderful, Mum,' Adam softened. It was hard not to protect her, to step up like he did when his father died. 'Anyway, Mum, there's a crowd of photographers outside my building.'

Winsome laughed with delight… a breathy, girl-like laugh. He heard her telling Stephanie before returning her attention to him. 'Well, that worked. I just needed a decoy, Adam, or else they would be here and Steph thought the chase might be fun if we casually mentioned that I was visiting you in Brisbane.'

Adam reigned in his anger. 'Great. Do you want to get *Steph* to give the media a call and mention you are not in Brisbane so my patients can get into the office?'

'Hold on.' He listened as Winsome moved away from the phone to speak with Stephanie. 'He wants to talk with you.' She returned her attention to him. 'Bye, Adam. We should do lunch soon, maybe on your birthday – you could fly down. I hope you are enjoying the present,' she reminded him.

He heard her hand over the phone. *Do lunch soon*, he ground his teeth.

'Hi Adam, how are you?' his ex-wife's dulcet tones came down the line.

'Stephanie, I'm fine but I seem to have a media scrum here.'

She laughed. 'We thought you might like the publicity for your new business. I'm sure Nate will love it, even if you don't.'

'Unless you've forgotten, I'm a psychologist… so my clients don't want people to know they are seeking help, they don't want media hanging around as they come and go from the building… nor do I need fake clients for a week trying to ask me about my childhood instead of telling me about theirs! Unlike you and Mum, I'm not seeking exposure.'

'Oh, lighten up, Adam. It'll blow over… besides, think of it as doing your mum a favour.'

Adam hung up. *No bloody idea.*

*****

'They're gone,' Nate said, closing the office door behind him. 'I told you you'd pay for that car – although I'd put up with more than that for a Mercedes for my birthday.'

Adam shook his head. 'She's unbelievable. Hopefully that's it now, it's old news for crying in a bucket, who's interested?'

'Me!' Jessica squealed, and then shrugged as Adam looked at her confused. 'Your mum's a star and even if it happened a long time ago, she's still got a huge profile.' Jessica turned to Nate. 'Did you get any good publicity out of it?'

'Well if we didn't, it's not from lack of trying. I stood right next to the business sign and phone number, while suggesting to the photographers they move on and maybe try Sydney. That set them off asking if you had told me that, so of course, I said you let it slip.'

'Whatever it takes,' Adam agreed, 'thanks, Nate.'

Jessica grinned. 'You big ham, Nate.'

'Hey, it's cheaper than advertising,' Nate said, and if Winsome is going to use us, we may as well make the best of it.'

'So, is she really in Sydney or did you just say that? Is she coming here?' Jessica asked, with a hint of excitement in her voice.

'She's not even in the State,' Adam said.

'Oh,' Jessica said, disappointed. 'It can't be easy to see images of your mother looking cute and scantily dressed sitting on the ex-P.M.'s lap.' The look on Nate's face made her realise she had said too much.

Nate jumped in. 'Winsome's a star… like all people in the spotlight, they think everyone else wants to be as well.'

There was a knock at the door, and Nate moved toward it, moving the louvres aside. He opened the door to Danielle.

'Any press down there?'

'A few hopefuls, they're talking to our business neighbours asking about you, Adam, and if your Mum's been seen around here,' Danielle said.

'I hope you didn't get photographed,' Nate said to Danielle. 'You'll be no use to me on surveillance if you're posing in media pics.'

'Give me a break, I'm better than that. I slipped in like a ghost. Having the coffee orders helped, I think they thought I worked at the café,' she said, handing them around. 'Speaking of ghosts, you should have come last night, Jess, it was fun,' Danielle said, enthusiastically, moving to her customary spot, leaning against the end of the reception desk. 'We saw the hanging man!'

'Really?' Jessica gasped. 'So, what happened to… you know, the body?'

'I'm sure it was just a dummy. They can be pretty real these days,' Adam said.

'We went back and it was gone,' Nate summed it up. He took the large flat white and took a seat in the waiting room.

'Looked real to me,' Danielle agreed.

'Do you think it was a ghost?' Jessica asked.

'Yes, Jess, I do, case closed,' Adam teased her. The group laughed.

'Here, you need this, grumpy,' she pushed Adam's coffee towards him. 'Were you scared?' she asked the two men.

Nate pushed his hand through his blonde hair and his green eyes widened. 'Hell yeah. But every time we heard something, Adam ran towards it.'

Adam grinned. 'There was a moment when my torch blacked out; I had to tell myself to keep it together,' he confessed. 'That place... it's like everyone just walked out yesterday and all the bad history is still there, alive, ready to smother you!'

'And did the guy have the *'Truth'* sign pinned to him, like last time?' Jessica asked. 'Do you think he's seeking the truth or trying to expose the truth of what happened there?'

'Good question. I think he's wanting to disclose what went on there,' Adam said. 'That institution has an amazing history... it's been in use for well over a hundred and fifty years and supposedly more than fifty thousand people passed through it, including our Joe. Allegedly,' he stressed the word, 'there's been torture, murder, electric shock treatments, beatings, medical experiments... it's a cruel place. The truth could mean any number of things.'

Danielle shuddered. 'So sad.' She stopped, glanced toward the door and listened, expecting another media intrusion, but it was a key being inserted into the office next door.

'I read they had some forensic patients there for a while,' Jessica said.

'What's that mean?' Danielle asked.

'The criminally insane,' Nate said, swinging his legs from the chair beside him and sitting upright. 'You know, not guilty by reason of insanity.'

Jessica grimaced. 'Do you think one of them, a former patient, could be doing this? Maybe they heard you guys have found something there or are investigating the place and they want to bring it to your attention?'

'That's one explanation,' Adam said, 'or they're connected to Joe and his solicitor, or hanging man might even be a descendent of a victim.'

'It wouldn't be anyone from that ghost tour place trying to get some publicity?' Jessica asked.

Danielle shook her head. 'Harry Bond seemed genuinely surprised by it. Not sure he's clever enough to pull something like that off anyway,' she looked to Nate for his agreement, and he nodded.

'I don't think he'd risk losing his licence if he was found out pulling that stunt,' Nate said.

'It's a valuable piece of land the hospital is on... maybe someone is trying to attract attention to the place, trying to stir up something, or deter us,' Adam suggested.

'The Truth,' Nate said more to himself than the group.

'So, what does it mean, detective?' Adam asked Nate. 'Who's doing it, where's your ghost, what's it got to do with us and Joe, and who wants us to find the truth?'

Nate rose. 'Mm, tough one.'

'The truth is out there,' Danielle said as she stood.

All three looked at her.

'It's from the *X-Files*,' she said. 'You know – FBI Special Agents Mulder and Scully. Come on... really?' Danielle sighed. 'They were brilliant; they would knock this stuff over in no time if we could get them on the job.'

'They weren't real, Dan,' Adam teased her.

'They were real to me,' she said, following Nate into his office.

'You've got a client in fifteen minutes, she wasn't put off by the media,' Jessica turned to Adam. 'It's that really skinny girl,' she whispered diplomatically. 'She always makes me feel huge.'

Adam looked surprised. 'She makes me feel hungry.'

'It's weird though, isn't it? That she can't see how thin she is.'

'It's a complex disease,' Adam said, 'and a distorted body image is just scratching the surface.'

'I can imagine. We dealt with a lot of strange people in the police service... and that was just the cops,' she said, and smiled at her own joke.

Adam lowered his voice and glanced towards Nate's office. 'What was Nate's strength when he was a cop... you know, what did he do best?'

Jessica thought for a second. 'In his reviews, his boss always said he was an excellent judge of character. I would have added that he was headstrong, brash and full of himself.'

'Yeah, but he's matured since then though,' Adam said, defending him. 'He's not that brash anymore.'

Jessica laughed. 'Funny!' She looked to the clock; it was just on eight-thirty. 'I'd better turn the phone on then,' she said noting the flashing message bank. She no sooner turned the switch from night to day and the phone rang. Jessica answered it; 'No, I'm sorry Dr Murphy is fully booked for the next week. I can put you on a waitlist?'

She shrugged and put the phone down as the caller hung up.

'You're going to get a bit of that today,' Adam said, just as the phone rang again. He left Jessica to it. Everyone had returned to their rightful places.

# Chapter 16

**Then…**

Adam rolled onto his stomach and propped himself up on his elbows. Nate lay beside him sucking on a long blade of grass. They watched Joe as he drew a sketch of the two of them.

'How did you hurt yourself, Joe?' Adam asked.

'Hurt myself?' Joe said, and looked up from his sketching. He looked confused.

'The red marks… you have one on each side of your head, just here,' Adam rubbed his own temples.

'Yeah, you do, Joe,' Nate said, looking closer at the man on the other side of the wire fence.

'Ah, that,' Joe nodded. He rubbed the sides of his head absently. 'I got burnt, but I'm okay.'

The boys didn't speak for a moment then Nate filled the silence.

'My mum won't let me in the kitchen; she says I'll burn myself. I'm allowed to cook toast and that's all,' he said.

Joe smiled. 'Yes, well I should take your mum's advice young Nate. Very good advice. I mustn't do any more cooking either.'

'What were you cooking?' Adam asked.

'Cooking?' Joe looked confused again. He looked to the door and back. 'I suppose I should go back inside.'

Adam changed the subject. 'Hey Joe, there's a girl here, she said she'd see us next time, but we haven't seen her... Kelsey... that's her name.'

'Ah Kelsey,' Joe said, and nodded. 'She's gone, lads.' He didn't elaborate.

The two boys looked at each other.

Nate nudged Adam. 'We'd better go too Joe, or we'll get in trouble. We've got work to do... Dad said he'd pay us if we wash the car.'

'Yeah, Joe, we'll see you again soon,' Adam said.

'Sure lads, thanks for coming by,' Joe said, his voice slow and measured.

Nate nudged Adam and they skidded back down the bank, out of sight of the fence line. Nate looked back over his shoulder.

'He's still there,' he said.

'Maybe he wanted us to go. Did you think he was kind of weird today?' Adam asked.

'Yeah, like he was one of those robots in slow motion,' Nate agreed.

'Weird,' Adam said, again.

*****

**Now...**

'Delaney and Murphy', Jessica answered the phone again. 'No, I'm sorry, Dr Murphy is with a client, and booked out for several weeks. Would you like to make a future appointment? No? Okay, thanks for calling'. She hung up. 'I hope you get help, you nutter', she mumbled.

She opened her browser to check up on the local news and there was Adam's photo from this morning... his hand covering his face; another shot of him getting out of the car; going up the stairs; a shot of him on the phone; and... she stopped. There was a photo of Winsome—still beautiful, cute and making headlines—on the arm of the tall, handsome superstar singer, Jack Bernham.

'Wow, Jack Bernham...' the door opened behind her and Adam came out. She sighed; *sprung again researching his mother.*

'Did you know your mum is seeing Jack Bernham? What am I saying, of course you know! I love him, my mother loves him. We saw him perform live three times and that was after his farewell concert!'

'Yeah, they've been going out for a while,' Adam said.

'Have you met him?' Jessica asked, sounding starstruck.

'He's my godfather...' He looked over her shoulder at the photo on her screen, '...and probably my soon-to-be stepfather I'm guessing. So, how's it going?'

Jessica groaned. 'Two genuine appointments, the other twenty-something callers were time wasters. But at least your clients can come up the front stairs now.'

'Sorry to put you through that, Jess,' Adam said. The phone rang again and she held up her hand for him to wait.

'Delaney and Murphy... I'm sorry Dr Murphy is booked out for a couple of weeks and has a waitlist.' She waited for the caller to hang up but instead, a gravelly voice said: 'I need to talk to him; he'll want to take this call.'

'Um, okay, then let's see when he can call you back.'

'No, it has to be now. Tell him the hanging man is on the line.'

\*\*\*\*\*

118

**Extract from Joe's diary:**

*I didn't see them coming; it's been a while since they took me and I had got comfortable. I forget to be on alert, and they were here right now – these two men pulling me out of my seat, pulling me along. They had a tight grip on my arms, and I would have walked but they were going too fast and my feet dragged behind every now and then. Everyone's eyes were diverted; who can blame them?*

*I recognised the room, I told them I wanted to talk with my own doctor, my lawyer, anyone I could think of to call on, but they ignored me. It was as if I had no voice... that I was the only one who could hear my words.*

*They pushed me roughly onto a bed and began to strap me down. I tried to get up but it all happened so fast and they were so much stronger. Why was this happening to me? Why was I getting this treatment?*

*The hospital's doctor entered, I had met with him once or twice before, I couldn't remember his name. Sinclair. Sinead. Sinnett. He looked down on me. I asked him why. I asked him who had authorised this. But all he said was that I needed to relax. My heart was beating so loud and fast I could hear it.*

*He put electrodes on my temples while I asked my questions over and over, and then he pushed a wad of rubber into my mouth and told me he was giving me a muscle relaxant. The needle went into a vein in my hand and I was gagging but he told me to count back from ten in my head. I couldn't think of the numbers, I was too terrified. I tried to fight it, but that's all I remember.*

*When I woke, I was in my own bed, in my dorm. I was the only one in the dorm; it must have been activity or meal time. I lay still for a while trying to assemble my thoughts. I said my* name, my birth date, my mother's name, my brother's name. I tried to recite some of the poems I knew by heart:

'The woods are lovely, dark and deep...

'The time has come, the Walrus said...

I couldn't remember them all, I couldn't find the lines, they were somewhere in my mind. I slowly sat, my head was thumping.

It was time to leave; I had to leave this place, now. That thought was clear.

I heard screaming, piercing screaming. I was on a knife's edge; so much screaming; I just wish it would stop. I need to go now, go back to my place, to my family home. I can close the door and feel the quiet. I could do that; I could live there the rest of my life, just me, my drawings, maybe the radio sometimes for company. I could walk to the park and I could go to the shops when they are not busy, when there's not many people around. Maybe I could get deliveries so that I don't have to go out if I don't want to. I could just live quietly, inside. It's time, I have to do that. I have to go now.

Chapter 17

Meeting them was a risk; Ron 'Mac' McIntyre knew that. They might try and charge him for break and enter, or try and commit him again. But they'd been here twice now and that girl had called out Delaney and Murphy; he wrote it down. He checked out their details online at the library; no-one would sit next to him while he was at the library computer, but he was used to that. He looked like a homeless guy and he smelled like it too on his off shower days. So, Delaney was an investigator and Murphy a psyche. They could be useful.

Mac walked through the rooms again... he had his exits planned if they became a threat, he knew every corner of the asylum – a clear blueprint in his head. But they were doing some type of investigation and he had decided to get back on the horse. Maybe, just maybe, the timing was right, at last.

*****

'Why the hell does everyone want to meet here, and at night?' Nate asked, glancing to Adam in the passenger seat of his car. 'Seriously? Why don't people want to meet for a beer anymore? Even a coffee? Once upon a time...'

Adam groaned. 'No! Please, not the once upon a time lecture. Start that and I'm going to give you the *why-I-hate-SUVs* lecture again,' he said, with a glance around the inside of Nate's large SUV, '...because you know I hate SUVs, you can't see around them, can't see past them... they never go off road so why do people have them in suburbia? Besser blocks on wheels, frigging ridiculous. And—'

'Fine then,' Nate cut him off. 'No *once upon a time* or car lecture. But if we walk in and he's hanging, I am out of there.'

Nate pulled his SUV into the now-familiar street.

'The gate's unlocked if you want to drive in,' Adam pointed out. 'Who is this guy that he has a key?'

'Looks like you and me are the only ones that haven't been given one... yet. You ever get homesick coming back to the old neighbourhood?' Nate asked.

Adam smiled. 'I never lived in here,' he joked.

'You know what I mean,' Nate said, with a smirk.

'Sure. We had a pretty good childhood as childhoods go. Lived on our bikes, had a heap of freedom... you only have to run a few prison counselling sessions and you'll know what a bad childhood was all about.'

'Nature or nurture?' Nate asked, as he pulled up and cut the ignition.

'Tough question.'

Nate parked the car just outside the entrance gates. 'Don't want to get locked in,' he told Adam. He turned off the ignition and they sat momentarily looking at the gloomy building.

'Did you hear back from your police friend?' Adam asked.

'Burnsey, Matt, yeah. He's playing hard to get. Told him we could share info but I think it will be me sharing and him holding out. I told him about Joe and the will.'

'Remember that time when Joe had the burn marks on his face… on his temples?'

Nate turned to look at him. 'I'd forgotten about that. Christ… that's right.'

'What do you think that was? Shock treatment?'

'I'd say so, yeah. He was dazed, kind of out of it, remember?' Nate shook his head. 'This place is unbelievable.'

The two men alighted; they made their way to the entrance of the abandoned asylum. It was eerily quiet and dark. No visible lights could be seen and there was no movement in the grounds.

'He's got to be here if the gates are open. C'mon.' Nate led the way in as Adam reached for his torch in his jacket pocket, and followed close behind.

In the middle of the hallway, a tall, wiry man stood, his arms folded. He wore all black and behind him, suspended from the ceiling, a figure dressed in a white straitjacket and pants hung from the ceiling. The *Truth* sign was pinned to it.

'I'm out of here,' Nate said, turning. Adam grabbed his shoulder and they moved forward.

'Just play it out,' Adam whispered.

Nate sighed and imitated Mac's stance, crossing his arms across his chest. 'So, you're the truth guy!' Nate stated the obvious. 'Pretty lifelike hanging man.'

'Masks today can be pretty realistic,' the man answered.

'So why the theatrics?' Nate asked, his impatience obvious. Adam ribbed him.

Adam introduced himself and Nate; the man in black nodded.

'Ron McIntyre,' he said. 'Prefer to be called *Mac*.'

The two men nodded. Adam studied the man before him;

mid- to late-sixties; rough complexion, thin and scarred. He had tattoos on both arms and his yellowed teeth indicated a history of smoking. His hair—what little there was—was white and cropped close to his scalp.

'So, Mac, why contact us?' Adam asked.

Mac cleared his throat; his chest rattled. 'I contact everyone and anyone who'll listen. No-one really cares. You'd think someone from those ghost tours might be interested in investigating the truth, but nuh. No-one cares. But you guys are investigating somethin'… aren't you?'

'How do you know that?' Nate asked.

'I've seen you come here a few times now,' he hesitated. 'I live here,' he explained, with a nod to the ceiling, 'up there.'

'Here?' Adam asked. 'That was you we heard above us on the first night we were here?'

'Yeah. Thought you were kids and I'd scare you off but then you started chasing me,' he gave a chuckle. 'What are you investigatin'?'

Adam looked to Nate, who spoke up.

'When we were kids a friend of ours was in here… and we want to know what happened to him.'

Mac nodded. He turned and moved to the wall nearest him where he released the rope; the hanging man fell to the ground. 'I might know him.'

'You were a patient here?' Adam asked, his voice laced with caution.

Mac nodded. 'I was brought here 'cause they said I was a troubled teen. Street kid,' he said, and spat on the ground. 'Stole a few things, got into a few fights. The judge said he didn't want to put me in prison. Would have been better off in prison.' Mac took a deep breath. 'Who was your friend?'

'His name was Joe O'Connell,' Adam said.

Mac nodded. 'I knew Joe. Quiet, good at drawing... only person I know who spent two weeks in solitary confinement here and seemed to prefer it.' He reached down and rolled up the hanging man dummy.

'Know what happened to him?' Nate asked.

'Maybe. I know a lot of things. What I want to know is will you tell the truth about this place? Lots of us... who used to be here, we want it to come out; we deserve justice.' He rocked on his heels as he spoke, holding the hanging man tight to his chest, but his voice never rose.

'Why don't you hit up a journalist?' Nate asked.

Mac scoffed. 'Yeah, we've tried that. We've sent letters to the State Government... you know, to the Minister, the Premier, and we've done media interviews. Somehow it always gets buried again... funny that.'

'How many people... patients, are we talking about here?' Nate prodded.

'There's a dozen of us, so far. We were all *patients* here. Victims more like it.' He sighed and seemed to lose his bravado, his body untensed.

'What sort of help did you have in mind?' Adam asked. Unlike Nate, he stood in open body stance... his arms at his side, facing Mac, showing his interest. He'd had enough patients to know how to get the best out of them.

'We want one of those class action things,' Mac said. 'We want someone to take our stories seriously, to write them down and represent us. Joe's story too.'

'That sounds fair,' Adam said. 'What is Joe's story?'

Mac looked away from the men and down the hall. 'That room down there, the last one on the right... that's where they did experiments.'

'Shock treatment?' Nate asked.

Mac nodded. 'More than that… in my group, some of us had shock and we had other stuff injected into us. Lots of stories. Joe was one of those too.'

Adam looked to Nate; they read each other's look. This was getting bigger than they had expected.

'Do you know if he died in here?' Adam asked, returning his attention to Mac.

Mac shook his head. 'No, he got out. Had a bit of help.'

'He got out, alive, and never came back?' Nate exclaimed.

'Well, can't swear on a stack of bibles but he got out; don't think he ever came back. I know someone who can tell you more about that if he's prepared to,' Mac said. 'I could ask him to meet you here if we come to an agreement. See, we've got no money but you could work on that no-win no-fee type of thing that some of the lawyers do. I've heard it on the radio. You could maybe sell the story if you needed to, we could come up with something.'

'Don't worry about the money,' Adam told Mac. 'We've got that covered, and we've got a lawyer on side.' Adam looked to Nate. 'I know a retired psychologist who would come on board, he's open to projects and he's had a bit of experience with hospitals,' Adam chose his words carefully.

'Rob Ware?' Nate asked.

Adam nodded. 'Mac, if your group will meet with us, we can look at what's involved. But it has to be about Joe too. That's our priority right now, and we'd really appreciate meeting this contact of yours who knows more about Joe.'

'I'll talk to them,' Mac said. 'They're not real comfortable around authority, got to be sure no-one is going to be, you know, re-committed.'

Nate pulled out a business card and gave it to Mac. 'That's okay, we get it. No police, no-one with white jackets…'

Mac put the card in his pants' pocket.

'Are you okay here?' Adam asked looking around. 'I could find you somewhere to…'

Mac cut him off. 'I'm good, it's all I know,' he shrugged. 'It's home.'

\*\*\*\*\*

'I'll drop you home and then I'm going back to the *Bishop and Rose* pub,' Nate told Adam. 'Dan's there on surveillance and I told her I'd drop in if we finished early. Come for a drink if you want?'

'Thanks, but I'll go in and call Rob. I'm getting way behind on all this stuff… the more we dig, the more we find.'

The two men spoke about Mac and what they were getting into.

Nate shuddered. 'I'd go insane living in that place at night.'

'I'd be homeless anywhere but there… interesting that it's cathartic for him,' Adam agreed.

'That normal?' Nate asked.

'Nothing is anymore,' Adam said, with a shrug.

Nate pulled up outside Adam's house; it was dark, no-one there to put the night lights on. 'Call me later, after you talk to Rob,' Nate said, and with a salute, drove off. He was at the hotel ten minutes later, after giving the police boys at a random breath testing station a wave as they moved him on. He parked in the hotel carpark. He saw Danielle as soon as he entered; sitting at the bar, her foot tapping along to the music. He watched her in action as she swirled the ice in her glass and drank down the last mouthful of her coke. In the mirror, he saw her eyes never left the pasty, middle-aged man with his young date, even while she pretended to return a text in order to snap a few shots. The kissing shots would get her over the line and a cheque in the mail from the wife. Job done. She glanced at her watch and then up.

Nate caught her eye and joined her at the bar. 'Come here often?' he asked, as she turned to greet him. He dropped down onto the stool beside her.

'Sadly, yes,' she said.

'No rum with that?'

'I'm working, and like a good employee, I don't drink on the job,' she pushed the glass towards him.

'Mm,' he grunted and grabbed the bartender's attention. He ordered her another of the same and a beer for himself.

'How'd it go?' she asked about their asylum visit.

'Bigger than all of us.' He ran her through it. 'So, how'd you go tonight?' Nate asked. He manoeuvered himself so he could see their subject over her shoulder.

'Three offers of a date, two free drink offers, and enough to bury your client,' she said, raising her new glass of coke for a toast. 'A toast to clients who are too stupid to be discreet'.

'I'll drink to that. According to his wife, he's supposedly at a fundraising event tonight for sick kiddies. What a guy. So, how'd you get rid of the suitors? The lesbian excuse again?' Nate took a long draw on his beer and sighed. 'Needed that.'

'I told them I was waiting for my parole officer,' she said, with a grin.

Nate laughed. 'Yeah, great, thanks. Perhaps if you didn't look quite so sexy,' he eyed off her leather pants and fitted top.

'There's a uniform for surveillance?' she asked, eyebrows raised. 'I wasn't trying to blend in, and as you can see, I didn't need to,' she returned her gaze to the client who hadn't noticed anyone else in the bar. 'This one was too easy, I feel bad taking your money.'

'Really?' Nate said, 'sounds promising'.

'Don't worry, I'll get over the guilt,' she assured him. 'It's pretty boring watching two people at it when you're not getting any action yourself. How's your new girl working out?'

'Jess? She's fitted right in,' he said, taking off his jacket.

'Is she in love with you yet?' Danielle teased.

'If not, it's only a matter of time,' Nate said. 'But seriously, not going to happen. I've known Jess for years... we both worked for the cops. I think she's over her crush.'

Danielle grinned. 'She's too doll-like to be a cop. Can't imagine her arresting anyone... managing the kissing booth maybe.'

'Meow, bitchy!' Nate shook his head.

'It's a compliment!'

'Whatever. She wasn't a cop, she was in admin.' He turned his face away as their subject rose and came to the bar to buy drinks. 'What are you like at lifting deceased records from archives?' Nate asked.

'I'm good at everything I put my mind too,' she said, teasingly.

'Mm,' he grunted again. 'I don't doubt that. We need to find a death certificate for Joe, if he ever died, that is.'

## Chapter 18

John Liberman had promised Adam and Nate the relevant paperwork he had collected on his client, Joe. He didn't realise until he went to his law firm's archives just how much he had collected – three large boxes sat shelved bearing Joe's name. John slid one box off the shelf and placed it on a bench; he lifted the lid on the first box and saw the file on top with his own neatly printed handwriting. He had a sudden longing to be back there again – those years when he was less jaded, at the prime of his success and still enjoying the industry. Now, he was at the top and not much gave him a rush these days. In equal measure he felt envious and annoyed by the young bloods in his firm, with their ambition and enthusiasm.

John had emailed Nate after lunch to let him know Joe's ex-wife, Donna, would see them, and Nate had shot back his thanks and a subtle reminder they'd appreciate anything else he had… that was his motivation to finish up early and spend a few hours in archives, packing a box for the two men – Joe's friends.

He sighed as he read back over some of Joe's letters—gentlemanly requests, queries, sometimes poems and drawings, and letters seeking assurances that his mother was cared for and receiving his earnings—all written in a copperplate style of handwriting. John created several piles: letters, clippings, contracts, and general. He pulled out a faded news clipping, and remembered the controversy like it was yesterday:

## BEST-SELLING ARTIST SPENDS HIS DAYS IN A LUNATIC ASYLUM

*By Douglas Reed, Arts and Entertainment Writer*

Joseph O'Connell, 37, Agnew Road Gallery's best-selling artist, can't be found in a den or in a studio like his contemporaries. For the past decade, his depiction of streetscapes, landscapes and portraits largely done in pencil, have transported the viewer to the scene, capturing the essence of the moment like no other artist. But Joseph O'Connell is creating many of those works from memory, from a dormitory of the River Park Lunatic Asylum or as it has recently been renamed, the River Park Hospital.

Declared 'Affected by mental illness' by government doctors after his court appearance in 1985 for the murder of his father, O'Connell remains in the River Park facility where according to insider sources, he draws prolifically.

Doubts over his ability to physically kill his father, the role of his brother, stories of child abuse and the family's story that O'Connell's father was hit elsewhere and came home to die, made for a sensational court case at the time. Since then, he has been all but forgotten, except by the art world, where the strange events may have increased the value of his drawings.

Agnew Road Gallery owner, Justine Applecot, would not be drawn on his present arrangements except to say that she received the occasional piece from him and his work was always in demand. A recent streetscape went for $325,000 at auction.

Several of O'Connell's drawings which the newspaper obtained show patients strapped to beds, images of angels through windows and in one particular portrait, a patient apparently undergoing some form of shock treatment – attachments to his head and a wedge-like object protruding from the mouth.

A spokesperson for the River Park Hospital said 'Mr O'Connell was encouraged to draw and express his artistic talents, and any treatments conducted were done so with the full authority of the patient, the patient's family and their doctor.'

O'Connell's agent, Avery Polson, could not be reached for comment.

John placed the news story on the clippings pile. He knew that Joe's father never liked Joe drawing; said it was a waste of time and 'sissy'. John was fairly confident the staff at the asylum didn't like it either, especially Joe's depiction of the acts going on under their roof. But Joe had become skilled at hiding his work and funnelling it to the outside world.

John picked up a self-portrait that Joe had sketched a year after his arrival at the asylum and gifted to him. He had humorously named it: '*The artist as a lunatic*'. John knew he was joking; Joe never lost his unique way of looking at the world. Several hours later, John put the lid on the archive box, grabbed a black marker and addressed it to Adam and Nate. In a way, it felt like a goodbye.

*****

'Another day, another night, another trip to the bloody asylum... two nights in a row, I'm going to book a room soon,' Nate sighed. 'Want me to drive?' he asked eyeing Adam's black Mercedes SL convertible.

'Nope, unless you want to take her for a spin? Drive home then,' Adam said, as he unlocked the doors and they slid into the cream leather interior. They belted up and Adam steered the car out of the office carpark.

'You know I saw another one of these driving past just the other day... they're as common as...' Nate teased.

Adam grinned. 'Yeah, a specialist at the Greenslopes Hospital drives one. I've passed him on the way to work a few times.'

'How do you know he's a specialist? He might be a male nurse with his dream car and in hock up to his neck.'

'His rego was IFX-HRTS. I'm guessing he's a cardiologist.'

'Mm, probably paid for it with cash. It's not like you to accept something from Winsome,' Nate turned to look at Adam.

'She insisted that she had a right to give me a big gift for the pending thirtieth birthday. I *almost* ruined her figure, remember? So, she wants to commemorate my not-so-auspicious arrival in the world.' He grinned. 'I would have given it back but...'

'But, why should you? You'll hurt her feelings, besides, you've earned it,' Nate said.

'Knowing Mum, I'll be earning it for a while.'

They drove in silence for a while, before Adam spoke again.

'You've got one minute,' Adam said.

Nate glanced at him. 'What for?'

'To stop the tapping, drives me nuts. I'm going to get an eject button on that seat.'

'If you let me drive I won't be able to tap, because I'll have both hands on the wheel,' Nate said. He wiped his hands on his pants and sat still. 'Where are you at with your Joe stuff?'

'I've left a message for my banker friend about that private account, but I haven't had much luck finding any resident or visiting psychologists who practised at the asylum who'll talk. The first one I tracked down died a decade ago, another won't speak with me, and a third has onset dementia.'

'Thought as much. I've had no luck with a death certificate for Joe, and if there was one, I'm pretty sure Dan would find it. But, Joe's wife said she'll see us,' Nate announced.

'Really? Why didn't you tell me earlier?' Adam said, taking his eyes momentarily off the road to look at Nate. 'That's great.'

'I only heard early afternoon. John got clearance and Dan managed to contact her in Dubbo.'

'Road trip then,' Adam said. 'Have fun.'

Nate laughed. 'Right, so you're not coming?'

'C'mon, you and Dan will have a ball. But I don't mind a good drive,' Adam said, almost to himself.

'Yeah, remember the school holidays when you came away with us on that road trip? Every other year we went to Straddie, but that time Mum and Dad decided to hit the highway,' Nate shook his head. 'If they weren't lost, they were fighting about being lost, or arriving in small towns too late to get into the caravan parks. Dad always wanted to drive one town further.'

Adam laughed at the memory. 'You were car sick most of the way, and remember that night we had to set up tents in a bush area because we drove for too long and then couldn't get a hotel room anywhere, and the next morning we woke to the Hare Krishnas' singing?'

The two men laughed at the memory. Nate continued. 'Mum swore we were all going to be murdered, and loaded us into the car so fast, she almost left Dad behind. The poor peace-loving Krishnas were happy to share their lentils!'

'Least it was Straddie or Bribie pretty much every year after that,' Adam said. 'It was good of them to take me along.'

'C'mon, they had an ulterior motive; it kept me out of their hair so they could drink and play cards with their camping neighbours,' Nate said.

The asylum came into view and Adam drove the now familiar route towards the front gate. He shuddered. 'It doesn't warm on you… still freaks me out every time.'

'You said it. What did Mac say in his message about this guy we're meeting?' Nate asked.

'Nothing much more than what he said on the night. Dave used to work there as a warden or something like that, and was prepared to meet with us… he knew Joe, and he had some stuff that might help us. That was it. He gave me Dave's phone number and hung up. When I rang Dave to lock it in, he said even less.'

'Least he wants to meet at dusk… still a bit of light around,' Nate said.

'He must want to show us something here,' Adam suggested. 'John knew this guy's name too, from Joe's will. He'd left him something, allegedly.'

'Joe did alright for himself given what he went through,' Nate said. 'Hard to make a living as it is without trying to support your mother and create art while inside an asylum.'

Adam parked where they could see if someone approached them, and outside the gates for a quick exit. 'Back again,' he said.

'The River Park Lunatic Asylum,' Nate muttered looking around, 'welcome home.'

*****

The derelict asylum looked a little better in the red and orange tones of dusk; not much better, but at least the sounds and shadows weren't as accentuated. They sat for a few minutes, studying the area. A man came from inside the grounds towards them to unlock the gate; he held a keyring laden with keys.

'Still thinks he's the warden,' Nate said, breaking the silence.

'I guess that's him. Looks small to be a warden... can't imagine he could control anyone who went off the rails.'

'And that'd be most of them. Let's go,' Nate said, and pushed open the car door. He raised his hand to the man who met them at the gate. 'Don't know why they bother locking up... seems more people are getting in than out these days,' Nate said in a low voice.

Dave Trigg was a slight man, a little hunched, and a head shorter than the two men. His face said he had seen a few things in his time; he was marked with distinct ageing lines; his eyes were rheumy and his face downcast. But he looked sorry, not cruel. He stood aside, allowed them to enter and locked the gate behind them.

Nate did the introductions.

He nodded. 'Trigg,' he said, 'Dave.'

'Been a while since you've been here, Dave?' Adam asked.

'You can say that again,' he looked towards the building. 'Still got some contacts though, a few privileges,' he jangled the keys. 'Miserable bloody place, they should pull it down.'

'Why exactly are they leaving it up?' Nate asked.

'Beats me. Not bloody heritage-listed, that's for sure,' he sighed. 'I'll give you boys a tour, hey? Then, we can talk about Joe. C'mon.' He walked ahead with the two men in tow.

Adam fell slightly behind. He could do without the tour… historic misery never did much for him. Nate on the other hand loved the scene of a crime.

'So, you were a warden, Dave?' Adam asked.

'God no, I was a nurse. Did that lawyer tell you I was a warden?'

'John? No, I don't know where we got that idea from,' Nate said, with a confused look towards Adam. He was careful not to land anyone in deep water. 'We probably got it wrong. It was Mac who originally said we should meet with you… that you could help us solve the Joe mystery.'

Dave sighed. 'Joe, a gentle soul. I remember him like it was yesterday. Some people, well they didn't belong here; he was one of them.'

'Who was in charge when Joe was here, do you remember?' Adam asked.

Dave made a snorting sound. 'Who could forget. Digby, Superintendent Gregor Digby. Arsehole to work for, arsehole to the patients. He had his mates in high places, in the government, nothing stuck to him.'

'Is he still alive?' Nate asked.

'Don't know,' Dave said. 'Don't see why not… he'd only be in his sixties or so. Probably still working and creating misery somewhere else.'

'I'll add him to my list,' Nate said with a glance to Adam.

They entered the hallway, this time seeing it clearer in the afternoon hues. They stopped momentarily as the overwhelming smell of the first room hit them.

Dave turned to them. 'You haven't already had a tour have you because we can skip it if you have?'

'No, we'd like a tour, thanks,' Nate assured him, open to Dave's insider take on the place.

He nodded and continued, stopping to swear as the stale odour hit him. 'Jesus,' Dave muttered. 'This was the mess hall. Didn't stink then, but you get these bloody kids larking in here… pissing against the wall, doing their graffiti art if you can call it that.'

Nate nodded, trying not to breathe in as they followed Dave through the room. The next area had large chunks of the roof missing; the ventilation helped.

'This is where the women slept… and the room next to this…' he continued to walk at a quick pace as though he was on the clock, '…this room will interest you. This is where they—we—performed medical treatments.' He swallowed and looked away from the men.

'Experiments?' Adam asked.

'Sometimes,' Dave nodded, not meeting their eyes. 'I was a graduate nurse – young, stupid, did what I was told… but no excuses. Most of the time, I handed out medication, sedated, did the basic stuff… and sometimes, I assisted in here.' He moved away from the room and into an area that both men recognised.

'Joe's ward,' Nate said.

'Just by the wall there,' Dave agreed. 'I heard you found his diary...'

'We did. How did you hear?' Adam said.

Dave tapped his nose. 'I have my sources.' He gave them a wink.

'Is there anything else we should have found?' Nate asked, not happy that Dave had some information that couldn't be placed.

Dave nodded. 'Yep, come this way.'

Nate and Adam exchanged looks. Nate gave a slight shrug and followed, with Adam close behind. They followed Dave down the hall – he seemed to become more shrivelled the further they ventured into the asylum. He casually called out locations and purposes; Adam glanced through empty window frames to the outside. In the light of day, he imagined being inside and wishing for that freedom.

'This is it,' Dave said, and entered an abandoned room not much bigger than a cupboard. Shelves still lined one side of the wall. The reverse side had several iron frames, the balance of the shelves were gone or broken in pieces on the floor. Above them was a small skylight, not big enough for an adult to pass through. 'This is where we kept the medical supplies, and this is how I helped Joe get away.'

Nate looked around. 'Did you hide him in here?'

'Nope.' Dave leaned down and slid a small square of masonite away from the wall. It had created the effect of a fake wall, behind it was an opening to the outside. 'Coming?' Without waiting Dave sat and slid through. Nate looked at Adam, and turned to follow suit. Adam followed, his feet hitting earth moments later. He smiled when he saw where they had come out.

'This looks familiar,' Nate said, reading his mind. In

alignment was the wire fence where Joe once sat talking with them. The men wandered over and Dave followed.

'At night it's easy to get over the fence if you're a bit agile. There's no real security… it wasn't a prison, just a secure hospital. My car was parked just there,' he nodded to the nearby carpark.

'Joe waited in your car for you?' Nate asked.

Dave nodded. 'Well he was supposed to.'

'But he didn't? What happened?' Adam asked.

'Why did you help him?' Nate added.

Dave took a deep breath and shoved his hands in the pockets of his grey pants. 'I owed his brother a favour,' he said.

'The brother that disappeared…Stephen?' Nate's eyes narrowed.

'Yeah, that's him,' Dave said. He turned and began to walk back toward the building and the two men followed. 'I met him when I was working on a building site, I was only a young bloke then, left school early… it was before I decided to do nursing,' Dave explained. 'This was in the days before they had all that workplace holding-your-hand stuff, and being a skinny little runt, I was the brunt of all jokes and beatings. Until Stephen O'Connell arrived. He was strong and he knew how to fight, said he learned it from his father.'

Adam and Nate exchanged knowing looks.

Dave stopped outside the main entrance to the building and crossed his arms across his chest. 'Yeah, well he said he had a brother about my size, and told the rest of the boys if they wanted to pick on someone, make it him or else. A few of them tried it on but you can't work if you've broken an arm or leg, so they quickly learned to leave us both alone.'

'So… how did you meet Joe?' Adam asked.

'Just a coincidence really,' Dave said, with a shrug. 'Stephen had spoken about Joe every now and then… he was kind of proud of him; said he was an artist and nothing like himself. It was about three or four years later when I graduated and came to work here that I met him. I knew right away… sure O'Connell is a common enough name, but a Joe O'Connell, a slight guy who was an artist with a brother Stephen… it had to be him. And he should never have been in here; just got himself a bit mixed up with his history I think.'

'So, you broke him out?' Nate asked.

'I'd befriended him, got him the arty stuff he needed. I guess, eventually he trusted me. Then, he came to me one day with a plan. I was only too happy to oblige. Stephen was a good bloke, and his younger brother, Joe, deserved to get on with his life. And as I said, I owed my life to his brother, I've no doubt of it.' Dave looked to the hole in the wall they had slipped through. 'And that's how I got him out of the building… but our plan went off the rails,' he said, and scoffed. 'I didn't exactly get him off the grounds,' he said.

'Hold up… so he was supposed to wait in your car, but you didn't get him out of here? So, could Joe have still died here? Did he drown?' Adam asked.

'Not on my shift,' Dave confirmed, 'I'm sure I would have heard. I left here about a month after I got him out of the building, never heard from him again, and no-one ever put two-and-two together. Why are you two looking for him?'

'We knew him when he was in here…' Nate started.

'You're those two kids,' Dave smiled, looking at them with trust for the first time. 'The two boys he drew and talked about. That you?'

'That's us,' Adam agreed.

'Took your time looking him up.' Dave said, matter-of-factly.

Nate ignored the comment. 'So, you don't know where he is or what happened to him after you got him out of there?' he said with a nod to the escape hole.

Dave started walking towards the gate where Adam's car was parked.

'That I couldn't tell you. The day of the breakout, he said he wanted me to drop him back at his family home. I told him that would be the first place they'd look for him, but he said he didn't care, he wanted to be dropped at the front gate. I offered him some money, but he said he had all that sorted.'

'So, he mightn't have actually gone into the house; he could have just taken off,' Nate mused.

'Our plan didn't get that far,' Dave said. 'When I left work and came back to my car, ready to smuggle him out, he was gone.'

'What do you mean?' Adam asked, trying to read how much of Dave's story held truths; his body language didn't match the whole story and the car seemed to be a sticking point.

'Gone… he'd bolted. He didn't wait for me in the back of the car like planned.' Dave shrugged. 'And before you ask, I don't know why. I don't know if he got cold feet and just took off in case he got spotted, or whether someone found him in there… but I never saw him again.'

'Crap,' Nate said. 'So, he could be out there anywhere; or he might have drowned in the river; or he could have been in solitary confinement for months!'

'Yeah, that's the strength of it. Never heard from him or Stephen again.'

Nate exhaled loudly. 'Chasing our tails some days.'

'That symbolic?' Adam asked nodding at the broken crucifix pendant hanging around Dave's neck.

Dave reached up and touched the pendant.

'Am I losing my religion, you mean?' he said, with a grin. 'Nuh. My Mum gave me this and I couldn't part with it even though I broke it.' He shrugged. 'Still got my faith… need to know there's something after.'

'Hope you're right,' Adam said. He cleared his throat, surprised at the wave of loneliness that just overtook him. He continued. 'Not that it's any of our business, but we're trying to eliminate leads… did Joe set up a regular bank transfer to you into a private account?'

Dave laughed. 'No, I didn't do that much for him. But he did leave me a small amount in his will; I just found out. More than I'll be able to leave any of my kin. He was like that, Joe was, always grateful for the little things. All I did was bring him pencils and art paper when he ran short, and…' he stopped and swallowed the words he was about to say. 'He was always grateful,' he left it at that.

Adam exhaled and looked at Nate, frustration written all over his face. 'Two steps forward and one step back,' he said.

# Chapter 19

Adam stormed out of his office, startling Jessica at reception. Close on his heels was his patient – a man in his late twenties, well-dressed and looking equally as annoyed.

'Would it kill you to give me an interview since I'm here and paid for your time anyway?' the man asked.

'Yeah, it'd kill me,' Adam said.

Nate stuck his head out of his office, hearing the raised voices. 'Okay?' he asked Adam.

'Jason, who works for *The Times* is just leaving,' Adam said.

'Don't suppose I can get a refund?' he asked, with a glance to Jessica.

'No sorry,' she said. 'You've taken up Dr Murphy's time and the place of a patient... so maybe you should have used the time more wisely for some... self-help?' she said with a raised eyebrow. 'Want a receipt?'

Nate grinned, as he leaned on the door frame, arms folded and watched the show.

Adam opened the door for Jason, who turned his attention back to Adam and smirked at him.

'You know, I reckon it's true... I've seen the photos and you look nothing like your father, more like the Prime Minister...'

Adam lunged at the reporter; Jessica gave a yelp of surprise and Nate moved at the speed of light to come between the two men. He pushed Adam back against the wall and the reporter out the door.

'I could have you for assault,' Jason sneered at them, straightening his collar.

'We could have you for impersonating a patient,' Nate answered, cutting Adam off. 'Get the hell out of here.'

The reporter smirked at Adam and headed down the stairs. Adam shook himself free of Nate and slammed the door.

'I'm sorry, Adam,' Jessica said, 'He sounded so genuine.'

'Not your fault, Jess. It's another leftover from Mum's performance last week,' Adam said, and sighed. 'Thanks,' he said, with a glance to Nate, and a barely discernible nod. He returned to his office and closed the door.

'The perils of fame,' Nate said to Jessica.

'They're idiots,' she said. 'Do they really think Adam's going to give them an interview just because they've gone to the trouble of getting in to see him? I'm going to become much better at being a bouncer,' she said baring her teeth.

Nate shuddered. 'I believe you.'

'Is he close to his mum?' she asked, with a glance to Adam's closed door.

Nate shook his head. 'She wasn't around much when we were kids. Adam's grandmother pretty much raised him. She had a granny flat on the property and moved into the main house every time they were away, which was a lot. She's great, Audrey, a real character. But when his dad died, Adam and Winsome got a bit closer.'

'Sad really. Why have kids if you don't want to have a family?' Jessica said.

'Beats me. I'd like more kids, a sister or brother for Matilda,' he said, in an unguarded moment.

'Really?' Jessica said, surprised.

'Yeah, well, it's a good gene pool, why waste it?' he said, putting himself back on comfortable territory.

She rolled her eyes. 'So, when are you leaving for Dubbo?'

'In about thirty minutes, as soon as Dan gets here,' he said.

'They've got a zoo there,' Jessica teased him, 'You'll fit right in.'

*****

Danielle yawned, stretched and glanced over at Nate behind the wheel. 'Want to sing some show tunes?'

'God no... like what?'

'You know, something from *West Side Story* or *Sound of Music* or...'

'God no,' Nate said, again. 'How do you even know those songs?' he asked half amused, and half fearful she would burst into song.

'My sister loves musical theatre... I mean loves it... lives and breathes it. She's hoping to break into the scene,' Danielle said.

'Right, well good luck to her.'

'Or we could do some rock classics...' Danielle continued. 'My music list is pretty cool. At least think about it,' she said.

'Okay...' he narrowed his eyes as he thought, then shook his head. 'No, no show tunes or sing-alongs in any genre!'

'Such a spoilsport,' she said, and started singing a song Nate recognised.

'Who sings that?' he asked.

'Amy Shark.'

146

'That's right, let's leave it to her, hey?' Nate teased, and Danielle thumped his arm, 'Well, what do you want to do?'

'Nothing. I want to be there now.' He glanced to the reverse mirror. 'I love a road trip for about an hour, maybe two, then it's just so boring.'

'Well you've called everyone you know, twice,' she said, '…we could play one of those games… you know 'What am I?' or 'I Spy'… you must have played them when you were a kid, travelling.'

Nate sighed. 'I was too busy throwing up from car sickness.'

They drove in silence for a while. Then Nate spoke again. 'So, you know where to go when we get there?'

'You've asked me that twice already,' she said, gruffly with a roll of her eyes. 'I know where she lives and as soon as we enter Dubbo, I'll be sure to direct you.'

'Right.'

Silence again.

'Jessica seems to be working out well,' Danielle said.

'Yep, she's good,' Nate agreed. 'and Adam's nice too.'

Danielle grinned. 'Smart arse.'

'I know you want to talk about him,' Nate teased. 'Strong, silent type he is… single, just waiting for the right woman… wow, could that be you?'

Danielle punched his arm again. 'Shut up. Fine then, we won't talk about our *colleagues*,' she said, emphasising the word. 'I've got a friend that you might like…'

'Nope.' He shut the conversation down.

'When do you think you'll get back on the horse then?' she asked him.

Nate frowned and said nothing. He grabbed the steering wheel a little tighter as a road truck thundered past on the other side of the road, followed by a caravan and a stream of cars stuck behind it.

'Right then,' she continued. 'So back to something you can talk about...'

Nate sighed. 'I'm not trying to be an arsehole,' he said, considering what to say next and how to say it. 'I just don't need to be thinking about all that shit... I'm in that headspace enough in my own time, I'm tired of analysing myself to death and feeling sorry for myself.'

'It will pass, you know that,' Danielle said.

'First-hand experience?'

'Unrequited love,' she said, then made a sound between a snort and a laugh.

'Yeah, I've heard all the consolation sayings: it'll pass, you'll realise it's for the best, what doesn't kill you will make you stronger, you're not the first and won't be the last, her loss, it won't always be like this, and my favourite... God loves you.'

'Ha, I'm sure he does,' Danielle agreed and patted Nate's knee. 'I get it, sorry, no more motivational thoughts. So...' she changed the subject back to work, '... why do you think Joe befriended you two... I mean why would he bother with two kids or was there a connection?'

Nate looked at her and back to the road. 'I don't think he befriended us intentionally... he was there, we were hanging around, we talked. There weren't too many other people visiting him. It must have been a pretty isolated life in that place... probably hard to strike up normal conversations.'

'Really?' she asked suspiciously. 'Just random?'

'Yeah really. You watch too many soapies – this is not *Home and Away*.'

'But it could be! You don't think he could be connected to you or Adam, or your parents?' Danielle pushed.

Nate frowned. 'So, you think he was hanging out there, waiting for Adam and me... two kids he didn't know from a bar of soap who could tell him nothing and give him nothing?'

Danielle shrugged. 'He's not… related?'

'Neither of us is adopted if that's where you are going; he's not our real father languishing in there, trying to get a glimpse of one of us, and I don't think he's Uncle Joe.'

'I'm just putting some theories out there,' she said.

Nate put on the indicator, and with a glance to the side mirror, pulled out, overtaking another long road train. He pulled back into the lane and put some distance between them. 'Damn, there's two bloody caravans ahead. We shouldn't have had that coffee break… I'm sure we've already overtaken them earlier.'

'They should only be allowed on the road between midnight and 6am,' Danielle agreed.

Nate laughed. 'Yeah, don't say that around my folks… they're about to do the grey-nomad thing. Dad's getting a van designed for their needs.'

'Yeah? What if they hate it?'

'He's not expecting to. Guess he'll just sell it if it doesn't work for them.' For a moment he envied them – a long and mostly happy marriage, now content and travelling together in retirement. If only he could hit the road and forget everything.

'Anyway, don't change the subject,' Danielle said, bringing him back to the now. 'Could Joe have known who Adam is… you know, the kid of a rich and famous mother? Did Joe know Winsome? Did he paint her?'

Nate thought about it for a moment. 'It wasn't common knowledge that Winsome lived in Brisbane, half the time she didn't anyway; you didn't see Adam's parents around much. Like I was telling Jess, Adam was more or less raised by his grandmother who lived with them… well in a granny flat at the back of their place which was bigger than our whole house. But that's a good thought. Look up who did Winsome's portrait.'

Danielle grabbed her phone and opened the search engine. 'No-one called Joe,' she said, after a few minutes. 'An artist by the name of Angelo Salvatine.' She put her phone away. 'Do you think Adam could be the former Prime Minister's—'

Nate cut her off. 'No! And don't ever raise that with him; he'll freak out. He hates that shit. No, I think meeting Joe was just a coincidence. He liked to sit on the boundary, where he could see the river and draw it… we used to hang around the river playing in the trees and in the water.'

Nate slowed down as the speed limit dropped at the entry to the town. The sign read: 'Welcome to Dubbo'.

'Thanks, great to be here,' he responded. 'Right navigator, step up… where to?'

\*\*\*\*\*

The house that Joe's ex-wife Donna lived in was small, city small… unusual in a country town. It sat tucked between two larger properties like an afterthought. Nate drove past slowly and saw all the space was in the backyard… a long narrow block. The roof was a rusty red, the front timber wall looked in good enough condition, but the sides of the house missed out on the lick of paint the front enjoyed. Nate drove to the end of the street—a dead end—and returned to the house to park opposite. He saw the curtain move slightly.

'As my grandmother would say, get your best china out, we're here,' he said. 'How did Donna sound on the phone?'

'Okay… curious, open to talking with us,' Danielle said.

'Mm, interesting,' Nate said. 'C'mon.'

'Now be nice…' Danielle said.

'When am I not nice?' Nate asked, surprised.

'You can be a bit, well, abrupt, you know, impatient… have the offered cup of tea, compliment the curtains, take a biscuit, that kind of thing.'

He scoffed. 'Garbage, I'm always nice.' He exited the car.

She followed him out, mumbling 'I rest my case.' Danielle swung her handbag over her shoulder and took the lead up the pathway. She smiled at the woman who opened the door before they got to knock.

'Donna? I'm Danielle, this is Nate, thanks for seeing us,' Danielle said, extending her hand.

The plump woman in front of them smiled and nodded. She straightened a clean frock that was tired and pale from washing. Her tied-back, grey-toned hair looked the same – clean and neat. She gave Danielle's hand a limp shake and extended her hand to Nate to do the same.

'Thanks for seeing us,' he said, again. 'Guess our call was a bit of a bolt out of the blue.'

'You can say that again. Come in, please.' She held the screen ajar, leaving Nate to close it behind them as she led the way down the hallway which ran right down the centre of the house. Two small rooms peeled off either side until they came to the kitchen and dining room at the back of the house. It opened onto a small deck and overlooked a yard and creek.

'How lovely,' Danielle said.

'I live at this end of the house,' Donna agreed. 'It's really nice of a morning when the sun streams in. I'll put the jug on. Tea?'

'Love one, thanks,' Nate said, with a smirk to Danielle.

'That would be great, thank you,' Danielle said. 'I'll help.'

'Milk's in the fridge… there's a milk jug if you like…'

'No, it's just us,' Nate smiled and she returned his smile. 'You have a lovely home,' he attempted and was rewarded with a nod from Danielle.

'It's comfortable, does me just fine,' she agreed. 'Needs a bit of money spent on it, but you know how it is.'

'Do I ever,' Nate said.

Donna continued. 'It was my grandparents', they once owned the entire corner. Then my parents got into a spot of trouble and subdivided. This is what's left, but I was never much for mowing so I don't spend any time regretting that.'

'I hear you,' Nate agreed, taking the suggested seat at the dining room table as Danielle placed the milk and sugar in the middle of the table, and Donna shook some Iced VoVo biscuits from an open tray in the fridge onto a plate and put them in the centre. Nate reached for one straight away.

'Men, always hungry,' Donna smiled and encouraged him.

'Can't fill him up,' Danielle agreed.

Nate accepted the tea with thanks and dived straight into his topic. 'I knew Joe, I met him when I was a kid.'

Donna's eyes widened. 'Oh…' she looked to Danielle, 'you mentioned you are investigating Joe's past and patients from the hospital… but…' she turned back to Nate. 'How did you… were you one of the boys… those two boys?'

Nate smiled and nodded.

'Wow.' She looked at him with a new fondness. 'I think you saved him you boys, gave him something to look forward to, or made him feel a bit human.' She gave a slight shrug. 'I remember the lawyer telling me that.'

'John Liberman?' Nate asked.

'Yes, John Liberman,' Donna confirmed. 'The other lad, what was his name?'

'Adam,' Nate answered.

'Yes,' she nodded, 'Adam, that was him. Well, imagine that. I heard Joe thought you were both destined for great things.'

Nate chuckled. 'Yeah, well don't know about that, but nice that someone thought so.'

'How did you meet, Joe, Donna?' Danielle asked, reaching for a biscuit.

Donna accepted the sugar bowl from Nate and stirred a spoonful into her tea. 'I met him in his early thirties, he'd been a bit of a lost soul, I think. He didn't talk about it much,' she said. 'We worked together. I'm a nurse at the hospital here, was a nurse before I retired. Spent a lot of my early career here… the hospital was good for me, good opportunities, good hours. I was in my early thirties when Joe arrived. He was handsome, and gentle, kept to himself,' she smiled, looked at her tea.

'Bit like me,' Nate said.

Danielle laughed and rolled her eyes. 'So not like Nate,' she told Donna.

Donna grinned. 'He worked in the wards, just taking patients where they had to be, and helping out as required. Always charming and helpful. Soon, he was helping me out a lot, always on my ward,' she smiled at the memory. 'We had a bit of whirlwind romance; married within a year.'

Nate leaned forward, keen to cut to the chase and ask Where was Joe; What happened to him? Danielle nudged him under the table, and instead, he took another biscuit and sat back.

'Our son came pretty soon after,' she said, her voice dropping. Nate suppressed a cough as he nearly choked on his biscuit.

'You had a son? I'm sorry, we didn't know Joe had a son, or for that matter, a wife,' Nate said. 'I don't know why he left a gift to Adam and I if he had a family. We don't need it of course…'

Donna put up her hand to stop him. 'We had a son, Thomas… Tom,' she said, tearing up. 'Joe liked traditional names,' she looked from Nate to Danielle. 'Never liked those trendy names, like Paris and Serendipitii with two 'ii's.' She smiled at her own joke; Danielle smiled and nodded.

'Another tea?' Donna lifted the pot, as a look of impatience flashed across Nate's face.

'Yes, that would be lovely, thank you,' Danielle offered her cup. Donna filled it and turned to Nate.

'I'm good, thanks,' he said.

Donna filled her own cup and reached for the milk, stirring in a little. She sighed. 'Joe didn't cope with the pending birth of Thomas… not one aspect of it. He would lie awake at night when I was pregnant, worried he'd be like his father. That he'd be violent and awful. I tried to help him, tried to make him see that he wasn't like that now, why would he become that?'

Nate nodded. 'I understand that. Adam, he's a psychologist, so he'd know more about this than me, but kids can learn aggression and then it becomes part of their behaviour pattern too. You would have seen some of that nursing?'

Donna nodded. 'Research studies have shown violent patterns of behaviour are transmitted from generation to generation. But Joe, you know him, he was so gentle.'

'I was only a kid when we knew him,' Nate said, 'but he was kind, and artistic, seemed gentle…'

'He was,' Donna agreed, 'he was just that. But the closer we got to the birth, the more unstable he became. He'd have these panic attacks, he'd wake up from dreams where he failed us, and he would disappear for days.' She sighed and reached for her tea.

Nate and Danielle waited. Nate expected the worst.

'What happened?' he asked, eventually. He noticed Donna's hands were shaking slightly.

'He disappeared.'

Danielle groaned, and Donna nodded.

'About two weeks before I was due, he disappeared. I never saw or heard from him again, except through the lawyer. He said Joe had set up a bank account for me and our pending child and that we'd never want for anything.'

Nate's eyes widened; was Donna the owner of the private bank account? No, can't be, he realised, because John knew Donna… he'd know if she was the recipient. His head was spinning with thoughts.

Donna continued. 'I told him I never wanted anything from Joe from the start except for Joe himself. I didn't know where he was getting the money from or that he was wealthy. When John explained, I wanted it even less. I swallowed my pride for Thomas's sake, I'd do anything to give him a good life, what parent wouldn't?'

'But there's a private account out there that someone is still living off,' Nate said, then softened his words. 'We were hoping it was you; that you had a good income and were provided for,' he finished. She shook her head.

'My account isn't private, John knows all about it.'

'And Thomas?' Danielle asked.

'He went the way of his father,' she said.

# Chapter 20

Nate wrapped the towel around his waist and grabbed his ringing phone. He swiped to answer.

'Where are you now?' Adam asked.

'Hey, I'm in a hotel in Gilgandra… or verandah, as Dan keeps calling it,' he moved to the hotel room window and moved the curtain slightly to look out over the carpark.

'Why didn't you stay in Dubbo?'

'We like the look of Gilgandra… got a good oval and grandstand for a morning jog. I'll call you back when I get to the pub… I've got to meet Dan in five minutes for dinner, and I'm just out of the shower.'

He hung up and finished getting dressed.

Minutes later he heard a knock at the door, grabbed his room key, wallet and phone and opened it to greet Danielle.

'We should get a decent meal tonight… a real steak, nothing fancy,' she said.

'Counting on it,' Nate agreed. 'Remind me to call Adam after we order.'

*****

Jessica saw Adam's last client out and locked the door. On hearing it click, he came out of his office.

'It's a wrap for the day?' he asked, walking to the door to close the office blinds.

'It is. Fancy a drink?' she asked.

'Sure, if you want to have it in the office. Nate's calling me back in 10 minutes.'

'Crack open that chardy,' she said, and Adam grinned. He made his way to the minibar in the kitchen, as Jessica found two clean wine glasses.

'You know you don't have to stay back if I've got a late client, I can see them out,' he said, filling the glasses halfway.

She glanced to the clock; it was nearing 6pm.

'It's not that late. Besides, I like to stay back a couple of nights a week just to catch up, so I'd rather do it while someone's here,' she said.

'Is the job okay, what you expected?' Adam asked as he brought their wine glasses over to the waiting room chairs and they sunk into them.

'It's great. I like being out of the city, and I like a small office environment.'

'And there's Nate and me of course,' Adam added.

'Goes without saying,' she said, with a smile.

'Apparently,' he smiled at her. No sooner had they toasted, Adam's phone rang. He put Nate on speaker.

'It's schnitzel night, but Dan and I are having steak, and you?' Nate asked.

'Of course it's schnitzel night,' Adam said, 'isn't it always in country towns? You're on speaker phone and Jess and I are having a glass of white wine with an assortment of cheese and condiments.'

'Really?' Danielle asked her tone far from indifferent.

'No,' Adam answered, 'you'd be lucky to find a stale biscuit in this office.'

'The chardy part is true at least,' Jessica piped in. 'Nate, you had a few bookings today, I've emailed you.'

'Thanks. Missing me?' he teased.

'Hell yeah,' she answered. 'Lucky that with all your backdated invoices, and Adam keeping me busy, I forgot to notice you were gone.'

'Mm, you'll keep.'

'So, you two, what did you find out about Joe?' Adam sat back in the chair, expecting the worst.

Nate ran through their meeting with Donna and the breakdown Joe had before becoming a father. 'But we don't know if he knew anything about his child, because Donna never heard from him again and that was just before she gave birth,' Nate finished.

'A boy or a girl?' Adam asked.

'A son, Thomas,' Nate continued. 'In the end, when Thomas was old enough to start asking the right questions, she told him his father was dead.'

'Christ,' Adam muttered. 'So, where's Thomas? He'd be about ten years younger than us?'

'Six to be exact,' Danielle informed him, 'so he'd be about twenty four now.'

'His mother said he went the way of Joe,' Nate said. 'That's all she'd say… couldn't draw another word from her about Thomas.'

'What does that mean? He's dead, he's artistic, he's in an asylum?' Adam asked.

'And why didn't Joe leave the child his fortune? He knew Donna was having his kid,' Jessica asked.

'He did set up an account up for them through John the solicitor, but Donna initially didn't want it. She accepted it for Thomas of course,' Nate said.

Danielle continued. 'Donna told us that after watching Joe's deterioration, she was scared in the end – scared that maybe Joe or his brother Stephen had murdered their father, scared that madness ran in the family, scared Joe or Stephen would try and make some claim on Thomas and take him. She said that when she first met Joe she knew his history, but it was only after he started to breakdown, and he deserted her that she began to think she was naïve… I guess she was also pissed off.'

Nate picked up the conversation. 'She said she become hyper-vigilant watching Thomas for signs of a predisposition to mental illness… she's a nurse, she's pretty cluey. So, she changed their family name, organised a fake death certificate to show Thomas had died at birth, then they moved to Newcastle and started over. But she came back to Dubbo a few years later to nurse her dying mum and stayed.'

Adam took a deep breath. 'So where is Thomas now?'

Nate sighed. 'She wouldn't tell me and won't say anything more about him until I produce a death certificate for Joe and Stephen, or could show her a body.'

'Seriously?' Adam set his wine down, stood up and paced. 'She hasn't seen or heard a word from Joe or Stephen in years and now she wants evidence they're not coming back? I'd say the odds are pretty good, she's safe.'

'I asked her why she contacted John to have Joe declared legally dead now, and she said the timing was right,' Nate said. 'She wouldn't elaborate.'

Danielle jumped in: 'She had pencil sketches stuck on the fridge with magnets. They were good, really good.'

'By whom?' Adam asked.

'Well that's the thing,' Danielle said, 'there was a squiggle in the corner and a date. I could see it was this year, so they were recent, but it was just initials.'

'It's anyone's guess,' Nate said. 'It could be Joe or...'

'I wonder if Thomas really does take after his father,' Adam added.

## Chapter 21

The irony was not lost on Robert Ware as he waited in the boardroom of Adam and Nathan's new office. It had been adapted for him so he could join them a couple of days a week and help prepare the potential class action. But there was a time when he was the hotshot; when he was Adam's advisor during the young man's PhD. He glanced out the window that looked onto the building next door with a glimpse of the parkland behind, but what he really saw was his own reflection in the window. His thinning grey hair, his thinning body… he had his son to thank for that. He was a man grateful to come out of retirement for a while and feel needed.

He had known the boys most of their life; he was their junior rugby league coach for a few seasons and their cricket coach. They played in the same team as his son, Luke. The very same son who was now in prison for white collar crime.

Thinking of Luke always made Rob wonder where he had gone wrong. He was there for the kid, as much as any other father. Maybe Luke had it too easy, he thought. Luke was brilliant with numbers, probably too brilliant. He was Chief Financial Officer for a bank and did a bit of creative embezzlement… got away with it for a long time. But something told Rob that Luke wanted to be caught. Guilt or grandstanding? He admitted it was impossible for a psychiatrist to try and analyse his own son when all he saw was his own traits. Deb, Rob's wife and Luke's mother had suffered a stroke after Luke was sentenced and needed part-time care, it was the impetus for Rob retiring.

Onward, he thought, filing away that history. With Nate and Danielle back in town, he agreed to drop in at the end of the day to meet the team. He turned when he heard the office door opening. They had returned.

Adam's eyes widened. 'Rob, why didn't you come downstairs and join us?' he said, embracing him. Nathan pushed him out of the way and did the same.

'I thought there'd be plenty of nights for that. I took the opportunity to check out my new digs and bring in some of my things,' he said, with a nod to the coffee cup and a couple of pens.

'So, the delivery van has just left?' Nate joked.

Adam introduced Jessica and Danielle and as no-one was in a rush to begin their evening, they sat around the table, the men reminiscing before Nathan and Adam filled Rob in on their expectations.

'So, a class action…' Rob said, thinking aloud. 'You'd need at least seven patients to do that.'

'I think that's realistic; I think it will be a lot more,' Adam said. 'We don't know the extent of it, but you've done this before… basically, we're thinking you could interview and record anyone who wants to be part of it, starting with Mac, and manage the process. I don't know how many hours they'll need; I can probably take on an extra two clients a week if that helps.'

'Two would be full capacity for your diary at the moment,' Jessica piped in, 'especially if you're working with Nate too.'

'Okay,' Adam said. 'We've got John Liberman from Liberman & Clarke Solicitors who will help with any legals and do it pro bono. I didn't mention a class action to him, but if it involves Joe in any capacity, he'll help if we can bring it all together.'

'And if we find there is a case to answer to,' Nate added, 'John will do it no win, no fee.'

'Sounds good. Big firm Liberman & Clarke, what's in it for him?' Rob asked.

'He's a friend of Joe's too,' Adam said. 'Joe left him a little inheritance so he's investing his time and inheritance if needed.'

'Great. This Joe had some interesting friends. Who was he?' Rob asked.

'We don't really know,' Nate continued. 'He was our friend... a small, quiet, artistic guy who sat on the other side of the wire fence and sketched us in pencil, and told us we could be anything we wanted.'

'Then left you what he had to make that a reality,' Rob said, with a sigh. 'Poor fellow. So, what's your role in all this?' he asked Nate.

'I'm investigating what happened to Joe and his brother... we don't know how either of them died, or if they are even dead,' he shrugged. 'Adam's working through Joe's diary, looking for a private bank account and past asylum staff; we've got a few leads,' he said to Rob. 'Dan will back us up with research, Jess with admin.'

Danielle nodded. 'I can do any follow-up, research, fact-checking, surveillance, whatever, on anyone you see or on any of their stories, Rob.'

He nodded. 'Great. All sounds great. But...'

'We can meet your rate,' Nate said, 'well, within reason.'

'I'm very reasonable, in fact, I think my wife would pay you to get me out of the house,' Rob smiled. 'Perhaps we can work on a success fee instead.'

Adam and Nate visibly brightened; there would be few funds coming in, especially from the claimants.

'That'd be brilliant,' Nate said.

'And, I'd like to meet with John Liberman as soon as possible.'

'That's easy,' Adam said.

'What I want to say though,' Rob continued, 'is that doing something like this—as Adam will remember—is huge. Remember when you did your placement with my firm and we were doing the victims' statements for the rural fire class action?'

Adam nodded. 'It was full-on,' he agreed.

'It was worse then because we had to do the groundwork in Queensland but then the law firm had to run it through the Federal Court of Australia, and for one particular class action through the New South Wales Supreme Court. Crazy stuff. Now, that's changed and the legal eagles can do class actions here.'

'So, what's the worst-case scenario?' Danielle asked.

'We will be seeing a lot of very angry, distressed, victims, who may not be the easiest people to deal with… they've been through a lot. There'll be a lot of admin work… recording statements, cleaning them up, filing them, looking for parallels across all stories… a lot.'

Jessica piped in, 'I'd like the challenge and it will be good for my CV.'

'Are you thinking about your next job already?' Nate asked.

'No Nate, I'm going to stay with you guys forever,' she said, sincerely.

'Good,' Nate said, and smirked.

Adam continued for Rob. 'Most class actions have an opt-out option, so we might do a lot of work and then someone decides they don't want to go ahead with it and pulls out. Frustrating but that's how it is… it can be very traumatic to revisit a lot of old stuff.'

'Exactly,' said Rob. 'Most won't have a dollar to their name, so a win could help them towards a better retirement. As long as we have it in our minds that it might be an unhappy ending and not have huge expectations… the State can pull out all their resources.'

'We might find ourselves needing security,' Nate added. 'If the truth has been hidden… if there's anything to dig up, perhaps there's someone or a group who want to keep it hidden.' He turned to Danielle and Jessica. 'You need to be sure that you know and accept that risk. We'll understand if you don't and we'll work around it.'

'Perhaps we should all sleep on it then,' Adam said, 'make sure we know what we are in for and if we want to take the ride.'

'I'm in,' Jessica said.

'Me too,' Danielle added.

They all looked to Rob.

'Glad to join the team,' he said.

# Chapter 22

Adam closed the door, threw his keys on the stand near the door and flicked on the lights. He didn't rush home of an evening... he was still not used to the complete silence of being alone; it had taken him some time to remember what he did when he was just one.

Stephanie had been loud, colourful... she had filled the house – most of the time though, he was glad it was over. For now, he wasn't keen to get straight back into a relationship; he couldn't be bothered to do the work required. Clubs and pubs weren't his scene; it only took a drink or two to become maudlin in those situations, and soon he found himself wishing he was home on the couch with the remote, the footy on the TV, and a beer in his hand. He wasn't interested in phone swiping or internet dating, but he figured he might have to get with 21$^{st}$ century dating sometime soon.

Some days he just wanted something physical. A friend with benefits would be ideal like Danielle had joked about, but he knew only too well that in Dan's case, he'd have to deal with expectations the morning after. Still, he was open to the idea.

He thought about getting a dog for company; a dog he could run with and that could come to the office as well – the patients would probably like that. It was three years since his dog passed away, he was almost ready to commit again. Sometimes, he thought Nate was lucky to have Matilda… sure, it meant he was forever connected to his ex-wife, but he also had someone to look after and invest love in.

He moved down the hallway into the bedroom, stripping off layers as he went. He hit the shower, standing under the stream of hot water, before turning off the hot tap only for a final cold shock. Drying himself down, he threw on a pair of jeans and a long-sleeved T-shirt and moved out to the kitchen to consider dinner. Adam's phone rang and he looked at the screen, surprised.

'Jess? Everything okay?' His new office manager had never called him after hours before.

'Yes, no… not sure,' she said. 'It's Nate. Just as I was leaving, I think his divorce papers arrived.'

'Oh. Where is he?' Adam asked.

'I don't know. I think he was heading home, but he looked… angry, devastated, I couldn't tell… I've only ever known him when he's happy or smart-arse. He barely said two words as we left, and he got in his car and just sped off.'

'Hey, thanks for calling me. I'll try him now,' Adam said. 'Really appreciate it, Jess.'

'Sure. See you tomorrow,' she said and hung up.

Adam took a deep breath and finding Nate's number in his mobile, called it. The number rang out. He went back to his room, slipped on his runners, pocketed his wallet and keys on the way out, and headed for Nate's place.

*****

**Extract from Joe's diary:**

*My friends, this won't make sense to you now, and it shouldn't… that's a very good thing. But when you grow up you have to* remember to be a little kind to yourself, and to other people too. It's like Atticus Finch said in 'To Kill a Mockingbird' (that's a very good book if you get a chance to read it): "You never really understand a person until you consider things from his point of view... until you climb into his skin and walk around in it." I try and remember that every day in here because there are people that are in charge who seem insane, and people who are insane who seem to have a sound grasp on life. Most odd.

One day you may learn of what I have done and why I am in this hospital; I make no excuses but understand that it is a half-true. What I did and what I do for love is much more important and I would do it again in a heartbeat. So, hoping that you won't judge me, I try not to judge the man next to me who keeps trying to fly or the nurse who insists on telling him that he can't. I try not to apologise to the kind nurse who will do little things to make our lives better when patients are ungrateful and tar him with the same brush as everyone else; and I try to forgive my father for his hatred and brutality because I don't know where he learnt that, but perhaps he experienced it firsthand and knew no better.

So my lads, just do your best to stay open-minded about people, about life, and about me too. I assure you, I try hard to be a person of good character, although it is hard to keep faith in humanity some days in this odd abode of mine. You will have days like that too, but remember you are wonderful young men, full of goodness and heart, and you can make a difference. Of that, I have no doubt at all.

Your friend, Joe.

\*\*\*\*\*

As he drove down the street, Adam could see that Nate's place was in darkness. He pulled into the driveway and made his way to the garage. Looking through the window, he saw Nate's car housed inside. He went to the door and knocked; no answer. He knocked again.

'Nate, it's me,' he called, and waited, his hands in his pockets, rocking on his heels. He rang the phone number again and heard the phone ringing inside the house.

'Crap,' Adam muttered. He was debating whether to force the front door when it opened. Nate walked away, waving a beer in one hand.

'Help yourself, I'll have another too,' he said, and fell back onto the couch.

Adam entered the dark house, closed the door, and put on a lamp in the lounge room. The pale blue walls that Adam remembered Nate's ex, Erin, proudly showing off as her Cambridge blue colour scheme, now looked cringeworthy against the remnants of furniture that Nate had assembled in a motley assortment of colours. Adam saw the legal papers on the coffee table and headed to the kitchen. He returned moments later, with two beers, handing one to Nate, he sat down opposite.

'Jess call you?' Nate asked. He took a large drink of beer.

'Yep. You okay?'

'It's official,' Nate said, looking at the papers.

Adam nodded.

Nate gulped another mouthful of beer. 'You didn't have to come over, I'm okay.'

'We're blood brothers,' Adam reminded him. 'Want me to take you to the outback?'

Nate put his head back and laughed. 'Hell yeah, I remember that... I wanted to go to the big red rock and you wanted to go to Melbourne or something?'

'Sydney,' Adam said.

Nate shook his head. 'Geez, life was a bit simpler then.' He sighed. 'Bloody outback... not a bad idea right now.'

'Yeah, you'd last about a week without your Foxtel sport and coffee hit at the corner. You know that you can crash at my place for a while until you next have Matilda... if you didn't want the space.' Adam frowned, trying to find the balance between friend and counsellor.

Nate shrugged. 'Thanks, I'll get through... you know what it's like.'

Adam lowered himself down further into the chair. 'Bit different for me though; in the end, I wanted it over with Steph. I still felt like a huge bloody failure though.'

'Yeah, thanks counsellor,' Nate said, and both men chuckled.

'You've got a little girl who idolises you though...'

'Don't worry. I'm not going to do anything stupid,' Nate said.

'Yeah? If I had a dollar for every time you said that and then did something stupid, I'd have a holiday house on the Gold Coast with a Porche in the garage,' Adam reminded him. He hesitated and looked to the ceiling.

'What?' Nate asked.

'I'd probably have a private chopper as well,' he added.

'Shut up!' Nate smirked at him.

Adam leaned forward and grabbed the papers. 'Want me to read through and check it's all legit?'

Nate nodded. 'Thanks. We agreed on 50-50 everything including time with Matilda.'

Adam nodded and began to read, occasionally glancing at Nate who sat motionless, staring at the window... at the reflection of the room – his usual energy was sapped; every now and then Nate raised the bottle in his hand to have a mouthful of beer. When Adam finished, he put the papers back on the table and turned the last page to face Nate, and tapped on it.

'All above board. Why don't you sign, and we'll go out and get a steak, have a few more drinks, taxi home and I'll crash the night here? We'll get Jess to send the papers back in the morning.'

Nate nodded, and putting down his beer, he accepted the pen Adam presented, signed, and gave him the pen back. Adam put the papers back in the envelope.

'I'll put these in my car,' he said, wanting them out of sight for when they came home later. Get changed and we'll go.'

Allowing Adam to take charge, Nate rose, taking off his suit jacket en route to his room. Adam sent Jessica a quick text message to let her know all was okay. His mind started on the familiar groove about his own marriage and his part in it. He stood up to clear the empty bottles away and stop the track playing in his head. After all, he thought, we have *Expectations*; Joe must have thought we were alright.

# Chapter 23

**Extract from Joe's diary:**

*Today, the boys asked me about a drowned person they saw in the river; I lied to them, to protect them from the evil I am exposed to every day. I did know the drowned man, Andrew was his name, and he was brave. You see they do some terrible things in this place especially to the women. One poor young lady underwent shock therapy, and while she was unconscious, three men took turns at entering her room. I saw them come out one at a time, adjusting themselves. Sickening. I don't know how she'll feel or what she'll feel when she comes around, but the violation is deplorable. Several women have fallen pregnant while they have been here… after a while, they get sent away somewhere.*

*We all saw the three men smirking and taking advantage of her. I did nothing… I dreamt in my head of all the heroic things I could do. Andrew, well he challenged them. He screamed at them, tried to shame them and when they laughed, he ran at them. When they restrained him, he yelled that he would tell someone and they'd be found out. I don't believe he took his own life or drowned trying to escape; I think he was shut up. I do that now, shut up; I can't help anyone from raging, so I have lost my moral compass in my defeat.*

It was raining heavily outside, a rarity of late. The grey day did little to cut the glare; Nate winced as Jessica opened the blinds in the office. She turned to study Adam who had come in behind Nate, unshaven and looking a bit green. He groaned at the sound of a loud horn down below on the street – the peak hour traffic made worse by the weather.

'Big night, guys?' she asked.

'I'm out of practice,' Nate said. 'Or getting old.'

'Or both,' Adam agreed. 'Jess, how soon are you doing that coffee run?'

Jessica rolled her eyes. 'Immediately. So, did you get laid?'

Nate feigned shock. 'What sort of question is that?' He looked to Adam. 'I can't remember. Can you?'

'I'm sure we were brilliant if we did,' Adam said. He lowered himself into one of the waiting room chairs.

'Hmm.' She eyed them both, before continuing around the office and opening the blinds.

Adam moved slightly so she could reach the control behind him. He was conscious of her proximity, her perfume, the cut of her fitted black dress.

'Are you thinking of changing out of those jeans into a suit?' she asked as she leaned behind him to snap the blinds open.

'Sure, it was just what I was thinking about,' he said.

'Right then, coffee and something greasy to eat. I'll get you both an egg and bacon burger,' she said, grabbing the coffee tray and accepting the money Nate passed her.

'I think I love you,' Nate told her.

As she opened the door, Rob entered.

'Can you say that in the workplace these days?' Rob asked.

'Welcome, first day at school!' Jessica teased him, opening the door wider to allow him entry. 'Best to keep the noise down,' she warned him. 'Coffee?'

Rob took advantage of the offer and entered to find the two boys in slow motion. He lay his suit jacket over a chair and looked from Nate to Adam.

'What's happened?'

'We had a very out-of-character night commiserating the signing of my divorce papers,' Nate said. 'Good thing I've only got one wife, ex-wife... couldn't do that too often.'

'Well, I'm sorry to hear that, Nate, but it looks like you did the papers justice,' Rob said.

Adam nodded. 'Had to be supportive, you know how it is. Probably should have stopped being supportive about three vodkas and two beers earlier.'

Nate groaned.

Rob grinned. 'Boys, just like old times, then. Thinking of a shave and getting changed?'

Adam sighed and rose. 'Rugged is supposed to be in. Fine then, getting changed.' He read between the lines that Rob wanted five minutes alone with Nate.

Rob sat down opposite Nate. 'You know there's going to be a few darker times ahead even when you think signing the papers is the end of it; you can't hit the bottle every time.'

Nate nodded. 'I know, I won't.'

'You know you can call me or drop in any time,' Rob continued. 'If your house is too quiet or you start getting a bit overwhelmed by everything. Come around, I've always got the footy on and Deb is often out at her community meetings.'

'Thanks,' Nate said. He glanced to the door willing Jessica back.

'And clearly, you're completely uncomfortable talking about this,' Rob smiled at Nate, 'but if you want to talk about it with someone other than Adam, just find me... okay?'

Nate nodded. 'Thanks, really.'

'Are you sleeping and eating okay?' Rob asked.

Nate thought about his home time; he kept the radio or television on all the time so he didn't have too much thinking time. At night, sleep was a game of hit and miss; it was either just on the edge of his consciousness but out of reach, or he slept deeply and dreamed of his former life, only to wake up in an empty house.

'Yeah, fine thanks Rob,' he cleared his throat. 'It's been...' his voice trailed off as footsteps approached and Danielle appeared at the door.

*Another ten minutes would have been great*, Rob thought. But at least he got his message across. Rob rose and opened the door for her. Danielle looked around for somewhere to put her wet umbrella and decided on the bin behind Jessica's desk.

'Did I interrupt something?' she asked, sensing the solemnness in the air.

Nate rose. 'No, we were just talking general stuff. Adam's in the shower, and Jess is getting coffee. Did you want one?'

'I saw her, and ordered,' Danielle said. She had killer heels on; Nate had forgotten she was a shorty; with the three inches of boot heel she wore, she could almost look him in the eye.

'You okay?' she studied him.

'Sure,' he said, turning away.

Danielle moved to the window to look down at the street below. Rob joined her.

'That's some serious rain,' he said. Passing cars sprayed arcs of water in their wake, and across the road, a pool of water prevented access to the front steps of the library. The streets didn't cope well with a deluge of that magnitude.

'Makes me miss home,' Danielle said, and sighed.

'Where's home?' Rob asked. He leaned against the windowsill and crossed his arms.

'Darwin. When we were kids and it rained, or when we got the big storms, we'd be out having a great time in the downpour; Mum would be yelling at us to come inside. I've got to make a trip home,' she said, more to herself.

Adam appeared, doing up his tie; he moved to open the door for Jessica as she juggled with the coffees and food.

'Take Nate home with you, Dan, introduce him to the family,' Adam suggested. 'He needs a holiday. Tell your folks he's your boyfriend and scare the hell out of them.'

'I'm sure I could win them over,' Nate said, accepting the egg and bacon roll and beginning on it immediately. He closed his eyes. 'Chewing is so loud,' he mumbled.

'So, what would he have to do to win your parents over?' Rob asked, accepting a coffee.

Danielle smiled. 'Well, Mum loves her music, we all play an instrument.'

Nate shook his head. 'Can't play anything and can't hold a note.'

'Right,' Danielle pursed her lips while she thought. 'Dad loves fishing...'

Nate brightened. 'We've fished a bit,' he said, with a glance to Adam.

'A piece of string in the creek might not cut it,' Adam said.

'Fishing is so boring though,' Nate continued. 'You sit there for hours in the quiet, nothing happening and then you get a tug on the line, get all excited, the fish swims off and the bastard next to you pulls it in.'

Adam laughed. 'Yeah, sorry Dan, you're going home alone.'

'I think the whole idea of fishing is to slow down and enjoy the peace and quiet,' Jessica offered. 'Are you going away, Dan?'

'Not for a bit,' she said, looking out the window again. 'Just homesick for the rain and the sunsets, family, friends, Darwin time…'

As she said it, the office phone rang bringing them back to Brisbane time. Rob glanced at his watch.

'We'd better go,' he said to Adam. 'Don't want to keep our new ally, Mac, waiting. And I'd better drive.'

'Okay, but don't drive too fast,' Adam said, rubbing his forehead. 'Please, no sharp corners… no loud music… no—'

'Just go!' Jessica ordered them.

'So bossy!' Adam said.

She gave him a smile and he returned it. It didn't go unnoticed by Danielle.

'C'mon Dan,' Nate pushed himself up off the chair. 'We've got an appointment with former Superintendent Gregor Digby.'

# Chapter 24

Wiry, restless Ron 'Mac' McIntyre pointed to a couple of chairs that were solid enough to hold Rob and Adam's weight. They were in a room inside the asylum with several windows missing and a large hole in the roof; the natural ventilation meant the smell was barely noticeable.

'Is this where you live?' Rob asked.

Mac shook his head. 'No, but it's good to meet in here… airy.' He had no intention of showing anyone his residence in the building; it was his place alone, his safe place.

The two men sat as Mac paced, sat, then rose and moved to the window frame. His hands constantly moved – he rubbed them on his pants, rung them, pushed them into his jean pockets, then began the process again.

'So, the P.I. guy from your office said I never have to come into your office if I didn't want to, and there'd be no cops, no doctors … we'd just talk and you'd let us know if we have grounds for getting them,' he said.

Rob nodded and sat back. He and Adam had left their jacket and ties in the car; Mac didn't respond to authority.

'That's absolutely right, Mac,' Rob assured him. 'We're working for you… here to take your story, listen to what happened and fight for you. I can personally promise you, everyone who talks to us—here or at the office—can leave when they are good and ready. But...' Rob stopped and leaned forward, '... if anyone is not well or wants our help, we'll look after that too, okay?'

Mac's eyes narrowed, he looked to Adam and back to Rob, before he reluctantly nodded. Rob pulled a note pad and pen from his pocket and gave Mac a look of encouragement – a smile and nod.

'There's ten of us, willing to talk. I've given them the girl's number,' Mac said referring to Jessica.

'That's fine,' Adam said, 'Jess will look after them. Want to begin? You can stop anytime you want to... you don't have to tell us everything today. I'm going to record this like we discussed, okay?' he said, putting a small tape recorder on and wedging it against one of the window frames near Mac.

Mac nodded. 'You'll think I'm insane... you'll think I deserved to be in here.' He hesitated and looked to the grounds outside; the men leant forward to hear his words. They waited. After a while, Rob spoke.

'You know Mac,' Rob said, 'I'm not a young man anymore, and I can tell you four lessons I've learned over time and in some cases, learned the hard way...'

Mac nodded. 'Tell me.'

'First, everyone is a product of the choices we make or our parents make.'

Mac thought about that statement for a moment and nodded. 'Yeah, I'd agree with that.'

'Two,' Rob continued, 'I've heard enough stories over the decades that I've been doing this, that nothing you're going to say will shock me, I promise.'

A hint of a smile appeared on Mac's face.

'Yeah?' he said. 'Don't know if that's a good or bad thing.'

Rob gave a small smile and nodded in agreement. 'Three... we don't all deserve what we get or give.'

'Hell, that's the truth,' Mac said. 'Yeah... that's the truth... and what's the last one?'

Rob took a deep breath. 'My most important learning,' he said, solemnly, ensuring he had Mac's attention, '... sanity's overrated, Mac.'

Mac laughed. A loud involuntary laugh and Rob joined in. He wondered when was the last time Mac had laughed about anything.

*****

Danielle drove Nate's car; she wasn't sure her old vehicle wouldn't overheat with the stop-and-start traffic along Kingsford Smith Drive and the airport route.

'I'd love an office near the airport; right near the runway where you could watch the planes all day,' Nate said.

'You're easily distracted now, that'd be hopeless,' she teased him.

He smirked in her direction and she gave him a smile.

'What? You look like the cat that got the cream,' he said.

'I had a good day yesterday,' Danielle said. 'Got a result.'

'Me too,' Nate said. 'Bet mine's better than yours.'

'Doubt it,' she scoffed. 'I think I've got a lead on your friend.'

'Joe?' Nate said, suddenly attentive despite the fog in his head.

She nodded.

'Well cough it up.'

Danielle took a deep breath. 'I think I tracked Joe's brother, Stephen's movements, indirectly through Dave's movements.'

'Dave…' Nate repeated.

'Dave Trigg… the nurse… that bloke you told me about who smuggled Joe out because he owed Stephen a favour. With me?'

'Always,' Nate said. He held up his hand. 'Okay, I'm a bit slow today, but I'm hanging in there. Did you talk to Dave?'

'No, but he's a nurse, right?' Danielle waited for Nate to catch up.

'Right.'

'So, in your notes, Dave said he met Stephen when he was working on a building site and Stephen stopped Dave from being picked on all the time.'

Nate nodded. He wished he could lie down, but tried to look attentive.

'So, I went back through Nurse Dave's working history to find where he was working when they met – where that construction site was and I got a lucky break. The builders are Talinson.'

'Big company and still around,' Nate said, and brightened.

'Exactly, I contacted them about Dave and Stephen. They brushed me off at first, then when I mentioned the widow, and that we were trying to reach Stephen because Joe's been officially declared dead, they softened. The staff dude…'

'Is that his official title?' Nate teased.

'Yeah, it's on his business card,' Danielle grinned. 'Staff dude told me that he remembered Dave and that he'd left them for a gig at a hospital – he gave me the name. So, Dave must have gone back to nursing not admin, and according to Talinson's HR records, Stephen left not long after and we know they stayed in touch. So, I rang the hospital and I've got an appointment tomorrow with the Human Resources Manager to see if there's any chance they both went there.'

'Fantastic,' Nate said, 'nice digging, sleuth. Whereabouts?'

'Toowoomba,' Danielle said. 'It'll only take me an hour to get there. I'm thinking that if Dave was looking out for Stephen, he might have tipped him off about jobs at his new place of work, might have even gotten him one. If all that works out, the hospital might have some old contact details, next of kin if he married, anything.'

'Good on you,' Nate said, and closed his eyes. 'What's Dave Trigg's work history like?'

'Got lucky again,' Danielle said. 'He was a bit of stayer... he's had about three jobs and stayed there for decades.'

'Thank God someone's a stayer,' Nate said.

He pointed to a building that looked like it was made completely of glass. 'That'd be it then. There's a couple of guest parking spots underneath, allegedly.'

*****

Mac sighed. 'They were just waiting for me to lose it, so they had an excuse, to jab me. Not that they needed one... hell, people were dragged away and restrained all the time here, but sometimes they liked to look like it was all above board,' Mac told the two men. He stared out the window as he spoke, Rob leaned forward to catch his words, Adam stood against the wall nearby, his hands in his pockets, relating Mac's words to Joe's experience.

'Could you tell anyone?' Rob asked.

Mac shook his head. 'I never had any visitors; my family don't want to know me. So, no-one was around to question where the bruises came from or why I was more whacked out than normal, know what I mean?'

The men nodded.

'Did they do it to the men and women who had visitors?' Adam asked.

'No, they wouldn't dare. Unless the patient needed it of course... but you know, they could justify anything... everyone in here needed it.' Mac turned and spat on the floor. He took a deep breath and continued. 'I didn't know what they were doing the first few times but then some of us started talking amongst ourselves and it came out; we were part of an experiment – a truth serum drug.'

Adam took in a perceptible breath.

'They actually told you that?' Rob asked.

'No but Dave did, you know, Dave the nurse. And, we had a group, a few of us who stuck together. One of the guys had some medical knowledge... we used to call him Doc Jock... he was Scottish. Doc Jock said some drugs affect the nervous system or something like that,' Mac waved his hand dismissively. 'And when your nervous system is affected, you might talk more. I used to joke they could give us a bottle of rum and we'd do that for them without having to tie us all down,' he grinned.

Adam and Rob smiled, joining in the joke without enthusiasm.

Mac sighed. 'We were just guinea pigs... no-one gave a shit that we were here, no-one cared that we were being experimented on. They thought we were trash, not worth anything... you can't tell me the staff didn't know what was going on.'

'How long did this go on for?' Adam asked.

'As long as I was here, and that was years. It wasn't always the same drug or the same test; who knows what they shot into us and what they were testing for.'

Adam moved in line with Mac to look at the same view

from Mac's side of the building. 'Tell us what happened when they administered the truth serum.'

Mac nodded. 'At first, whatever they gave me, made me nauseous. Thought I was going to throw up but I couldn't lift my body to spit out. They kept trying to get my attention and I didn't answer much that time. I remember a question about if I'd ever killed anyone, but I think I laughed. The next thing I knew I was waking up in my room. I don't know if I said anything worth saying; I don't know how long I was out for… most days in here were pretty much the same anyway.

'They took Joe the next time, poor bugger. He always looked terrified, he wasn't as hardened to the system like some of us were. We'd been in it for years. I didn't see him for two days after that and when I next did, he didn't look at me. He just kept to himself, shuffling out to the fence to breathe the fresh air and doing his own thing. Never thought he'd survive this place.'

Adam cleared his throat from the lump that had formed thinking of Joe at their mercy. 'Did he ever tell you what questions they asked him, what happened to him?'

Mac nodded. 'Eventually but not right away. It was about two months later that we talked about it; don't know how that convo started, but Joe agreed with Doc Jock that it was some sort of truth serum experiment. Joe said they started by askin' him where his brother was, what happened the night of his father's death, if he'd knocked off his old man. Next time, cause there's always a next time, they asked him a lot of questions, like if his brother was alive and if he or his brother had murdered their father. I didn't ask him what he answered, but Doc Jock said they'd be checking against his statements to the police and seeing if they matched because with the truth serum, you're supposed to forget your lies, and that's why you tell the truth.'

'In the long run, did you remember any truths you gave up?' Rob asked.

Mac shook his head. 'My truths weren't worth knowing. But I know they took blood from me.'

'Without consent?' Rob confirmed.

'Never consented to anything in here… ever,' Mac said, and turned to look back outside to the freedom he now had.

*****

Rob glanced over at Adam as they drove back to the office. 'What do you think?' he asked.

Adam exhaled. 'I think we're scratching the surface.'

'Agree. What a place,' Rob said, and shook his head. 'What a bloody nightmare.'

'What are the odds of getting those files… where would they be?' Adam said, thinking out loud.

'Bet you the management destroyed them, but the original psychologist or doctor on duty may have kept a copy.'

'I've started on that path, not much luck yet,' Adam said. 'If we can get Joe's police interview transcript… Nate should be able to swing that.'

'Be interesting,' Rob agreed.

'That it would.'

'If the other claimants go ahead with their stories, boy, have we got a case. I wouldn't mind giving your solicitor friend, John, a heads-up already,' Rob said.

'Sure, I'll connect you,' Adam said. 'What's your take on Mac, do you think he's alright?'

Rob took a deep breath. 'Don't know how, but yeah, for what he's been through, he's pretty together. But if he had to front court and say any of that, well that's a whole different ballgame.'

# Chapter 25

'I hate suits,' Nate grumbled just as the elevator doors opened into the lobby of a small private company. The sign behind the receptionist's desk read 'WHAS: Workplace Health Advisory Service'. Danielle spared the receptionist Nate's grumpiness and advised they had a meeting with Mr Digby. They were shown to a small room with a round table, a jug of water and half a dozen glasses, four chairs and a view of the shopping complex opposite.

Nate poured them both a glass of water, drank his quickly and refilled.

A large man, easily Nate's height and carrying considerable weight entered the room. The irony was not lost on either of them... Gregor Digby was not the poster boy for workplace health.

He exhaled as he sat down and got straight to business.

'I know you want to talk about the River Park Hospital, but I've got to be honest... it was a minute in my life really, and I'm not sure what I can contribute,' he said.

'I understand,' Nate said, 'and given that, I appreciate you seeing us.' His words rang hollow with insincerity. *A minute in your life, a lifetime for your victims, arsehole.*

Digby shook his head. 'It was a shame about the records, not one survived the flood I heard. All that history,' he said.

'Yes, all that history,' Nate said. *Flood, huh? Must tell Adam that one.* Patience was not on today's menu when he already felt like crap and he knew the man sitting opposite was most likely the agitator for so much pain. If he was honest with himself, he wanted to lean over the desk, pull Digby up by the collar and knock him out clean. He might have done that once or twice in his past profession; not so easy to get away with it now.

Danielle stepped in. 'When he was a kid, Nate met one of your patients and now that patient's son is working with us to find out more about what might have happened to his father,' she said, embellishing the truth a little. 'Joseph O'Connell. Do you remember him?'

Digby exhaled again and looked skyward as he thought. Nate watched him; unsure if Digby was sweating due to pressure or because he was uncomfortably unfit, or both.

'Well, a few Josephs and Joes came and went during my time. Got a photo?' he asked.

'He was an artist. Small, bearded, gentle...' Nate said.

'Ah, that Joseph,' Digby said, and webbed his fingers across his stomach. 'I do remember him, quite a talent. Got discharged from memory or did he escape and we never found him?'

'Do you know why he would have been left for weeks in solitary confinement or given unnecessary shock treatment?' Nate snapped.

Digby held up his hand. 'Well let's just stop there shall we? Where's your information coming from because I can assure you, nobody got mistreated during my time or got any treatment that wasn't beneficial to their recovery.' He chuckled as though the very idea was ludicrous. It increased Nate's blood pressure.

'We have some testimonies, diaries and other information that points to widespread mistreatment of patients,' Nate started. He knew he was going too far, but he couldn't take his eyes of Digby's throat and the pleasant thought of his own hands wrapped around it.

Digby scoffed, the cruelty evident in his face. 'Every patient there will give you some hard luck story. Best you remember what they were in there for in the first place... because they were mentally unstable or insane. You couldn't believe an account from any of them' He wiped his sweating hands down the sides of his trousers. 'Now, I've got a busy day and I really don't know how I could be of any more help.'

'You haven't...'

Danielle cut Nate off. 'Thanks for your time, Mr Digby. If you do recall anything about Joe that might help his son have a little closure, here's our card,' she said, offering it. He took it, shoving it in his suit pocket without looking at it.

'Perhaps you can direct any further queries to my lawyer; email me if you want their details. I'm sorry I couldn't be of any more assistance.' He rose, and Danielle did the same, nudging Nate to his feet.

Digby opened the meeting room door and watched them, making sure they left the premises.

Outside Danielle gave Nate a look and sighed.

'I know, I know, sorry. But we both know we were never going to get anything from that dick,' Nate said. 'I should have left him to Adam.'

'Mm,' Danielle said. 'Maybe you should just do paperwork for the rest of the day... don't want you offending clients.'

'Yeah,' he said, in agreement. He lowered himself with a grunt into the passenger seat of his own car and turning to

Danielle as she put on her seatbelt, said, 'You'd better take my car up to Toowoomba, yours won't make it up the range. Just drive me back to the office; Adam can drop me home.'

'Thanks,' she brightened. 'That'd be great. You know we're going to get a lot of this… stonewalling… no-one's going to admit to taking part in any of the shit that went down there.'

Nate nodded. 'Digby's in so deep he can't see the tide coming for him, and I'm going to get him.' He glanced up at the building and could just make out the silhouette of Digby looking down at them as Danielle steered them away from the building.

*****

Jessica rose from her desk to meet Adam at the office door as he entered. The waiting room was empty and just the sound of the radio drifted in the background.

'Where's Rob?' she asked looking behind him.

'Dropped me off and gone. What's up?' Adam asked.

She glanced at his office. 'There's a man waiting for you in there. I tried to get him to wait out here for you but he said he had information for you and couldn't be seen here. He just barged in there while I was on the phone.'

'Information about the asylum? Or is he a former patient?'

'He wouldn't say but he was really assertive. Said he could wait a short while only but couldn't let anyone see him,' Jessica said. 'Sorry, I know he could be going through your files and—'

'No, it's fine, all the files in the office are locked or password protected, so he can't do any damage. Besides, it's better you diffuse the situation than fuel it… especially when you're here alone. Are you here alone?' Adam said, glancing at Nate's closed office door.

'Yeah, he's on his way back, I called him about ten minutes ago.'

'Did you tell him to step on it?' Adam asked.

Jessica shook her head. 'No, I'm okay.'

Adam's eyes widened. 'We need to talk about this… two of us always need to be here – Nate, me or Rob, even Dan.'

'Do you think it's a journo again?'

'No, more likely to be someone involved in the asylum history.' Adam slipped his jacket on as he walked to his office door. He opened it, walked in and closed it again. He looked around; no-one was sitting at the desk or on the couch. And then he heard a voice from behind him.

'Hello, Adam.'

*****

Jessica looked at Adam's office door, to the phone and back to the door. She picked up the handpiece and dialled Nate. It went to message bank and she asked him to call her back as soon as he got the message. She shook her head; just like Nate, always missing in action when she needed him. His Sergeant could never track him down half the time either. He even partnered Nate with the team's model police personality; a third-generation, tick every box, big on following the letter of the law cop. Nate corrupted him; had him smoking, drinking, fighting, and as Nate said, 'loosened up' in a matter of months. She found herself smiling thinking about him when the ringing phone snapped her back to the now.

'Delaney and Murphy', she started.

'It's me,' Nate cut her off. 'What's up?'

'We might have a Code Two.'

'On my way,' he hung up. Her phone rang again moments

later. Before she could do her normal spiel, Nate cut her off.

'What's a Code Two again?'

Jessica sighed. 'You're a dill…'

'Is it? I don't remember that,' he teased her.

She laughed, then dropped her voice. 'Code Two: Urgent matter – risk of injury to person or property. This is police drill 101… remember?'

'Mm, vaguely,' he said.

'So, are you coming?' she asked.

'Oh, you're serious?'

'Of course I'm serious,' Jessica's voice rose. 'Do you think I've got nothing better to do than interrupt you on a job with inane code messages. Give me strength,' she said, channelling her mother. Jessica lowered her voice and looked towards the closed door to her left. 'Adam's got someone in his office that wouldn't announce himself and wouldn't wait in the waiting area… he's in there with him and he's a bit weird, the other guy, not Adam, you know what I mean… I have a good radar for this sort of thing.'

'Okay, okay, I'm about five minutes away and hurrying. I'll get Dan to put her foot down.'

Jessica heard the click in her ear. Next time, she decided, she would call Danielle or Rob first.

****

Adam froze. He scanned the face of the man now blocking the doorway. He was in his fifties, a head shorter than Adam, stocky, rough, and his cheeks were pocked with scars. Adam's mind went into overdrive. *It's not Joe, is it? No, not Joe, can't be Joe. Is it a patient from the asylum…but how would he know me? One of my former patients… don't remember him. Someone in Mum's life? Is he a risk?* Adam noted the man was clean, in need of a haircut, and solid enough to hold his own.

'I can't believe it's you; I would have known you anywhere,' the man said, crossing his arms across his chest, a genuine smile on his face.

'How long has it been?' Adam asked, prompting him for information.

'How long? How long...' the man said, and laughed. 'You would know better than me. You were a boy, look at you now.'

*A boy. Can it be Joe... no, who? If I say I don't know him, will he flip out?*

Adam smiled at him. 'Been a while then. Let's sit...' Adam indicated the couch but the man didn't move. Adam moved there, half turning so he had him in his sights. He sat in the corner inviting the man to sit opposite.

The man moved towards Adam and sat down opposite in the middle seat clasping his hands in front of him.

*How does he know me?*

'Dr. Murphy, hey? Well, well... good for you, Adam,' he said, and looked around. 'That's something to be proud of isn't it, hey? I've never seen a shrink, you know. Never much believed in it.'

Adam ruled out university and his patients; he was particularly relieved he wasn't a former patient.

The man exclaimed in a loud voice. 'You don't seem surprised to see me,' he said to Adam and then looked slightly over Adam's shoulder.

Adam resisted the urge to do the same; it was killing him. Then he saw the scars on the stranger's wrist and recognised the nervous habits; he had to tread lightly here. The man studied Adam.

'You've taken me by surprise,' Adam agreed. *More so because I have no idea who you are.*

'Still the quiet type, hey?'

Adam smiled. 'I leave the noise to Nate,' he said, waiting for a reaction.

'Yeah, Nate,' the man said, and nodded. 'How is he?'

'Good, yeah, very good,' Adam said, frowning. *Better if he was here.* 'So, where have you been?'

The man took in a deep breath, stretching his body to full sitting height, and then exhaled. 'Where haven't I been?' the man asked. His leg began to shake and he rubbed his hands down his worn trousers. He reached into his pocket and pulled out a pocket knife. 'Sometimes,' he said, 'I feel like where I've been is in the shadows forever, you get me?'

Adam nodded. 'I get that.'

He continued fingering the knife, rubbing the handle, polishing it and then he put it away and pulled out some chewing gum. He took a few pieces, offered it to Adam, who declined, and then sat back.

Adam thought he heard Nate's voice outside, and glanced to the door. *Thank God for that, hurry up.*

'I've got things I need to do, so better cut to the chase, hey?' The man said to him, his hand rubbing over the knife in his pocket.

'Sure, of course. Can I help?' Adam asked.

The man laughed. 'You've got absolutely no idea who I am, do you, Adam?'

Adam frowned and studied the man's face. 'You found me. Did Joe tell you how to find me?'

The man took a deep breath. 'Joe,' he said, the word hissing out between his teeth. He rubbed his wrists.

'Did you do that… cut yourself?' Adam asked.

'Once, when I was young, trying to get out of a situation,' he pulled his long sleeves further down over his wrists. He looked up at Adam. 'So, you've been looking for me?'

Adam glanced to the door again; *where the hell was Nate?* As he thought the words there was a sharp knock on his office door and Nate walked straight in. He sized up the men and the situation.

'Well, this is a surprise,' Nate said, looking to the man.

# Chapter 26

He had his favourites, hard not to… the compliant men, the pretty, young girls. Gregor Digby thought about the private investigator and his sidekick. He noted the make and model of their car and wrote down the registration.

'Just what I don't need – two crusaders,' he muttered.

That history was buried, he'd seen to it, or thought he had. He returned to his chair and lowered his bulk into the seat. Those patients were lucky they were born now and not in past centuries, he stewed; the conditions would have been much worse. The Nazis would have just euthanised them, he assured himself of his good intentions.

The mental image of his private room at the River Park Hospital came to mind. It hadn't been renamed when he worked there and Digby liked the original name… the River Park Lunatic Asylum, it said it all. He'd done some good work there, and he shared the spoils. All of his staff had been complicit; no-one complained about helping themselves to a bit on the side when it was on tap. The experiments though, that was something else. He'd made a tidy sum from trialling some of those drugs for the pharmaceutical companies… set him up nicely. Kept him in fine wine, upmarket cars, business class travel and paid for his mistress. He didn't have to work if he didn't want to, but then he'd have to stay home with the wife and the relationship worked better when he was off being in charge anywhere but in their house.

He remembered the artist; he had the drawings but they'd been destroyed, he'd made sure of that too. The artist was supposedly destroyed as well. Clean. Problem solved. He rose again, grabbed his mobile and looking for a number, he dialled.

He could hear the fear in the voice of the man who answered.

'Been a while,' Digby said, and laughed. 'Well the dead have risen, I have a job for you. Need you to give a few people a bit of a fright.' He briefed the man on what he needed to be done.

Hanging up, he leaned against the window frame, looking down at the street. He thought back to those days; he had power then… and respect, or at least he was feared.

He didn't feel sympathy for any of the victims then and he sure as shit didn't feel sorry now, but hell would freeze over before he paid for what he'd done.

\*\*\*\*\*

'Stephen,' Nate said. He moved towards the man and offered his hand; Adam looked from Nate to Stephen, unsure of what was going on.

Stephen grinned and shook it. 'Steve,' he said, 'don't stand on formality here. I think I had your mate here confused.'

'Steve, Joe's brother! Really? I thought you were some unbalanced former patient, and I was stringing you along waiting for clues,' Adam admitted, looking a bit sheepish.

'Why didn't you say, "*Mate who the hell are you?*"' Stephen joked.

'I've been in this situation before and the last person I said that to had a bit of an inferiority complex… it didn't help,' Adam said, with a grin. He scanned Stephen's face, then looked to Nate. 'How did you know?' He turned back to Stephen before Nate could answer. 'We never met you or even saw a photo of you when we knew Joe.'

Nate answered. 'Joe's wife showed me a pic of a younger you, the two brothers together.' Nate narrowed his eyes as he studied Stephen. 'We saw you once or twice…'

Adam shook his head. 'You're a freak for faces.'

Stephen sat back down, this time next to Adam. He crossed his arms across his chest and grinned. 'I was in disguise… do you remember as what?'

'Challenge accepted,' Nate sat opposite and studied him. 'As a woman.'

Adam's eyes widened, and Stephen laughed.

'Bingo, you've got it,' Stephen said.

Nate turned to Adam. 'Remember that ugly woman that visited Joe?'

Stephen chuckled. 'Yeah, I was no oil painting. Had to keep reminding myself to keep my legs closed when I sat. But I got away with it.' Stephen looked at Adam's face again and laughed. 'You look like you've seen a ghost.'

'You've been off the radar for years,' Adam said.

'Yeah, well I'm hard to find if I don't want to be found,' he boasted. 'But I heard from a source that you were looking for me,' he tapped his nose like it was a secret. 'Wouldn't have come back in the past either, but I had to look after Joe then.'

'That's when you made plans with Dave?' Adam asked. 'Did you know he worked there when you dropped in to see your brother.'

'Nuh, couldn't believe my luck. Scared the shit out of him too when this woman started talking to him like a man in drag,' he laughed again at the memory. 'He was putty, poor old Dave. So skittish… just had the feeling he would have done anything to save his own skin.'

'Anything? Think he's capable of murder?' Nate asked.

Stephen scoffed. 'No. Man's scared of his own shadow. I mean he seemed as frightened as the patients. He wouldn't have survived in there without being on someone's good side.'

The two men took in Stephen's words.

'So, where's Joe?' Nate asked.

Stephen looked from one man to the other. 'That's why I'm here,' he said. 'Where's Joe?'

Adam groaned and leaned back.

*****

Sitting in her car in the Toowoomba General Hospital carpark, Danielle took a deep breath and went over the questions she intended to ask. She didn't like hospitals, including the administration blocks.

Just as she had psyched herself to go in, Danielle's phone beeped with a message; she grabbed it seeing it was from Nate. 'What the…' she mumbled as she read: '*Found Stephen, come home.*' Danielle sighed… at least she didn't have to take the meeting now, even though she had driven an hour to get here. She rang the number, cancelled the appointment and rang her aunt to tell her she'd be dropping in earlier.

*****

**Then…**

'Do you reckon if we said we were Joe's sons or nephews, they'd let us in?' Nate asked. 'We could really visit him then… like that woman. She's pretty ugly.'

198

Adam chuckled.

'Well, she is,' Nate said. 'Hope she's not Joe's girlfriend.'

The two boys watched the woman walking beside Joe as they strolled along the perimeter fencing. She was ungainly, slightly rough.

'Yeah, maybe,' Adam said. 'But what if we got sprung while we were in there. They might lock us up too.'

'Our folks would get us out,' Nate said.

'Unless they couldn't find us... what if they didn't tell them we were there and we stayed there until we grew up and were Joe's age!' Adam exaggerated.

'Nuh, we'd escape,' Nate said, scoffing at the idea.

'Yeah, we would. I wonder if that's Joe's wife or his girlfriend, or sister.'

'He seems pretty happy to see her,' Nate said. The boys turned and looked toward the road as they heard the sounds of a siren.

'Ambulance,' Nate called it.

'Betcha they're picking up another dead person in there.' Adam nodded towards the asylum.

'They wouldn't need the siren if they were already dead,' Nate said, his voice rising enthusiastically.

'Yeah, true.' Adam's eyes widened. 'I've got it... if Joe's still in here when we finish school, we could become ambos and pretend to come for a dead person and rescue him.'

Nate nodded. 'That'd work. She's leaving, that woman.'

The boys watched the woman put her arm around Joe and pull him close, then just as quickly release him. Then they both disappeared through the doors and into the building.

## Chapter 27

**Now...**

Danielle braked, again – she sat behind another driver in the right lane who didn't know that the left lane was for slow drivers, and another driver with a car that didn't come with an indicator! She sighed; driving down the range from Toowoomba to Brisbane used to be fun, she thought. Now the lower speed limit, the cameras and the increased traffic took all the fun out of it. If you weren't braking the whole way down you were stuck behind some idiot in the wrong lane who was braking. She passed a young blonde girl driving carefully in the left lane with her 'P' plates on display, and noted the huge truck bearing down on her. The young driver gripped the wheel and was concentrating with all her might.

Poor kid, hang in there, Danielle thought. She glanced to the edge, it was a hell of a drop to land below, not that she was intending to go there. The car in front of her moved out of the lane at last and Danielle accelerated to the speed limit. Driving Nate's car was easy... the SUV almost drove itself. She moved back into the left lane, leaving plenty of room between Nate's car and an old red Nissan sedan behind her that was going about the same speed but hadn't bothered to overtake since they started on the range; the driver weaving in and out with her.

Danielle glanced at the clock. She still had plenty of time, a couple of hours, until she was supposed to be at the team meeting; she probably could have stayed at her aunt's place a bit longer… operate on Nate time.

She followed the winding road around the next bend, and like every driver, glanced at the runaway truck bay… the sand bed to the right of her. No recent tracks, that's a good thing. She braked instinctively at the sight of it and felt Nate's car grab slightly to one side. She gave a nervous laugh… her defensive driving teacher said people always look at what they don't want to hit, and then hit it! It was a good course and a clever present from her Dad; he gave all of the kids in the family a safe driving course for their eighteenth birthday.

She took the next bend and pressed the brakes; the brakes that weren't there.

She glanced to the edge. Ice cold pure fear engulfed her; Danielle leaned forward, her foot pumped the floor.

'No, NO!' she pumped again and the pedal went flat to the floor.

The thought raced through her mind: *This is how I'm going to go. This is it, now!*

There were cars in front and behind her and nothing but descending steep road as far as she could see. She gripped the wheel, her adrenaline sending her heart racing.

She called out Nate's name… out of fear, because it was his car.

'Think! Don't panic!' She tried to remember what to do and pushed the car into a lower gear, then grabbed for the handbrake and put it on. At the decline she was on, it made no difference.

Another bend came into sight. She blasted her horn and

a car moved out of the way, the driver giving her the finger.

Her thoughts went to her mother; I might not see her again. She hurtled around the next bend, gripping tightly, she wanted to see her mum again.

A runaway truck bay was coming up on her right. *Thank God.*

But a driver was in front of her; Danielle would hit the car before she could get to the sand bed. She kept her hand on the horn.

'Move, move,' she screamed, and the driver moved over as well as a couple of drivers in front of it; Danielle's car almost clipping the rear of the retreating vehicle.

She braced for the jolt. The impact expected from the spinning wheels embedding in the sand.

*Better than going off the other side.*

The car raced straight into the sand bed, and a few metres up the incline, with the gravitational pull taking over…. then the sand slowed it down. The car stalled.

It was over.

Danielle leaned forward, resting her head on the steering wheel, her heart pounding and chest tight.

'Thank God, thank you God!' she mumbled looking skyward.

Danielle sat back. 'I'm alive', she moaned and then instinctively looked in the rear-view mirror. Was this an accident or… she didn't know whether it could be related to the asylum case or one of Nate's disgruntled clients. No-one was behind her… the red sedan was not in sight and the driver must have seen it happening. He could have stopped to see if she was okay, she thought, still, it was impossibly hard for drivers to pull up and help on the winding road.

She closed her eyes and allowed herself to sit and breathe;

she began to shake. In a matter of minutes, she heard a siren. In no time, a tow truck arrived. Must have been circling like a vulture, she thought. With shaking hands, she reached for her phone to ring the auto club to organise a tow and a lift back to Brisbane. The flashing lights of a police car illuminated the inside of Nate's car, and she opened the door to let them know she was still alive.

Shaken, freaked out, but still alive.

*****

Nate tried Danielle's phone again, got the message bank, swore and hung up. 'Where the hell is she? She knows we had a 4 o'clock meeting,' he said. He glanced at the clock as the hour neared 5pm. He whirled around as the door behind him opened and Danielle burst in.

'Sorry I'm late,' she said to Nate and the team sitting at the table – Adam, Rob and Jessica. 'Traffic was a bitch along Ipswich Road. I prefer the morning meetings… anyone else?' she said, and stopped to draw a breath.

'Where were you?' Nate asked, 'I've been ringing for an hour. I thought you'd met someone shady at the hospital. I was about to send out the cavalry.'

'Oh, shit,' she said, and reached into her handbag. Danielle turned the silencer off and saw his missed calls. 'Sorry… I went to see my Aunty and she hates technology. She goes off if a phone is ringing when someone is visiting her or if you have any screen time at all.' She looked back to Nate.

'Yeah, wasted all that energy. I need a beer. I declare it a drinking meeting.' He strode to the bar fridge. 'Anyone?' He brought back a round of drinks and placed them in the centre of the table, sinking down in a chair beside Jessica.

Adam grabbed a beer. 'The upside of an afternoon meeting.'

'Do you think we drink too much?' Jessica asked.

'No!' Nate and Adam said, in unison.

'Right,' she said, with a shrug.

Danielle sat down and took a deep breath. Adam looked at her and paused, his beer bottle raised midway.

'You're shaking… what's wrong?' he asked. All heads turned to look at Danielle. He rose. 'Is someone out there?'

Rob joined him and the men headed to the door.

'No, no, sit Adam, Rob, it's all good,' she said, and took a Coke from the selection on offer. She looked at Nate. 'I'm sorry, there's been an accident.'

'Jesus, are you okay? What happened?' he said. 'Why didn't you call?'

Danielle told them about the brake failure, and his car being towed back to Brisbane, and her lift with the tow driver named Rishi.

The mood was sober with everyone thinking of the consequences of what could have happened to Danielle.

'I'll call in a favour and get the cops to check the brakes,' he assured her.

'I spoke to them at the scene,' she said.

'That's terrifying, Dan,' Jessica said, and shivered. 'Thank God you're level-headed, I don't know what I would have done.'

'We need to take a fresh look at this now,' Nate said, addressing Adam. 'The situation has just become extremely risky.'

Adam nodded. 'Especially for you three,' he said, looking at Danielle, Jessica and Rob.

'Don't worry about me,' Rob said, 'I can handle myself.'

'Want some rum with that?' Nate asked, as Danielle sipped her Coke.

She smiled. 'No, I need to be clear-headed, at least until I get home.' She felt herself winding down for the first time in hours. 'I like Toowoomba, nice place,' she said, attempting to think of something other than what could have been – which she had spent considerable time processing on the trip back. 'I could live there.'

'Me too,' Rob said, sipping a beer, and understanding her need to talk. 'Remember when we took you boys up there a couple of times for footy matches. Some good rugby league teams up there.'

'Yeah, you got knocked out in one game, remember?' Nate said to Adam. 'In those days they let you go back on the ground as soon as you woke up… explains a lot now.'

Adam smirked at him, as the group chuckled, lifting the tension.

Jessica cleared her throat. 'So, our meeting, shall we declare it officially over?'

'Anything I need to know?' Danielle asked.

Adam, Jessica and Nate started talking at once. Nate and Jessica stopped; Adam summed it up.

'Yeah, 'we still don't know where Joe is… whether he's dead or alive… whether he was taken back, died on the run… who is doing the etchings that his wife got recently… if his son Thomas is alive… if we can get compensation for any of the asylum victims…'

'We're rooted then,' Danielle said.

'Not quite,' Rob said, playing his trump card.

# Chapter 28

Rob rose from the table, headed into his office and returned with a file. He sat down, flicked through the pages of a patient file before looking at the group who was watching him with interest.

'I saw this man yesterday – he's one of the class action victims that Mac has sent in to see me. It didn't click until now… Jess and I are a bit overloaded with transcripts,' he said, and looked to Jessica. 'You know the patient who mentioned the drawings?'

Her eyes widened. 'Yes, it's about the bottom of page six or seven.'

Nate looked impressed. Jessica explained: 'It was the last one I transcribed so I remember it.'

Rob flicked through and found it. 'Listen to this,' he said, looking from Adam to Nate. 'The client talks for a while about being strapped down and injected with something that makes him nauseous and wipes him out for hours. Then this bit… *"I was coming around when I heard voices, so I just faked it and stayed under. It was one of the doctors and a guard. They were talking about a guy they called the artist— don't know his name, they never said it—but he'd been doing drawings of the stuff that was going on. You see they used* to check our letters, listen in on conversations, pretty much censor everything we wrote. So, they were saying this guy was slipping out drawings of stuff that was going on and it could be dangerous for all of them. They said they had to deal with him, and whoever was helping him." That's the only part relevant to Joe,' Rob looked up. 'I'm guessing it's Joe.'

'The artist,' Nate said, 'I'd say so.'

'We need to know when this was in context of Dave Trigg smuggling Joe out,' Adam said. 'It sounds like Joe already got some drawings out, and management were in panic mode.'

'It does,' Nate agreed. 'We need to find out too if Dave knows about the drawings and was he the one filtering them to the real world.'

'I'd love to get my hands on those drawings,' Rob said. 'Did Joe have any other regular visitors that might have helped do this?'

Nate and Adam looked at each other. 'Well we were only there occasionally on weekends and school holidays, so a bit hard for us to say, but he didn't have a lot of visitors.'

'What would the authorities have done... you know if they found Joe and found the drawings or found he was smuggling them out?' Jessica asked.

'I wouldn't put anything past them, even murder,' Nate said.

Jessica exhaled. 'Can't believe it. I can't believe people get away with this stuff; it's like every patient was at the mercy of the staff, not there to be helped by them.'

'The patient's testimonies are certainly supporting that,' Rob agreed.

'What about Joe's agent... or the gallery owner who exhibited his paintings... would they have smuggled the drawings out for him?' Danielle asked.

'Yeah logical thought,' Adam said.

'Call Joe's solicitor, whatever his name is... he'll have Joe's agent's name,' Danielle tried to recall his name.

'John Liberman...' Adam said. 'I'm due to update him anyway.'

'And I'll have a chat to Nurse Dave again and see if he was behind it or has any insights,' Nate said.

Adam's phone rang and he looked at the screen. 'Sorry, just got to take this... I'll only be a minute.' He rose and answered. 'Hi Mum...' Adam walked away from the group.

'Winsome,' Jessica's eyes lit up. 'I hope she comes in here one day.' She watched Adam, now oblivious to the conversation around her.

****

Adam smiled as he listened to his mother's good news; he paced around the office.

'Congratulations, Mum... of course I'm happy for you... Jack's a good guy and he's really good for you. I don't know what took you so long.'

She laughed. 'So, you're really happy for me? You know that no-one replaces your father in my life though, Adam,' she said.

'I know Mum,' he assured her. 'But Dad's been gone a very long time, and he would want you to be happy. He'd approve of Jack; so will Audrey.'

'Speaking of which, I can't reach your grandmother,' Winsome said.

'She's walking the Camino.'

'Good grief. Does she know there's no cocktail bar at every port of call? They just do that wine and pilgrim's meal, or so I've heard.'

'I guess she did her research,' Adam said, 'but it is a bit out of character.'

Winsome sighed. 'I just wanted her to hear it from me first, never mind. I'll put Jack on.'

Adam spoke with his godfather, Jack, for a few minutes before hanging up and rejoining the group.

'How's Winsome?' Nate asked.

'Engaged, to Jack,' Adam said, with a smile.

'Great news,' Rob said, and the group offered their congratulations.

'So, are you happy about this? Do you like him?' Danielle asked.

'Of course,' Adam said. 'I want Mum to be happy, and be with someone decent, and she's dated some real dickheads since Dad died. Jack, aside from being my godfather, is a good guy, they're suited.'

'Wow, this will be a big celebrity wedding,' Jessica gushed. 'The *IT* girl and the *Voice*... think of the guest list. I can't believe she hasn't remarried since... well, it's been a long time since your dad's passing.'

'She's been engaged twice. Thank God she likes a long engagement,' Adam said.

'Long enough to discover they're losers,' Nate agreed.

'Will Nate get an invitation?' Danielle asked.

'Of course I will, Winsome loves me.'

Adam and Rob gave him a look.

'Okay, she likes me better now than she did when we were kids. She used to say I was a troublemaker, but once I became a cop...'

'You were still a troublemaker,' Jessica reminded him.

'Hopefully they'll elope,' Adam said, cutting in.

'You knew about this, didn't you?' Jessica studied him.

'Yeah, Jack rang and gave me a heads-up a few days ago,'

Adam said. 'Their agents are going to put out a statement tomorrow morning.'

'Their agents…' Jessica giggled, she stopped when she realised what that meant. 'Oh, so…'

'Yeah, only my regular clients for the next few weeks,' Adam sighed. 'I can brush off the media calls if they get too much.'

Nate held up his hand for attention. 'This might be a good time to put the message bank on for the day, clear the diary tomorrow, lock the doors,' he said, with a glance to Jessica, 'and Adam and I can go drop in on Joe's agent and Nurse Dave. Can we do that?'

'Sure,' Adam said, and looked at Jessica. 'Can we do that?'

'I'll try and clear both of your diaries,' she said, and frowned at them. 'You're both troublemakers.'

'Me?' Nate exclaimed. 'C'mon, nothing to do with me… my mother brings in cakes, and she doesn't let the media know when she's baked!'

'Will you both get to take dates to the wedding? Because if you need handbags, Danielle and I could help out,' Jessica continued. 'Just saying…'

'Excellent idea, because it's easy to pick up at a wedding, and if you take us, we'll be sure not to hang off you so you have a chance,' Danielle directed the comment to Nate.

Adam shook his head. 'Mum! See it's started already. Meeting over.'

'But we'd need plenty of notice though, to shop,' Jessica added.

'And a bonus to help with the shopping…' Danielle added.

'Maybe we should get something made,' Jessica said. 'If we were invited…'

Nate, Adam and Rob rose and headed in opposite directions.

# Chapter 29

The next morning, the men had discarded their suits and arrived dressed casual for their research day out of the office. Nate indicated for the keys to Adam's car as they walked towards the new Mercedes. Adam handed them over, continuing his conversation on the phone. Nate grinned; he'd been keen to give the new model another spin.

'You're giving them too much,' Adam said to his ex-wife, and his mother's publicist, Stephanie. 'Just give them a couple of standard lines…. I know it's your job… I know you're the expert on this, but I'm the one doing the talking, allegedly.' He slid into the front passenger seat beside Nate and rolled his eyes, listening as his ex-wife read him the statement she had prepared for him to give to the media.

Nate pulled the car out of the carpark and headed west.

Adam sighed. 'Just say I'm thrilled for both of them and wish them a… fine, why ask me then if I don't get a say in it? Yeah, bye.' He hung up and took a deep breath.

'How on earth were you two ever together?' Nate asked.

'Be buggered if I know,' Adam agreed. 'Probably helped that we were working all the time and never home.' Adam looked around. 'How did you get to drive?'

Nate grinned. 'Distraction. Handles very nicely doesn't she?'

'She does,' Adam agreed, with a grin. 'When do you get your car back?'

'Could be a while yet. It's sitting in the cop yard waiting to be inspected,' Nate sighed. 'That reminds me to follow up Burnsey about getting the brake report.'

'Speaking of Burnsey, any luck getting Joe's interview transcript from the cops?' he asked.

'Funny story about that… according to Burnsey, it appears to have disappeared from the file,' Nate said.

'Right,' Adam rolled his eyes. 'I wonder how many decades it's been missing.' His phone rang again and Stephanie's number came up. He took a deep breath. 'Stephanie,' he answered. 'Okay, go ahead,' he said; she had reworked his comment to make it a little less wordy. He listened. 'Fine, thanks… no, I'm not just saying that… I don't do that when I'm fed up… yeah, okay maybe I do, but it's fine, thanks, release it to the hounds. Yeah, bye.'

'See, she still cares what you think,' Nate said.

'Nuh, she's just smart enough to know it's in her best interests to maintain a reasonably good relationship with me since she's working for Mum. Christ, I hope Mum and Jack elope.'

Nate smiled. 'C'mon, Dan and Jessica would kill to go to that wedding with you.'

Adam turned to look at Nate. 'You don't see it do you?'

'What?' Nate asked.

'Jess is mad for you. That whole fighting thing is just foreplay,' Adam said.

Nate shook his head. 'Nuh, not seeing that.' He looked past Adam to find number twenty-four on the street, indicated and turned into a small art gallery's car park. 'Okay get your culture on. Perhaps we should have worn our ties.'

'Then they'd try and sell us something. Just don't touch anything... we don't want to go home with a broken interpretive sculpture,' Adam said.

'Yes Mum.' Nate goaded him. They exited the car and Nate pocketed the keys before Adam could get them back. They didn't notice the red sedan that had been following them since they left their office.

*****

Sergeant Matt Burns pushed his police cap off as he entered the Stones Corner office of Delaney and Murphy; he ran his hand through his thinning brown hair. So, this is Nate's new digs, nice, he thought. He'd been tempted to leave the service a few times but he couldn't think of anything else he wanted to do. Then he got promoted and got a few more interesting cases—the hanging man at the asylum was one of them—so he stuck around, for now. Even nicer than the office was the receptionist who was squinting at him.

'I know you,' she smiled.

Matt laughed. 'Jessica... you worked for the Deputy Commissioner,' he said. 'I'm Matt Burns.' he extended his hand and they shook.

Jessica ran an appreciative eye over him. 'Matt Burns, I remember you now. We saw your name in the press clipping but I couldn't put a face with it before.'

'Yeah, well unlike Nate, I tried to keep a low profile at work, especially where the Deputy Commissioner was involved. Nate did well to recruit you! So, is the private detective in?'

'No, but he won't be long. I can give him a message. I'm guessing you've got news on his brakes?' she asked.

Matt nodded. He pulled a folded slip of paper out of his jacket and handed it to her. 'The report... confidential of course.'

'Of course,' she agreed, 'thanks. Want a coffee or tea?' she tried to stall him.

'Love one, but I'll have to raincheck... I've got to drop in on someone just around the corner from here and I'm on the clock.'

Jessica rose and saw him out, making small talk. She watched him walk down the stairs. Good to see he hadn't gone to fat like some of the guys do once they get through the academy, she thought.

She returned to the desk and unfolded the report. She drew in a sharp breath then let it out slowly. There was nothing accidental about Danielle's accident.

*****

A bell announced the arrival of Nate and Adam as they entered the gallery. It was on split levels, pristine white, cool and calm. One other person wandered around the lower floor stopping to study the paintings. Adam and Nate moved to a small white desk that was currently abandoned and glanced around. Nate checked out a painting nearby, noted the price tag of just under $5000 and moved on. They turned at the sound of footsteps behind them.

'Hello, you must be Nathan and Adam,' a flamboyant, older man said, offering his hand to Adam first, then Nate. 'I'm Avery Polson, owner and agent.'

'Thanks for seeing us Mr Polson,' Adam said.

'Please, just call me Avery... so we're talking about one of my top clients, Joe, come on through to my office.' He waved them through with an effeminate flourish, stopping briefly to motion to a slim, attractive woman who appeared on the stairway near them; she nodded. 'Eloise can look after the shop,' he said to the men.

Nate noted she looked particularly capable. They followed Avery into a large white office, with numerous paintings covering one span of wall. In his bright tangerine shirt, yellow jacket and cravat, Avery looked every bit the artistic type.

'Ah Joseph,' he said, after offering them coffee. He slipped into his office chair. 'That's one of his there.' Avery pointed to a landscape watercolour painting depicting a Utopian scene of beauty. 'It's titled '*View from my vain hopes*'. Quite lovely.'

'Can't part with it?' Nate asked.

'It was a gift, I'd never sell it,' Avery said. 'It was when he was first put away for a breakdown… not in the asylum he ended up in, but a health care facility that was a little kinder.'

'Were you always his agent, from day one?' Adam asked.

'I was the first to sign him and I always believed in him. He truly was a tortured artist… so much talent, so much anxiety, and such a terrible childhood. What he might have become if his father had nurtured his talent instead of trying to beat it out of him.' He sighed dramatically. 'So, what's your interest in Joe?'

Nate straightened in his chair. 'We're his friends… well we were kids when we met him at—'

'Oh my God, you're the boys… the two young friends he spoke of and drew…' Avery interrupted him, clapping his hands together.

'That's us,' Nate confirmed.

'Oh my, I didn't make the connection. Well, that is something,' Avery said, looking from Adam to Nate and back to Adam. 'I saw drawings of you both. So why are you here? Are you trying to buy his work?'

'No,' Adam said, 'we're trying to find him. Or his son, Thomas.' He explained about the *'Expectations'*.

'Ah that is so Joe isn't it? *Expectations*,' he clasped his hands together again. 'Delightful'. Avery laughed, then stopped and frowned at both men. 'What do you mean though, that you are trying to find him? Isn't he dead?'

Adam looked to Nate; the two men looked deflated. That answered that question… Avery wasn't going to lead them to Joe.

'We think so,' Nate said, turning his attention back to Avery. 'But where is he buried? No-one knows what became of him after he left or escaped from the asylum, or if he ever did really leave.'

'Oh, there was a flurry at the time, I assure you of that,' Avery said. 'Myself and Joe's solicitor whose name escapes me now…' he looked skyward for inspiration.

'John Liberman,' Adam filled in.

'Yes,' he looked at the men, pleased to solve that puzzle. 'That's him, John. Well, we demanded answers when we found out he was missing. We were told Joe had run away of his own accord. Then they changed the story about three weeks later and said they found his body and he had drowned. They called it suicide,' Avery said, his face reddening with anger. 'I didn't buy that for one moment. Joe had many years and many times when he was driven to suicide and never did, he was quite religious and was scared that he wouldn't enter the afterlife if he took his own life. But they insisted and said that as he had no next of kin who could be reached, he'd been cremated. It was outrageous. We wrote to the State Government, spoke with the media, but it was like some strange conspiracy… no-one cared, no-one wanted to know about it. Then, the asylum management presented some ashes to John and wouldn't give us the time of day to investigate it any further.'

'We're finding a lot of brick walls like that,' Nate agreed.

'And you never heard another word from Joe?' Adam asked. 'Never got a drawing or a painting again?'

'No, he vanished,' Avery said, waving his hands in the air. 'I do hope you find out something though, it would be so lovely to give him a proper farewell.'

'Just a few more questions before we get out of your hair,' Nate said, and continued on. 'We have a contact who believes Joe might have been killed because he was drawing scenes of what was going on at the asylum… the human testing, the violence…'

Avery nodded. 'Yes, I received those. It was… well, it became quite dangerous.'

'Can you tell us what happened?' Adam asked, sensing the man's reluctance.

Avery swallowed before continuing in a quieter voice. 'It was an awful time; Joe's work used to be confiscated by the management. They said he could paint and draw, they even said they encouraged it, but they didn't. Joe needed to draw, it was a part of him. I used to visit and take some of his works home with me when he had completed something significant, but they started getting very narky about that,' he stopped for emphasis. 'They started wanting to inspect me and my satchel when I left. So, Joe organised an insider to slip the paintings and drawings out to me.'

'Can you tell us who it was?' Nate asked.

Avery shook his head. 'I never saw them. I would arrive at work, and the drawings would be wrapped in paper and slipped under the door. Some marvellous stuff. But then they started getting, well, like you said… alarmingly factual, and I started getting threats. First, a letter saying it was in my best interest to destroy the drawings, then a rock through the window, and on the final occasion, the gallery was completely trashed.'

'Did you involve the police?' Adam asked.

'I did but I couldn't mention the Joe connection… he was still in there and I had to protect him. They never found out who did it and it was before the days of CCTV. I was frightened; I went to see Joe and told him what happened and that I couldn't accept them.'

'How did he take it?' Nate asked.

'Oh, he understood. He was mortified that he had placed me in danger… he really was a very kind soul.'

'Did you get any further threats after that?' Nate asked.

'No, but Joe disappeared within a week of my visit, and I never saw him again or got another piece of work from him again.' Avery looked to Joe's painting on the wall. 'A terrible waste of talent.'

'Have you ever heard from his son, Thomas?' Adam asked.

Avery smiled and returned his attention to the men. 'A lovely young man, but he's no artist. Oh, he's tried, and he can sketch, but he's not an artist. He just doesn't have the originality and interpretive flair.'

'So, you've met him?' Nate sat forward on his chair.

'Indeed, he works right here in Brisbane.'

'We spoke with his mother, Donna, but she failed to mention that,' Nate said, also not mentioning that Thomas's mother wanted proof of Joe and his brother, Stephen's death, before telling them anything about Thomas.

'Oh, she's probably being very protective. But if you are discreet, I'll share the information given your intentions are noble. My how Joe would love to meet you both today,' he said, distracted. 'So, Thomas, you'll find him easily. It's odd—well I think it odd—he runs those ghost and cemetery tours. He takes one of them through the asylum of all places; must be some kind of way he feels closer to his father, who knows? He uses a stage name...'

Nate's eyes widened and his body tensed. 'Harry Bond?' Nate asked. 'The owner of River City Ghost Tours?'

'That's him,' Avery said, 'that's Joe's boy.'

## Chapter 30

Adam had to hurry to keep up with Nate as they returned to his car.

'You've got to kidding! All this time he's been right under our nose,' Nate said. 'Never said a word,' he unlocked Adam's car door and opened the driver's side.

'Hold up,' Adam pushed the door closed, grabbed the keys from him and pointed to the passenger side. 'You're not driving fired up.'

Nate scowled and went around to the passenger side. The men slipped into the car and Adam started it, putting the air con on full blast.

Nate looked at his watch. 'Let's ring Nurse Dave and tell him we'll be late. I want to go straight over to see Harry aka Thomas. I can't believe it... been chasing our tails... why aren't we moving?'

Adam sighed, 'Just breathe.'

Nate started to speak again and Adam shut him down. 'Seriously, just stop for a minute. Think back. How many times did you see Harry?'

Nate frowned. 'Once.'

'So, what did you tell him... did you mention Joe or why we were interested in the asylum?' Adam asked.

Nate thought about it. 'We'd gone in to speak with him about the hanging man that he saw, and his interview in the paper the next day when they got a hold of the story. I don't remember... hold up.' Nate grabbed his phone and swiped, found Danielle's number and called her. She answered straight away, and he picked her brain. Hanging up, he turned to Adam.

'She doesn't think we ever mentioned Joe... we just said we had a client interested in finding out more about the place.'

'Okay,' Adam pulled the car away from the curb. 'Call Dave, see if we can bump him to later and we'll head to Harry's... Thomas's shop, or can Dan handle Dave?'

Nate thought about it. 'Don't see why not.' He rang Danielle again and checked she was free; he gave her a briefing on what they needed to know. Hanging up, he rang Dave and told him Danielle was on her way. Adam went over the situation in his head as he drove the short distance to Fortitude Valley and Nate made arrangements.

Nate hung up. 'All sorted.'

Adam sighed. 'I can't believe it. I can't believe Joe's son has been in the same city all this time.'

'He looks nothing like Joe,' Nate said, 'you'd never look at him and be reminded. It is weird though. Turn down that laneway up ahead, you can park down there.'

Adam parked the car against the curb, relieved to find the office of River City Ghost Tours open. 'Okay, you need to tread carefully here, yeah?'

'Yeah, I know,' Nate said. Adam's eyes narrowed; he'd believe it when he saw it.

'You know, Joe's wife, Donna, said her son *went the way of Joe*... I thought she meant he was slightly unbalanced too...' he said and opened the car door to exit.

Adam shrugged. 'She might have meant he was an artist.' He alighted, locked the car and followed Nate inside.

*****

Danielle was meeting former nurse, Dave Trigg at 2pm at the Stones Corner Hotel, across the road from their office. He was late but not by much. She spotted him right away from Nate's description: slight, hunched, short and wiry with a worn face. He was hurrying down the street towards the hotel, talking on his mobile phone. He hung up, looked around and she gave him a wave. Dave pocketed his phone and came towards her.

'Dave Trigg?' she asked, rising from her seat.

'Danielle,' he said, and shook her offered hand. 'Sorry I'm late, got held up and then the traffic. Let me get you a drink. What will it be?'

'Ah thanks, mineral water with lemon would be great.'

She watched as he hurried to the bar, was intercepted by a waiter on the way, placed the order and returned.

'Waiting long?' he asked.

'No, a few minutes,' she assured him. 'Thanks for meeting me.'

'Sure,' he said. 'I used to work with one of your mob at the hospital up the road.'

'One of my mob?' she frowned.

'An indigenous lad,' he said, 'fine nurse he was too.'

'I've worked with a lot of your mob,' she said.

He smirked. 'Yeah, bet you have. Sorry, just meant… well you know, not a lot of—'

She interrupted him. 'Successful mob?'

He studied her. 'You've got a chip. Wasn't going to say

222

that. I was going to say, there's not as many aboriginals, indigenous people, your mob, whatever you want to call them, working in Brisbane. When I worked in country towns, the balance was better.'

She nodded. 'Yeah, sorry. It's just… you know…'

'No, but I can guess.' He took a mouthful of beer. 'Better get to your questions then.'

She nodded and thanked the waiter as he delivered her drink. She clinked glasses with Dave.

'Cheers, thanks for the drink.' She sipped it and pulled a small note pad and pen from her pocket and placed it on the table. She looked at it but didn't open the pad. 'Did you help Joe by smuggling his drawings out of the asylum?'

Dave looked startled. 'Yeah, well straight to the point, eh? Who wants to know and why?'

'Fair question,' Danielle said, and sat back in her chair. 'Adam and Nate were told by Joe's agent that he used to get Joe's drawings and then it stopped. Whoever helped get them out was probably in danger too or if it wasn't you, might have been hurt as well.' She said, and studied him for a reaction. 'Make sense?'

Dave nodded and thought about her words. 'You're right on all fronts. At the start, I was just taking his art to his agent, Avery. Arty name, hey? Then the sketchings of what was going on started to get mixed amongst them and Avery didn't know what to do with them; neither did I. Avery sent one to the newspaper and shit hit the fan; it was a storm in a teacup though and the management squared it up with the old lunatic excuse.'

'Then it became a witch hunt at the madhouse?' Danielle asked.

'Oh yeah. We were all hauled in and warned it wasn't in our best interests to be doing something like that. Then we were interviewed individually and warned again. I couldn't risk it after that. I don't know what Joe did with them, and you know Avery's place got trashed, so I think he destroyed the few he had.'

'Do you know if Joe kept drawing them?'

Joe shook his head. 'No, don't know and Joe would never put me at risk, he was like that.' He stopped, drained his glass and looked at Danielle. 'You know, that's not quite true... sorry I've got used to being shady about this stuff. It's true Joe never put me at risk, but he did keep drawing them, I just don't know what became of them. Or him for that matter.'

Danielle nodded. 'Well, thanks for talking with me.'

'Sure,' he said. 'Better hit the road. Want me to walk you to your car?'

'Oh thanks,' she said, but I've got a few calls to make so I'll finish my drink and head off soon. She rose and shook his hand.

Danielle sat down again and dialled Nate's number. It was engaged; she sat back, sipped her drink and waited. Then a few minutes later she saw him; Dave Trigg at the red light in a red Nissan sedan.

# Chapter 31

Harry Bond looked up from the book he was writing in at the reception desk, keen to greet a potential new client. He put down his pen and a slow smile graced his face as he regarded Nate.

'Ah, Mum said you'd be back, took you a while to work it out,' Thomas said.

'Didn't think to mention that you had a connection with the place because of your dad, or to follow us up once your mum filled you in?' Nate snapped, 'we're chasing our tails trying to get some kind of justice...'

Thomas cut him off, anger boiling to the surface.

'Yeah, I'm going to tell you and that other woman that I've just met two minutes ago, my whole history,' he snarled.

Adam stepped forward and put a hand on Nate's shoulder.

'Of course you're not going to,' he said, in a conciliatory manner. 'And we didn't give you enough information to let you know that we were friends with your dad. Did your mum tell you who we are?'

Both Nate and Thomas backed down slightly. Thomas took a breath. 'She said you knew my father and now you're trying to find me, him and my Uncle Stephen. She also said you were enquiring about the bank account, the private one.'

'That pays you a regular salary… interest from Joe's account,' Adam said.

'You found that out too, huh?' Thomas said.

Adam hadn't but he bluffed. 'I had someone looking into it. But I'm glad you have it… helps with this, I imagine.' Adam said, looking around.

Thomas nodded. 'Always wanted to run my own business; I didn't want to work for anyone and I like this. I don't believe in ghosts so I'm not spooked by them, but it's kind of fun freaking out other people and I get to be a bit theatric… since I'm clearly not my father's son when it comes to artistic talent,' he said, with bitterness dripping from his tongue.

'Can we sit?' Adam asked, and Thomas nodded. The office phone began to ring and Thomas excused himself to answer. Adam and Nate moved to the chairs and sat in the small reception area.

'Sorry I lost my cool,' Nate said.

'It doesn't matter,' Adam assured him. They listened to Thomas taking a booking for four people on his Saturday night ghost tour. When he hung up, he rejoined them.

'Did you want to read your father's diary?' Nate asked.

Thomas shook his head. 'I'm not interested, just like he wasn't interested in me.'

'Thomas…' Adam leaned forward.

'Don't start defending him!' Thomas snapped.

Nate cleared his throat. 'There's some drawings of us two in your father's diary. We were kids when we met him. He was good to us, treated us like we were important, you know like our opinion mattered.'

'Didn't do anything for me but leave me his money.'

'You know his story, don't you?' Adam asked. 'About the beatings he copped from his father—your grandfather—

and how he wasn't allowed to draw? How your uncle might have retaliated to protect Joe, and accidentally killed your grandfather?'

Thomas listened but didn't let on whether he knew or not. Adam continued. 'You know your dad never coped with that... especially when your uncle disappeared... he had to for his own safety.'

Nate took over. 'You know a lot about the stuff that happened in that horrible place he was put in. There are drawings... he captured some of it and we think his sketches might have put him in great danger.'

Thomas absorbed their words as he sized them up.

Adam continued. 'Your mum said, that when they were expecting you, Joe was so scared he'd hurt you... that his father's anger and his own insecurity were somehow genetic,' Adam finished.

Thomas rocked back and forward in the chair.

Adam studied the young man. 'He would have been so proud of you. You would have been his life's best work.'

Thomas covered his face with his hands and cried.

*****

Nate shuffled uncomfortably as Thomas attempted to get a grip on his emotions; Adam sat waiting – occupational hazard, he had seen this many a time.

'So,' Nate broke the ice, 'we want to find out what happened to your dad in that place and we've got some of the other patients who knew him, coming forward with their stories. We want the system held accountable... for how all of them were treated.'

'And we want to find your dad's remains and maybe give

him a proper burial,' Adam said. 'Do you know where he is?'

Thomas removed his hands, sniffed and wiped his face on his sleeve. He shook his head and Nate rolled his eyes.

'Someone knows something… he didn't just wake up and vanish,' he said, his voice laced with frustration.

'He had some stuff,' Thomas offered. 'A box or tin or something with personal stuff that might help.'

Adam brightened and sat up. 'Have you got it?'

'No. He wrote to his agent…'

'Avery,' Adam said.

'Yeah, Avery,' Thomas continued. 'Avery told me about it when he offered me some of the old sketches. He said since I didn't have any talent, did I want to gaze upon my father's work.'

'He didn't say that,' Adam said, with a smile and Thomas smirked.

'Yeah, well that's what he meant when he made the offer. My father told Avery that he'd hidden the box on the grounds and if anything happened to him, that he'd draw a map to it and he'd send it to him.'

'So, has Avery got it – the map? Did he give it to you?' Nate asked.

Thomas shook his head again. 'Sorry man, but I never got the map. But…' he began to get his showmanship back as he rose and strode in the small place between them.

'Now that I think of it, Avery said that my father had mentioned there was a simple version of it… he'd given it to his two friends.' Thomas's eyes widened. 'Have you got it?'

Adam looked to Nate, the two of them exchanged a knowing look.

Nate cleared his throat and looked guilty. 'He gave us a map for Christmas with a treasure hunt on it. Joe said he had some stuff there and… to be honest I don't remember much about it and then Mum put it through the wash.'

Adam gave Thomas an exasperated look. 'Yeah, he's still losing things. But, I don't think it was *the* map… this one had dragons and castles and all sorts of things drawn over it.'

'That'd be it,' Thomas said. 'When I studied my father's work at art college… I went for a while before I found out I had no talent…'

'Hold up,' Adam said, rising and going to the window to look down the alley. He turned and faced Thomas. 'You've got to let this hang-up go. You have skills your father didn't have… Joe was so introverted he could never have run this business or lead the groups you do with your theatrics. So, forget the art, do what you're good at. No-one expects you to be your father's son.'

'Hell yeah,' Nate piped in, seeing the look Adam gave him for back up. 'My dad was a great athlete, played State level footy and was an impressive track runner. I'm clueless at sport, but he'd be a crap detective… he's got no memory for detail and no patience. Couldn't solve where he left his car keys.'

Thomas gave the hint of a smile; listening, while he tried to maintain a look of nonchalance.

Adam studied him; he really was just a kid finding his own way.

'Anyway, I don't think it'd be the map in question,' Adam said, bringing them back to the point.

'Yeah, well you might be wrong on that,' Thomas said. 'Like I was saying, when I studied his work, he had a code for things in some of his paintings. I'm doing the same thing in the games I'm creating… you know, online games…'

'Ah, a code,' Nate nodded. 'So, I remember a castle, a dragon, a tree with a face…' He looked to Adam to continue.

'God, it was a hundred years ago. I don't know… there was that crest Joe created for us, and the sort of ancient looking compass,' Adam rubbed his brow and then his eyes widened. 'Nate, remember there was a time capsule… Joe told us not to open it until we grew up.'

'Wow, I'd forgotten that… a time capsule. And, oh yeah, one of the drawings was a tree with a door in it!'

'Yeah, but maybe Joe was prettying up the map to make it interesting for us,' Adam said.

'Doubt it,' Thomas said. 'In mythology, a castle represents power, authority or dominance; a dragon is usually good luck or good fortune; the tree with a door… well…' Thomas thought for a moment. 'The door's a portal but not just for travel…it can be for self-discovery or growth, you know consciousness to unconsciousness.'

'Right up your alley,' Nate said to Adam.

'Could you redraw it?' Thomas asked.

Nate scoffed. 'I looked at it for about three minutes and Adam even less. But it did start in that carpark area where Dave smuggled Joe out… remember?'

Adam shook his head. 'I just remember the big compass symbol and the river running through it. It was a good-looking map.'

Thomas interrupted their thoughts. 'Don't worry, this is great, we can draw something up and add whatever you can remember. We could solve this like a real mystery, the three of us.' He looked like a man with a new lease of life.

Adam and Nate exchanged looks as Thomas rummaged through his office drawer and produced two markers. 'Here,' he said, giving them one each. He strode to the corner of the office and pulled out a large board with sheets of paper clipped to it. The first sheet was covered with the words 'Company vision', and three attempts at coming up with it scrawled underneath. He tore it off to the clean sheet underneath. Thomas turned to the two men.

'So, draw the map… draw what you can remember but don't look at each other's drawings, 'cause it will sway you… just put what you think was there and we can compare.' He smiled at the men. 'Yeah, this is great.'

# Chapter 32

'The poor bastard,' Nate said, with a sigh.

Adam glanced over at him, as he pulled the car into the driveway of their office. 'Who?'

'The kid. C'mon,' Nate sized up the young journalist sitting on the stairs waiting for Adam. 'He's a kid – squeaky clean, looks fresh out of university and betcha his editor sent him here to get him out from underfoot and expected nothing back from him. Everyone else has left and he's still sitting… waiting…'

Adam thought by closing the office for the day he had successfully managed to avoid the media after his mother's engagement announcement. Except for that one journalist. Adam made a sound that fell somewhere between suspicious and not caring.

The young journo spotted Adam and his eyes widened. Scrambling up, he dropped his pad and recorder.

Nate continued. 'Give him a break, a quick interview… I'll take the pic for him.'

'Fine then, you big softie,' Adam said, and parked in the visitors' bay instead of taking the car underneath to his car spot. They exited the car as the journo ran over to them.

'Adam, hi, I'm Cooper Tarred from *All the News Today*

*Online*, can I have a quick interview?' he asked as quickly as he could, as though every captured moment counted.

'Sure,' Adam said, and Cooper's eyes widened more.

'Really? Wow, great,' he said, and smiled, then fumbled with his recorder. 'I'll just flick this on.'

Adam introduced Nate and leant back on the side of his car, waiting.

'Want me to get a couple of shots while you're doing that, Cooper?' Nate asked, eyeing the small camera. 'You know one of Adam alone, one with you interviewing him.'

'That'd be brilliant, thanks,' Cooper said. He handed the camera to Nate and placed the tape closer to Adam.

'Okay, so how are you feeling about your mum and Jack Bernham's engagement?' he started, with a glance to Nate as he snapped away.

'I think it's great,' Adam answered. 'Jack's a good guy and they've known each other for a long time; they'll be happy.'

'You're a psychologist, right? So, is that a professional or personal opinion?' Cooper asked.

Adam smiled. 'Both. But more personal... Jack's my godfather, and very grounded.'

'You didn't want to go into showbiz?' Cooper asked.

Adam grinned. 'No, can't sing, can't act, what would I do?'

'Model?' Cooper answered, 'like your mum. That would have got a lot of press.'

Nate laughed and Adam gave him a look. 'What? You don't think I could model?' he asked, folding his arms across his chest.

'Yeah sorry,' Nate said. 'That face could launch a thousand ships!'

Cooper grinned at their banter. 'Now that you're older than Winsome was when she brought down the government, what do you make of all that?'

Adam felt Nate stiffen beside him as he waited for the flare up but Adam took a deep breath and continued.

'Yep, good question,' he said. Cooper grew a few centimetres taller. 'It's hard to say because I've only ever heard a very small version of Mum's side of the story and read some of what was written in the media, and...' he cut off the inevitable question of what was Winsome's side of the story, '...I never really asked Mum about it. I suspect most kids don't talk to their parents about their past... too busy making our own. So, in terms of what I think about it, I see it every day in many guises. Success and power are aphrodisiacs in our society, now more than ever. People are still tempted, needing endorsement, vulnerable... it was just that the two people, in this case, were national figures and there was a family that got hurt.'

Nate looked at Adam with surprise; he'd never heard him say so much about it.

'Did you ever meet the former PM's kids?'

'No.' Adam glanced at his watch.

'Just one last question, and hey thanks, really super grateful for the interview,' Cooper said.

'You're the only interview he gave, be sure to tell your editor that you got an exclusive, and ask for your byline and pay rise,' Nate said.

'Yeah, great will do,' Cooper said, with a satisfied look upon his face. 'So last question, do you think the PM is your dad?'

'No. Right then, good luck, Cooper.'

Adam was gone before he had barely finished the sentence. Nate handed the camera back to Cooper. 'Good job kid.'

'Thanks,' he said, with a grin.

Nate caught Adam up. 'He had to ask it.'

'Sure, but that's why I don't do these interviews. It's just the same old bullshit. Next they'll be trying to get my DNA.' Adam bolted up the stairs, annoyed that he left himself be talked into it.

*****

At the top of the stairs, he fiddled with his keys in the closed office door; Jessica opened the door from the other side.

'You're still here? Everything okay?' Adam asked with a quick glance around.

'Yep, fine, just finishing some paperwork,' she said, and lowered her voice. 'Rob's still here too, he's got a client in with him.' She moved back to her desk. 'So, how did it go with Thomas?'

'Painful,' Adam said, following her inside. Nate was close behind. 'We had to draw our memories on a sheet of paper; now I know how my patients feel.'

'How'd you go today?' Nate asked.

'Good,' she said. 'The media gave up just after midday but the phone calls have been steady. I let them go to message bank and only answered the ones I thought were real clients.'

'Thanks Jess, sorry about that,' Adam said.

'It's all good… kind of exciting. Will you mum ever come to visit here?'

'Doubt it,' he said, moving to the window at the sound of a car horn below. The after-work commute was in full swing, and the wine o'clockers were filling up the tables on the sidewalk outside the hotel.

'Shame, it'd be amazing if she did,' Jessica continued. 'Anyway, Sergeant Matt Burns dropped in Nate, I did recognise him after all, and he left this for you,' she said, going behind the desk and handing Nate the folded report.

Nate realised what it was straight away and opened it quickly. He shook his head and looked at Adam.

'Deliberately tampered with... the brakes... crap. So, someone is worried we're opening this case up again, but did they think I was driving or did they know Dan was and thought it was a good way to get to us?' Nate asked, talking to himself more than anyone else.

As Adam went to answer, Rob's door opened and he stood aside to allow a woman to go in front of him. She stopped, seeing the people in the reception, and her eyes widened at the sight of Nate and Adam.

She backed up, running into Rob. 'You two,' she pointed at them, 'you worked there, at the hospital,' she said, 'you were on staff.'

Adam held up his hands. 'No, no, you're wrong. Look at us, we're your age, how could we have worked there.'

She looked from one to the other, took a deep breath and nodded. 'Right, of course... you're right. I'm stupid. I'm sorry,' she turned to Rob. 'It was just digging up all that stuff, you know.'

'I know,' he assured her.

'I'm sorry,' she said, again. 'I'm an idiot. I'm not here for counselling,' she hurriedly explained, as though that would be the worst thing to be caught in a psychologist's office. 'I'm just here because Mac said you needed as much testimony as you could get. I'm not interested in being a patient.'

'Sure, that's fine, thanks for helping out,' Nate said. 'You do know us though.'

Every head in the room turned to look at him. He studied the woman... tall, slight, thick red hair past her shoulders;

she had an edgy air about her. 'We met you once. You asked us to help you get out and told us Joe was in solitary confinement… but that's not the term you used. Casey.'

'Kelsey,' Adam corrected him. 'It's Kelsey isn't it?'

'Yeah, Kelsey,' she said, narrowing her eyes as she studied them. She crossed her hands across her chest and offered a small smile. 'The hole; he was in the hole.'

'Wow, you haven't changed much really,' Adam said, placing her in his memory banks.

She laughed. 'Oh trust me, I have. I'm a different person…' she stopped, not wanting to say any more in front of the audience. 'You were on the other side of the fence. I saw you a few times.'

'How long did it take you to get out?' Adam asked, 'we would have helped you, like you asked. We even thought of some ways to do it,' he said, with a glance to Nate, remembering their conversation. 'But we never saw you again.'

She shrugged. 'I was only there a few months. My stepfather deserted, so, my mother came and got me.' She started towards the door. 'Gotta go.'

Adam well recognised the look of someone avoiding the past.

Rob followed to see her out, and she stopped to look back at them once more.

'Huh, amazing,' she said, with just the hint of a smile before departing.

Rob closed the door behind her.

'That…' he said, and took a deep breath, 'was a harrowing tale… what she saw in a few months would stand your hair on end.'

## Chapter 33

**Recorded transcript of River Park Hospital former patient:** Kelsey Bickley

**In attendance:** Robert Ware, Psychologist

**Robert:** When you are ready, Kelsey, perhaps start by telling me how you came to be a resident at River Park Hospital.

**Kelsey:** Hospital… ha, yes, I've heard it called that; it's usually called the madhouse or as my mum called it, 'the sad house'. I was thirteen when I was sent there. I wasn't crazy or anything, I was angry and in trouble at home. I've started wrong…

**Robert:** Start again if you like, but there's no right or wrong, we're just talking.

**Kelsey:** Right, of course… okay, so Mum was a single mum; I don't know what happened to Dad, I never knew. Mum said I didn't have a father and that was that. But she always had to have a man, none of them wanted to be my dad though. Plenty of them wanted me to sit on their knee. I had to call them Uncle. Mum couldn't seem to hold any man down for too long. I think she was too needy; you could smell it on her. Men don't like that, they don't like being fitted up as a husband and father when all they want to do is have is sex on tap and not be nagged.

Anyway, Mum thought she knew so much about it… she'd give me advice on how to keep and get a man. Like something out of the 1950s… don't talk too much when they get home, always have the smell of something good cooking, make sure you always looked pretty for them, all that crap, seriously.

My favourite was to make sure you praise him especially in the bedroom and let him be the man – *you're the best, I've never had it better, you're so strong, of course I came and several times*. I didn't even know what went on in the bedroom when she was saying this stuff to me. But when I hit about thirteen, I realised pretty fast that plenty of her dates were keen to show me what to do in there.

I don't want you to get the wrong impression of Mum though. I'm just here to tell you what I saw happening for the couple of months they stuck me in the asylum… a favour for Mac, he had my back then, as best he could. I've never forgotten that. I just have to set the scene so you know why I was there.

**Robert:** Trust me, no-one is judging here… I've got my own family tree that would give yours a shake for its money.

**Kelsey:** Ha, thanks. So back to Mum – she wasn't a bad person, it's just that attracting a man was pretty much the only skill she had. She'd won a beauty contest when she was eighteen and living in the bush… Miss Cow of the Year or something, and she traded on it. I'm kidding, it was the Carnival Queen.

But when I was about twelve, she met a guy who decided he'd stick around and they got married about six months after they met. Geoff... and he wanted to be my daddy. The first time he came into my room at night, I just froze with fear; I knew a bit about sex by then, we'd all talk about it at school... you know girls' talk. My best friends Dana and Fiona and me, we'd read scenes and make up fantasies... one day it might be '*Pride and Prejudice*' where it is all very gallant, next time, something modern, dramatic and fun. But for losing our virginity, we had these romantic visions of what it'd be like; rose petals, dim lighting, a guy who'd say we're beautiful and gently take off the lace or satin lingerie we would be wearing. Yeah, Geoff came in and said something like 'he needed to give me the sex talk because soon boys would be trying it on and I needed to be careful'. Such a good guy.

He pulled his track pants down and he had this huge erection and I'd never seen one... ugly, dirty thing. Then, he pulled me out of bed, made me kneel on the floor and he pushed himself into my mouth. I can remember gagging and crying, the whole show, and he had his hands around my head, controlling the movements like I was some inflatable dummy. He came in my mouth. (*Gagging sounds, the sound of patient rising*).

**Kelsey:** Sorry. I thought after all these years it would be easier to tell.

**Robert:** We can break anytime you like Kelsey. (*Sound of water pouring*)

**Kelsey:** No, thanks, I want to get this recorded, like I promised Mac, and then I'm done.

**Rob:** Have you had some professional help?

**Kelsey:** No. I'm not interested in talking about it again or having therapy, I don't need that now. But I'll testify this is a true record if you need me to.

**Robert:** Thank you, that's appreciated. I see you're a librarian now?

**Kelsey:** I love books; they're reliable. I love libraries too, so peaceful, no-one constantly talking at you. Sorry, I'm ready…

**Robert:** So, how did you escape from Geoff?

**Kelsey:** Geoff. He came back maybe three nights over the next month and did the same thing. Mum was home most of the time, so he had to pick his moments. Then he said that next time, he was going to teach me another move, he was going to let me feel him inside me.

**Robert:** Did you tell anyone? Your mum? A teacher or friend?

**Kelsey:** Hell no. But you know, when I look back on it now, of course it showed. I started freaking out if anyone touched me, I was tired all the time because I never slept; I was either waiting for him or recovering from him. I hadn't had my period, but I didn't know enough to know that I couldn't get pregnant… Mum had given me a very sketchy version of the 'talk'. I almost told her, but she kept saying all the time how great he was, how happy she was, and that we were a family. Kind of like she was warning me not to say anything.

**Robert:** She had no idea?

**Kelsey:** I don't know. I've thought about that a lot. Eventually, Geoff came to my room to give me the next lesson as he called it, and he gagged me so she couldn't hear. Oh my God it hurt and he got angry because he couldn't get it inside at first and thought I was doing something to stop him. How? So, he pushed and pushed, I bled after that and Mum thought my period had started.

**Robert:** So, when did your mum find out? Did she find out?

**Kelsey:** I told her where the blood was really from and she slapped me; told me I was always after attention and that I'd gone too far. She kicked me out. Can you believe that? I was thirteen and I didn't know where to go or what to do. I had no grandparents in the country and no Dad. So, I went to my best friend's house but her parents rang Mum who came to pick me up. Geoff denied it of course and so I was back in the house with him, and with her. It didn't stop him; he did it one more time before I ran away. I think now when I look back on it, I had a bit of a breakdown and when I stopped eating and started attacking anyone who came into my room, well…

**Robert:** Instead of finding out the truth, your mum had you institutionalised?

**Kelsey:** Yes. You know the funny thing, at first, I thought that would be so much better being there; I'd be safe and have a bed of my own and could sleep at night. It wasn't better, it was worse because I was young, vulnerable, pretty, and I never knew when and where the attacks were going to come from. Some of the other patients did what they could to protect me, like Mac, but what could they do? I wasn't there very long, but I think I was… raped, maybe three times. Sometimes, I wasn't even conscious but I'd wake and I'd be wet between the legs and sore, or someone would tell me they'd seen it happen. There was a guy who stuck up for me once and then he disappeared.

**Robert:** Did you see anyone from the outside world?

**Kelsey:** Mum visited once but could barely look at me. Geoff came up once by himself and warned me that if I ever opened my mouth about anything he had done to me, I'd never get out of the place, and my school friends weren't allowed to come, thank God.

**Robert:** What other violations did you see while you were there?

**Kelsey:** How long have you got? I can't prove it, but they'd take patients in for what they called a health check; the patients were so frightened going down the hallway to the medical room they could barely walk or breathe. I saw patients strapped to beds, injected, given shock treatment. I saw people put in solitary confinement and they wouldn't come out for weeks. One of the nurses who liked me, said she put several of the female patients out cold before she left for the day so they didn't know what was happening to them overnight. She offered to do it for me too. Once they studied me after I woke and wrote things down; I don't know what they were looking for or expecting. This one guy, he was older than me but we'd talked – he couldn't remember his own name for a few days after his health check. Appalling… unbelievable… who's going to believe us?

**Robert:** Could you identify the staff members who did this? Were they following instruction?

**Kelsey:** I've thought about that too a lot over the years. Many, many a time, I'd stop somewhere, shaking, and short of breath because I thought I saw one of them. But most times, the violence didn't happen when I was lucid. They can all justify giving me needles, strapping me onto the bed… standard procedure, they'll say. The violations that happened when I was groggy or put under, I couldn't tell you who did what.

**Robert:** How did you get out?

**Kelsey:** After about two months, Geoff deserted Mum. He found someone else and got them pregnant so it was a little hard to fake that one. Mum came and got me out. She decided then that she'd believe me.

**Robert:** Did you stay with her, with your mum?

**Kelsey:** Yes, where else would I go? I went to a different school for the last year of high school… a place where they didn't know me and I just kept to myself. I'm sure they all thought I was an aloof bitch but I just wanted to get the certificate, get out, get a job and my own place. Somewhere where I could lock the door at night, where I could sleep safely. You know what I mean?

**Robert:** Totally understandable. And you've never told anyone about what happened to you in there?

**Kelsey:** Ha, who? No-one would believe that story, I've got no power.

**Robert:** You have now.

# Chapter 34

'Long day,' Adam sighed, as the team wound down, preparing to meet John Liberman—Joe's solicitor—who was due at their office at any moment.

'Must be happy hour,' Nate said, opening their small mini bar fridge. He waved a beer in the direction of Jessica who wrinkled her nose and nodded as he grabbed the white wine from the fridge rack. He handed Adam and Rob a beer.

'Maybe we do drink too much,' Adam said, accepting the beer.

'Nuh, a couple of drinks a day is normal, isn't it?' Nate asked, with a glance to Rob.

'You know, you lads should think about eating something every now and then,' Rob suggested, unscrewing the cap of his beer. 'They do a good steak across the road, there's Thai a few doors up, and a terrific Mexi-Indian place too.'

'So, we're not getting all we need from our liquid diets?' Nate asked, looking at the label on his beer.

Adam smiled. 'We go home after work every night and dine on meat and three veg, Rob, promise. Straight from the freezer, ten minutes in the microwave, and you've just got to remember to take the plastic off before you eat.'

'Ah, good to know,' Rob said, playing along.

'So, what happened… you know, with Thomas, Joe's son? Did he cop to it all?' Jessica asked, impatient to cut to the chase.

'He did, he's definitely Joe's son. Nate was so encouraging, Thomas couldn't resist spilling it all,' Adam joked.

Nate scoffed. 'Yeah, I might have started off on the wrong foot.'

'Not like you,' Jessica teased, as he sat down beside her at the table.

'Not at all,' he agreed. 'But he thinks he might know where Joe left his drawings.'

Rob's eyes lit up with interest. 'We could really use those.'

Nate continued. 'Thomas had us drawing this treasure map… Lord help us… and he's going to colour it in. He thinks the map might lead us to the etchings.'

Rob looked confused; Adam explained. 'Joe gave us a treasure map once… and we lost it. But he said something about two things being hidden: a surprise for now and a time capsule for later.'

'And you think that might be where the drawings are?' Rob asked.

Adam nodded and rose as John appeared at the door. 'Yep, we found out today that his agent took receipt of them for a while until he was threatened.' Adam opened the door and invited John in, introducing him around.

'Well this is nice,' John said, politely.

'Yeah, much better than your shabby digs on the river,' Nate agreed.

John laughed. 'Those shabby digs are just to impress the clients… I never get time to look at the river. Did it work?'

'You bet; we knew you were going to be expensive the moment we pulled up and saw your view,' Nate said.

John joined them at the table and took the offered drink. 'You've got something for me?'

'Ah straight to the point. Still on the clock?' Adam teased him, 'lucky we're pro bono!'

John grinned. 'Sorry, occupational hazard. I could attempt some small talk. How about this weather?'

Rob nodded in appreciation. 'Beautiful Brisbane days. Did the lads tell you that I think we're ready to go?'

John's eyes widened. 'Really? You've done it?'

Rob nodded. 'We've got testimonies from seven victims, and I've got another three to see in the coming weeks. We can expect a bit of fallout, and once the news gets out we're launching the suit, we'll gain a few as well.'

John nodded. 'Wow. I thought you'd struggle to get anyone to come forward, to be honest.'

'I don't understand why it's taken them so long to do this,' Jessica said. 'I would have wanted to bring the offenders to their knees years ago.'

'Maybe, maybe not. It's hard to relive this stuff,' Adam said. 'Many of them have probably spent years trying to file it away and keep it out of their daily consciousness, and then we ask them to bring it back to the surface.'

'It's complicated,' John agreed. 'Add to that that each State can differ in terms of legal limitations. For victims or patients who were underage when affected, the Limitations of Action Act 1974 basically stated that legal actions for personal injury must be commenced within three years from the date of the injury. So, underaged children had three years from the time they turned eighteen to start action, and let's face it, I doubt any of them would have been in a state to do so then.'

'Now that's insane. So, what's changed?' Jessica asked.

'The law! In 2016 the State Government removed the civil statutory time limit for child victims of sexual abuse. So now, it doesn't matter when or how long ago the event occurred, they can sue,' John said.

'But that's just child victims,' Adam said.

John sat back and exhaled. 'Exactly. For adult victims it varies depending on whether the case is considered personal injury or death, or corporate damages, or unconscionable conduct, and on it goes. It's a landmine. What are they like... the statements?'

'Brutal... horrendous... controversial,' Rob said.

'I've been typing out the transcripts,' Jessica said. 'The women's accounts are just... well, there's rape, abortion, beatings... just shocking stuff, you wouldn't believe it could happen here, seriously, it's like some 19th-century drama. And, some of them were just young delinquent girls, some as young as thirteen; nothing wrong with them mentally. They should never have been sent there. It's a horror story,' she shuddered.

Rob nodded and continued. 'Some of our claimants were routinely drugged... stuff like paraldehyde—it's a central nervous system depressant—it was used a lot in the sixties, and clearly was still being used as late as the eighties too,' he explained. 'Largactil's another drug they were injected with... it's an antipsychotic medication. Some of them lived in straitjackets for days, and valium was handed out like lollies. There's a baby cemetery there somewhere too, it's bad... truly bad.'

'And it's going to get worse,' Adam added. He filled John in on the car brakes' incident with Danielle and the suspicion that it wasn't an accident.

John exhaled. 'Do you think you should give the police the heads-up?'

'I'm onto it,' Nate assured him.

John nodded. 'As for the situation getting worse, if the victims are up to it, we sure as hell are.' He turned to Rob. 'Do you want to come by tomorrow with the files and I'll get a few of the team together for a briefing?'

Rob agreed. John pulled out his phone, checked his diary and suggested nine o'clock or two in the afternoon.

'Nine is good for me,' Rob said, 'Jess?'

'We'll be there,' she agreed.

John marked it on his diary and looked up at Adam and Nate. 'And you two will be Joe's voice throughout all this.'

'His son will be even better,' Nate said and filled John in on finding Thomas and the potential drawings.

'We need those,' John said, his face masked with determination. 'When are you meeting him for the map hunt?'

'At eight in the morning,' Adam said, 'on-site at the asylum… again. I tried to make it seven but I don't think he's ever seen that hour of the day.'

'Those drawings, if they still exist, will be amazing evidence,' John said. 'We have to find them.'

'And Joe,' Nate said, 'we have to find Joe… where the hell is he?'

\*\*\*\*\*

Adam and Nate were the last to leave the office. They sat for a while in comfortable silence, finishing their drinks.

'You alright?' Adam said, eventually.

Nate sighed. 'Yeah. Some days not so good, but better. Definitely better. I've got Matilda this weekend, that'll be good. I thought I'd take her to the museum… they've got this kids' section. Want to come?'

'Yeah, love to, but my sock drawer is out of control… you know how it is. Time to clean out.'

Nate smirked at him. 'If you had got to it and Stephanie had pushed out one, we could have managed our daddy weekends.'

'Yeah, remiss of me. But at least now I'm not connected to her for life,' he said, then looked up. 'Oh, sorry.'

Nate shrugged. 'Tilly's worth it.'

'She is,' Adam smiled. 'You're lucky. Oh, I forgot,' he said, and reached into his pocket. He pulled out an invitation and handed it to Nate. 'Mum's not eloping, unfortunately.'

'And I got a look in, I knew she liked me,' he said, with a grin, and checked out the invitation. 'Wow, this must be the thickest paper I've ever felt and gold trim… no expense spared.'

'No surprise,' Adam agreed and finished his drink. He watched as Nate opened it.

'Nice,' Nate said. 'St. Stephen's Cathedral… she's getting married here?'

'Yeah, Stephanie said it was a concession to me and her past. Whatever.'

'Cheaper for us at least,' Nate said, 'we don't have to get flights and a room. Mm, marquee reception at the gardens, big budget. How many invited, did Stephanie say?'

'About six hundred,' Adam mumbled.

'What the…?' Nate said. 'Have you got a role?'

'Not yet thank God. Grandad will fly up and give her away, again. Jack's got a big clan and there'll be a lot of industry hangers-on. Yep, going to be a long day.'

They sat in silence again for a short while, before Adam spoke. 'So, are you going to ask Jess to go with you?'

Nate sighed. 'I think she'd rather go with you.'

Adam shook his head. 'For a detective, sometimes you are clueless. She's not interested in me, she's keen on you. Ask her, you know she wants to go.'

'It's too soon,' Nate said, putting up another barrier.

'You're not asking her to marry you... just to go to the wedding as your guest. She knows your situation. And, if you do ask her, make it nice. Don't do the old dismissive 'handbag' or plus one stuff, you know, ask her nicely.'

'Yes coach,' Nate said, and rolled his eyes. 'Are you going to ask Dan, she's busting to go too.'

Adam rose, and grabbed their empty bottles, throwing them in the bin. 'That's a bit more complicated,' he said, turning to face Nate.

'How so?'

'I'm not into her, and if I ask her... I'm leading her on. She's great, just too Stephanie for me.'

'Yeah, I get that,' Nate said. 'So, did you have someone in mind?'

Adam crossed his arms across his chest and leaned back on the reception desk. 'I do, and it's something she would never have experienced. She'll either be excited or it will be overwhelming.'

'You going to tell me who?' Nate asked.

'She's not a client of mine, and she's made it clear she doesn't want to be a client of Rob's either... but I need to check with Rob if he thinks it's unethical,' Adam said, talking to himself more so than Nate.

'You want to ask Kelsey?' Nate said.

'Yeah, I'd like to ask Kelsey.'

'You had a thing for her back then,' Nate said, studying him.

'Get out,' Adam scoffed, 'we only saw her for five minutes.'

Nate shrugged. 'Sometimes that's all it takes.'

# Chapter 35

Arriving early, Adam and Nate looked like two men used to mornings. Clean-shaven, in T-shirt and jeans, they watched as a dishevelled Thomas O'Connell, son of Joe, alighted from his car— a car that had also seen better days—and joined them. He wore loose track pants, a long-sleeved T-shirt and his hair sported a fashionable bed-hair look.

'Not a morning person?' Nate greeted him.

Thomas grunted. 'I run nightly ghost tours for a reason.' He unrolled the sheets he was carrying and handed them one each. He looked up, squinted and pulled his sunglasses out of his pocket.

'Wow', Adam said, studying the detailed and elaborate map in front of him. 'This is amazing.'

Nate agreed. 'This is a work of art. Your dad would have loved this.'

'Yeah?' Thomas grinned. 'You can frame your copies when we're finished then.'

'I will,' Adam agreed, 'you need to sign it though.'

'Sure,' Thomas agreed.

The map was done in muted pencil colours; dragons, towers, trees with personalities and pathways filled the A3 size page. An old-fashioned compass was drawn in the far right-hand corner.

'This is the kind of stuff my father used to do when he was younger. I saw some of his originals when I did the assignment on him,' Thomas said. He looked in front of him and over Adam's shoulder. 'Not as scary in the daylight,' he said, looking at the asylum. 'Just as miserable though.'

Adam turned to look and nodded. He thought he saw a movement past a window on the top floor and imagined it to be their friend, Mac, the hanging man, still hanging around the upstairs floors of what he called home.

Nate looked to Adam. 'Mac?'

'Yeah probably,' he agreed.

'That the hanging guy?' Thomas asked. 'He's added some excitement to my tours.'

'Yeah, it's home for him, so keep that under your hat,' Nate said.

'Hell yeah. You think I'm helping the authorities? Hanging guy can hang there for as long as he likes. Even better if he wanted to become a part of my tour.'

Adam returned his focus to the map. 'Let's start. This way?' he said, with a nod to the fence where a gap in the wire seemed to have permanency.

'I can lead if you like, I've been studying it closely with the online maps of the area now,' Thomas said.

'Sure, if you're awake enough,' Nate teased him.

Thomas smirked at him. 'Would have been better if you'd brought coffee with you, but I'll do my best.' He folded his map in half and worked off the side closest to where he was standing. 'First things first,' he started, 'we're through the rabbit hole.' He indicated the wire fence. The two men followed and they ducked and went through the broken fence. Nate glanced back at the nearby open gate, but with a shrug, followed.

'Got to be in character,' Thomas said, seeing his expression.

'Sure. I'll play me,' Nate agreed. Adam laughed.

'Right then,' Thomas said, and looked at the map again. 'The first clue is at the tree, the largest tree near the river and I'm guessing because you remembered it had a crest in it, it's supposed to be the tree you guys used to hang out in.'

'This way, then,' Nate said, and the three walked across to the bank of trees where as two young lads they had often climbed and watched out for Joe. It seemed shorter now, a stone's throw; Adam and Nate looked around disorientated.

'That can't be it,' Nate said, pointing to the tree that was in the logical position for their adventures.

Adam looked at the tree, the river bank, and back to the empty asylum. 'Must be. It looks so much smaller.'

'It was huge in our day,' Nate told Thomas. 'A goliath tree to climb.'

'It's shrunk,' Adam agreed, and they grinned at each other.

Thomas circled around the tree and shook his head. He looked up, then looked to Adam who turned to Nate.

'The clue has got to be a symbol or something that Joe could see from where he sat at the fence,' Adam said. 'He couldn't get out here, so what's in his line of vision between our tree and his favourite position?'

'Or maybe the perspective is reversed,' Thomas suggested. 'My father.. Dad,' he tried the title out, 'Dad picked something in his world that he knew you could see if you were in your favourite position. Where did you guys sit in the tree?'

'We used to go to those two middle branches,' Nate said, pointing upwards.

'Well, up you go, I'll give you a leg up,' Adam said, rolling his map up and sticking it in the pocket at the back of his jeans.

'Hold up, why me?' Nate stepped back.

Adam sighed. 'You spent years of our childhood telling me that you're the better climber so you had to go first, so, you've earned it.'

Nate smirked. 'Fine then.' He pulled his mobile phone and wallet from his pockets and placed them on the ground next to his map. Sticking his foot in Adam's webbed fingers, he grabbed the lower branch and pulled himself up. Nate made his way quickly to where they used to sit, and deciding it would still easily hold his weight, pulled himself up and threw a leg over the branch. He looked around.

'Wow, you should come up, this is a fantastic view.'

'Great,' Adam said, 'anything else to see there?'

Nate stared out again at the district. 'It really is a different perspective up here; shame we stop climbing trees once we grow up.'

'Yeah,' Adam said, 'there's plenty of studies around supporting the idea of child's play for adults.' Adam started wandering around the base of the tree and widened his circle, looking up at Nate, then back to the fence line.

'You know...' Nate started, 'from here we are perfectly aligned with the clock at the front of the building... the clock that never worked, even when we were kids. Now that I think about it, there was a clock drawn on the map.'

'You're right! There was a clock drawn in the tree!' Adam exclaimed. 'I remember it now because the clock's face was an old man with a monocle and a bowler hat... sort of Victorian times.'

'Steampunk now,' Thomas added. 'That's got to be it then, the clue has to be the clock!'

'Time stops for no man,' Adam said, 'except with this clock it has stopped.'

Thomas frowned as he thought. 'Mm, and I think that's the clue. If that clock was stopped when you guys were kids, Dad knew it wasn't going to change in the timeframe that you were doing the treasure search. So what time are its arms set on?' Thomas asked.

'Five past four,' Nate said.

They stood silent mulling over their thoughts.

'It's not the time, I'm an idiot,' Thomas said, excited, 'it's the placement of the hands. If it is five past, then the hand is on one and the other hand is on four. So maybe we have to add them together and walk five steps, or put them side-by-side and walk 14 or 41 steps!' Thomas made a whooping sound. 'Bet that's it!'

'Really?' Adam said, less than convinced.

'Yeah, I've seen clues like that before… betcha I'm right,' Thomas said.

'As pleasant as this is up here, can I come down?' Nate asked.

'Sure,' Thomas said, already counting out steps. 'Guess it's got to be this way otherwise we head straight back to the asylum.'

Adam waited as Nate edged his way down the tree, more cautiously than he did as a youngster, and dropped when he got to his body length from the ground. He wiped his hands on his pants.

'I wonder if it is boy sized steps or Dad size steps… we'll go somewhere in between,' Thomas continued, and headed off, measuring out the distance as the men followed.

Adam followed and stopped when Thomas did.

'Five steps got us nowhere,' Adam said, looking at the grass around him. It all looked the same. Thomas had taken off and stood where 14 steps would lead them.

'Same here,' he said, 'nothing stands out.'

'Forty-one steps is going to take us straight into the river,' Nate said.

'Unless it goes around... and I'm guessing you guys don't remember if the footsteps on the map went around the river?'

They both shook their heads. Thomas sighed and started off.

'Let's make life easy on ourselves before we go swimming, and assume it does,' Nate said, '41 steps in a southern direction, going around the river.'

'I've lost count,' Thomas said, and returned to the tree to recount the steps.

*****

Rob and Jessica entered the lift, pulling a small suitcase of files behind them; Rob pressed the floor number for Liberman & Clarke solicitors.

'You know, I like John, but I hate lawyers,' Jessica said.

Rob gave her a smile. 'Yeah, you wouldn't be the first to feel that way. There's a joke about that... what do you call five hundred lawyers at the bottom of the sea? A good start!'

Jessica laughed. 'Cute.'

'So,' Rob asked, 'What's a lawyer ever done to you?'

'Not me, but my uncle. He died from asbestos poisoning after years of working with the material; lucky we're only travelling up a few levels or I'd bore you with the whole story. The lawyers who defended the company my uncle worked for had no compassion, you'd think the compensation was coming out of their own pocket. They were the walking dead... equivalent to those White Walkers on *Game of Thrones*, no heart, no soul...'

The lift doors opened.

'Right,' Rob said, 'I hear you. Better leave the talking to me then,' he teased her.

She grimaced at him and followed. Jessica lowered her voice. 'I know John's a good guy and he's going to help these people.' She shrugged. 'It's life isn't it? There's good folk and bad folk... same in the cops when I was there, same everywhere.'

'That's the truth of it,' Rob agreed and stopped at the front counter. Before he could press the bell at the empty desk, John appeared and shuffled them into the boardroom; a receptionist appeared behind him, greeted them and offered tea and coffee. As Rob opened and unpacked files, they were joined by a sensible-looking woman in her fifties; tall, neat and with a kind face, her greying hair neatly tied back. John introduced her as Margaret Todd-Hawkings and she shook Rob and Jessica's hands before taking a seat opposite them.

John nodded for her to take over and she addressed Rob and Jessica.

'John's given me an overview,' she began, in a well-modulated voice, 'and to give you a bit of my background, I've represented several cases like this, private cases, however, not class actions, and not pro bono.'

'It's good of the firm to do that,' Jessica said.

Margaret smiled at her and agreed. 'Each of our staff identifies an area that we're passionate about and we select several pro bono cases a year that fit with our moral principles.'

John stepped in. 'It's not entirely an altruistic act,' he said, with a smile. 'Don't get me wrong, I've long believed in the importance of social justice, but by doing this, we are also able to attract staff in the calibre of Margaret... high-quality legal experts who want the balance. And, we can also give the law students working with us a chance to contribute and cut their teeth on these cases.'

'It allows us to watch them in action to recruit for the future, too,' Margaret added. 'So, this case falls right into my area of interest. I've done a fair bit of mental health work over the years but I suspect this will take the cake.'

Rob nodded and tapped the files. 'We definitely have to tread lightly here, but you know the drill. One of the victims is still hiding and I don't want to see him moved from the only home he's ever known. There will be some who will pull out, unable to face it, and others who will be lost now that they've bared their souls but don't feel any better.'

'I understand,' Margaret said. 'We won't be rushing into anything here.'

'Thank you,' Rob said. He pointed to the different collateral. 'Hard copies here, and on this USB, the electronic copies and audio of the interviews.'

She nodded. 'I'll come back to you within a couple of weeks after I've gone through these... but if there's a legitimate action, and I accept that by the nature of you presenting these files, there is... I can give you an indication of where I think this will go if you like?'

'Yes please,' Jessica said, and leant forward. 'I've met every one of these people,' she said, looking at the files as if each had a personality, 'and I've transcribed their stories. I want justice for them so badly I can taste it.'

John smiled. 'We might have to headhunt you I think, Jessica. Mm, did I say that out loud?'

The group laughed, breaking the tension.

'Sorry, you were saying, Margaret?' John threw the conversation back to her.

'Yes, in past cases like this, we've rarely gone to court, and

I think that's a good thing, to be honest.' She saw Jessica's face and held up her hand. 'I know everyone wants their day in court and we want the truth to come out, history to be corrected, and for the offenders to be punished, but sometimes the victims are just not up to that. So, we'll see how it pans out. In several of my other cases, an independent, formal mediator was appointed and that person leads a reconciliation process.'

'Who picks that person?' Jessica asked.

'It would be mutually agreed upon… ideally a community advocate, someone completely independent who would lead the process and liaise with our clients who are seeking redress, removing them a little from the front line of confrontation.'

Jessica nodded. 'I can see how that could be better.'

'What about Joe?' John asked. 'Do we know what happened yet, where he might be? Is this case going to be more than abuse, may be unlawful killing, murder?'

Rob drew a deep breath. 'Without a doubt, there has been a loss of life at the hands of asylum staff… allegedly,' he said, with a nod in Margaret's direction. 'How we prove that now, or if we get that far, remains to be seen. As for Joe, Adam and Nate think he got out of that place… we just don't know if he came back, for good.'

# Chapter 36

Adam's phone rang and he frowned when he saw who was calling. He looked at Thomas and Nate.

'Sorry, I'll just be a minute,' he said. The other two men took the chance to look at the map and recount their steps.

'Stephanie,' Adam answered.

His ex-wife didn't bother with niceties either. 'You could have told me you had done an interview… that is my job you know, to manage the media,' she snapped.

'What interview?' he asked, confused.

'The one appearing online today… byline by Cooper Tarred and titled '*Winsome's son denies any connection to former PM.*'

Adam groaned. 'Ah, that one. It was a mercy interview… Nate felt sorry for the kid… this young reporter who had been waiting all day.'

'Well if you had called me, I would have had a word to the editor and massaged it, that's my expertise, and your mother recognises that even if you don't,' she snapped.

Adam took a deep breath. 'I won't be doing any more, and I'm not calling you every time I want to talk to someone. I thought you believed all publicity was good publicity.' His comment started Stephanie off on a tirade about responsibility and the media; he tuned out for a couple of minutes before interrupting her.

'Stephanie, you know, it's too early for this. Whatever...' He looked at the phone and saw she had hung up.

'Right then,' he said, returning to Thomas and Nate.

'Ah love, ain't it grand,' Nate said, with a sigh.

'This is it,' Thomas said and looked at Adam and then Nate. 'This is 41 steps. Any thoughts?'

'Shit yeah, none relevant to this moment,' Adam said, his positive mood for the day soured by his past invading.

Nate hit him on the back. 'Let it go, mate. She knows how to play you and you rise to the occasion every time.'

'Not every—'

'Yeah, every time,' Nate cut him off.

Adam groaned. 'Fine then.' He drew a deep breath, practising the techniques he preached to his clients, but he kept coming back to the seven years he'd spent with her – two years dating, five married. Seven years of his twenties and for what? What a waste. If he'd been counselling a client he would have said no time in a relationship was a waste... consider what you learnt, how you grew, what you got out of it. But in his own head, he wished she had stayed in Sydney with her publicity agency, and his mother had never introduced them.

He heard Thomas talking to Nate and refocused.

Nate walked around the stump looking for markings. 'Nothing here,' he said to Thomas.

'Was this a stump when you were kids or was there a tree here that's missing now?' Thomas asked.

Adam and Nate looked at each other.

'Christ, it was 15 years or more ago, I don't remember every tree,' Nate said.

'Yes, we do!' Adam said, and brightened.

'We do?' Nate asked, surprised.

'Remember when Joe was telling us how to count the rings to work out how old the tree was?' Adam said. 'We came here… to this stump to do what he suggested. We picked it because it was in line with where he sat and he could watch us.'

'Brilliant,' Thomas said and moved between them. He counted the circle rings. 'Fourteen… or near enough.'

'So fourteen… what now?' Nate sighed.

'Did we actually tell Joe there were 14 rings, so that's why he used it for one of his clues?' Adam asked.

'We might have,' Nate said, 'it was his suggestion to count the rings after all.'

'Unless the number of rings is not important at all and the stump's meaning is important,' Thomas said, 'but that doesn't get us any further than here.'

'Right,' Adam agreed. 'So what does a tree stump mean, Thomas? I'm talking in terms of myths and symbols; does it have any special meaning?'

'Hold up,' Thomas said, and he pulled the page of symbols and their meanings from his pocket and unfolded it. 'Okay, a tree means life, strength, protection… so if it is cut off, it can mean a life cut short, or cut down in victory… or loss of home, loss of security,' he read, then looked up at the men.

'Yeah, that helps,' Nate said. 'So, loss of home, cut down… is Joe saying we should look at where he started, his home? Or in the asylum where he was cut down from being the talent he could have been… and somehow, is 14 significant when it comes to that?'

Adam sighed, and turned full circle, returning his gaze to the tree stump in front of them. 'I think we're overthinking it. Joe gave this map to two boys… I remember there were lots of footprints on it, so we're meant to walk around the woods a bit. Maybe, we're just meant to take another fourteen steps.'

'Yeah, makes sense,' Thomas agreed. 'So, if we go that way we're wet, if we go that way, we're just in the middle of a field, so let's go this way,' he suggested and led the way towards another copse of trees.

'That area would have been part of the asylum farm before it closed, wouldn't it?' Adam asked looking past the copse.

'Yeah,' Nate agreed, 'so it would have been easy for Joe to hide clues there, but impossible for us to access them, so probably not too far that way,' he stopped. 'Just a thought… why don't we just go to the end of the map and try our luck? I mean, the chances of clues still being here are pretty remote and if all the clues relate to how many paces to walk, well, let's cut to the chase.'

'Don't be ridiculously sensible,' Adam said, and Thomas laughed.

'I think Dad would have been a little more creative than that… but okay, let's see,' Thomas said, and unfurled the map. 'So, the last thing you two remember was the picture of the skull near the gate.'

'Skull, pirates, swords, it was something like that,' Adam agreed.

'A skull can mean a cursed area,' Thomas said, 'let's go.'

They walked the half-kilometre to a broken gate that stood, unhinged and attached to a small stone wall, keeping nobody in or out. The land sloped downward and got marshy underfoot. .

'Great,' Adam said, lifting each leg with effort as his shoes carried a load of fresh mud.

'Seriously, we're idiots,' Nate shook his head.

'You won't say that if we find something,' Thomas reminded him. 'C'mon, let's break up and cover the area.'

They circled the gate, studying the stones, hinges, the earth around the area, looking to the sky above, the earth below and its angle to the asylum. Ten minutes later Adam spoke up.

'I've got nothing. This might not have been the end, it could have been a loop… I can't remember where the footprints ended on the map.'

'Me either,' Nate agreed. 'Why don't we go back to where we were at the tree stump and work on that second clue,' he said, with a smirk.

'There's an idea,' Adam said, with a smile and stomped past him, shaking mud off his shoes as he walked. When he arrived back with the men close by, he paced out the area. 'Fourteen steps, right?'

'Right,' Thomas said. 'Let's walk to where the asylum farm would have been.'

They found themselves in front of a circle of small rocks.

'Stonehenge,' Nate said, and got a laugh. 'Right then…' he dropped to his knees and lifted each small rock, running his hand over the earth, searching each rock for signs or symbols. Thomas joined in. After a time, they stood and wiped the dirt from their hands.

'Ha!' Adam said, and laughed. 'What do you know?'

'Nothing, clearly, what do you know?' Nate asked, looking in the direction that Adam was looking.

'Birds' eye view… these stones are laid out in the shape of a number eight,' Adam said, and waited for the other two to agree. 'Look over there, the trees are in the shape of an eight too, loosely,' he said, and pointed. 'Do you think that's a clue?'

'Yeah, brilliant!' Thomas said, 'this is brilliant. Wait up!'

He rose and pulled a small booklet out of his shirt pocket. He waved it at them and read its title. *Treasure Signs and Symbols Made Easy* – my bible when I'm working on games. I've read about the number eight… just let me look it up.'

'I don't know,' Nate said, dubiously. 'Joe must have thought we were two pretty smart kids if we were going to work this out.'

'Yeah, well the map probably had more clues, and I could be wrong about the eight,' Adam said, 'but sideways it's a symbol for infinity.' He drew in a sharp breath. 'Stop!'

Thomas and Nate froze and stared at him.

'I read that, just the other night in Joe's diary; I didn't make the connection. He said infinity will reveal his journey, or something like that, I just thought he was being profound. It's got to be somewhere around here then.'

Thomas grinned with delight, and returned to wading through his reference book.

'And infinity can represent eternal friendship,' Adam continued looking to Nate. 'Remember he said he wanted a long friendship between us? I read out a piece about that.'

Nate nodded. 'He said it in one of his letters. This is looking hopeful.'

Thomas agreed. 'Here it is, listen up,' he said, with excitement. He read from the book. 'The number eight has been known to fool many treasure hunters and is often misinterpreted. Some believe they have found the infinity symbol and therefore have reached the end of the journey, but it must be interpreted as requiring a doubling of the original number given.' Thomas stopped and looked from Adam to Nate. 'And since we haven't been given a number, except for the eight symbol itself, then we should go sixteen steps, that way.' He pointed to Adam's loosely arranged copse of eight trees. 'Onward!'

'Okay,' Adam said, with a glance to Nate who was far from convinced.

'Who writes this stuff?' Nate asked.

'There are thousands of books and blogs on this kind of thing,' Thomas said, 'I've got everything from how to read runes and hieroglyphics to interpreting stones and rocks.'

'You've led such a sheltered life,' Adam teased Nate.

Thomas led the way. He arrived ahead of the men and then he saw it. 'Over here, it's here!'

Adam and Nate hurried to him. Thomas pointed to another group of small rocks surrounding the base of the tree that was at the very centre of the figure eight.

'This has got to be it at the centre of the infinity,' he said, and pulled a small garden spade from his jacket. He handed Adam his map and bag and leant down to dig, pushing the spade into the dirt. Adam and Nate stood by, watching with anticipation.

He didn't have to go far before he hit a tin surface. 'Can't believe this,' he said, scraping dirt off the surface until he revealed a handle and pulled up a small tradesman's toolbox. He pushed it towards Nate. 'Here, it was for you two… your treasure hunt so you should open it.'

'I think your dad would be blown away that you were here with us now and opening it,' Nate said, not taking the box. 'You do it.'

Thomas nodded and walked to a tree stump, placing the tin on it. He pried open the hinges, hitting one with the edge of the spade, to loosen it; he opened the tin. 'Hey, look at this.' He reached in and lifted out two small wooden planes, hand painted.

Nate laughed. 'That'd be our Christmas presents then,' he said, taking them off Thomas. 'Fantastic. How'd he get them here?'

'He might have been allowed to roam, or he got someone to bury it for him,' Adam suggested.

'Yeah, great,' Thomas said, less enthusiastically. He looked back into the tin and picked out the only remaining item – a rusty key with a tag attached. It had a cross drawn on it, like a religious symbol and a few words that read 'Time Capsule'. He handed it to Adam.

'And that might be where his drawings are,' Adam said. 'Maybe even a clue to where Joe himself might be.'

'I know what that key unlocks,' a voice said, coming from behind them. They spun around to see Dave Trigg standing there.

'Holy hell, you'd make a good stalker, didn't hear you coming,' Nate said.

'How long have you been watching us?' Adam asked, narrowing his eyes.

'The whole time,' Dave said, with a grin. 'You learn to walk quietly when you're a nurse… patients think they're in a hotel sometimes and not a hospital ward, so you don't draw attention to yourself!'

'Yeah, we could use you in the agency on the surveillance team. Have you met Thomas?' Nate asked, with a nod in Thomas's direction.

Thomas extended his hand; Dave hesitated then accepted Thomas's outstretched hand for a shake.

Adam read between the lines; Dave was a nervy type, untrusting, probably always had been.

'Thomas is Joe's son and Stephen's nephew,' Adam said.

'Well, that's thrown me… Joe's son, hey? I knew your father and your uncle… didn't know about you though, sorry,' he said.

Thomas nodded, 'Yeah I didn't know either of them, so you're one up on me.'

'You know where that key fits?' Adam asked him.

'Yeah, I've got a fair idea. I always wondered where it was; thought it was gone for good. Come on.' He turned and took off towards the asylum; his small, hunched figure doing a cracking pace. The three men looked at each other, then hurried to catch up with the former nurse.

# Chapter 37

Jessica nearly stepped on Danielle as she raced up the stairs to the office, with Rob trailing behind.

'Oh my God, you scared me,' she said, pulling up, and putting her hand over her heart. 'You need a key, I'll organise it.'

'That'd be great, thanks,' Danielle said, and rose from the top landing she was sprawled across. She greeted Rob. 'I came to give Nate an update but no-one was here!'

Jessica stepped past her and unlocked the door. She picked up some mail that had been slipped under it.

'We've been briefing the solicitors,' Rob said, holding the door open for Danielle to go before him.

'Oh, it's really going to happen,' Danielle said.

'It's really going to happen,' Rob said. He took the offered mail and began to sort it.

'It's going to be huge,' Jessica added. She turned the phones on, listened for messages, jotting them down, and then began to open the blinds, Danielle helped.

'I've got to talk with Nate… I've got a hunch about my accident,' Danielle said.

'So has he,' Jessica said. 'Have you tried to call him?'

'Yeah, it went to voice mail. Where is he?' she asked.

'Traipsing around the mental asylum with Adam,' Rob told her.

'So many good lines… so little time,' Danielle sighed.

'I've got a few messages for him too.' Jessica picked up the phone to call him and Nate answered this time.

'Jess, what's up?'

'Hey,' she said, and gave him his messages. She finished with: 'Avery called, Joe's agent, and said someone tried to break into his gallery last night but the alarm went off and they bolted. So, can you call him ASAP. Hold up, Dan wants to talk to you.' Jessica handed over the phone.

'Nate, it's Dan. There's something else… when I was coming down the range, there was a car behind me for a while. I didn't think anything of it, but it wouldn't overtake, it was happy just to stay with me, but a few cars behind.'

'What model and make?' Nate asked.

'Red Nissan sedan, an older model, the squarer type,' Danielle said, 'but there's more. Last night I met with Dave Trigg as we agreed, and when he drove off, he was in that same type of car.'

'Right,' Nate said. 'Don't do anything Dan, I'm onto it.'

Danielle finished the call and handed the phone back to Jessica. 'He's on it, allegedly,' she said, with a shrug.

'You should lock the door, Jess,' Rob said. 'Let clients ring the bell to get in and let them in only if they're clients. I'll be in my office with the door open.'

Jessica nodded. 'Thanks Rob.' She felt chilled now.

Danielle read her body language. 'Don't worry about it. This stuff happens all the time. Nate and I are always getting threatened, especially by cheating partners.'

'Mm, but this is bigger than that, so much bigger,' Jessica said.

'Speaking of cheating partners, I've got a report for Nate,'

Danielle said, and fished it out of her bag. She entered his office to put it on his desk. Jessica followed her in with Nate's mail.

'Oh wow, have you seen this,' Danielle asked and pointed to the wedding invitation on Nate's desk.

Jessica stopped. 'Is that—'

'It is, and it's not in an envelope… no-one will know if we take a peek,' she said, with a sly grin to Jessica. 'So, expensive.'

Jessica moved to her side and they read the invitation.

'I really want to go,' Jessica said.

'Me too, but you've got more chance than me,' Danielle said, returning the invitation to the same place. 'Nate will ask you… he's hot for you.'

Jessica scoffed. 'Not likely. I thought you'd go with Adam.'

'That's the fantasy,' she sighed. 'Nate says I'm too out there for Adam, he needs someone boring. So, he's not going to ask me because he'll be worried I think I'm in with a chance. Adam's so different… and cautious… and conservative… perfect.' Danielle realised she revealed more than she meant to and shrugged.

Jessica smiled. 'So, beat him at his own head game.'

'What do you mean?' Danielle leaned on the edge of Nate's desk and gave Jessica her full attention.

'Just tell him you've seen the invitation and if he needs a friend to have on his arm for the night, someone he doesn't have to be concerned about, or make small talk with… not worry he's leading them on, then you're available.'

'Okay, that could work but then I'm saying I'm not interested,' she said with apprehension, 'or what if he still said no, that'd be an ugly day.'

'No, you're saying you have no expectations. But then, of course you'll look gorgeous on the night in formal attire and you'll be in with more of a chance than if you were sitting at home and someone else was on his arm,' Jessica said.

'You're brilliant,' Danielle said.

'Yeah,' she agreed, 'Adam should watch out, I might have a new career in psychology!'

*****

Nate hung up from Jessica and glanced at Adam.

'Everything okay at the office?' Adam asked as he kept pace with him.

'Yes and no. Jess and Rob are just back from the solicitors, Dan's in too. Jess said Avery left a message this morning… he had a break in at the gallery last night but the alarm went off and they bolted.'

'Seriously?' Adam stopped to look at Nate. He lowered his voice. 'Think we were followed there?'

Nate nodded and continued walking, Adam caught up. 'Dan also has a lead on the brake tampering.' He glanced at Dave Trigg and back to Adam.

Adam frowned as he tried to interpret Nate's thoughts. They caught up with Thomas and Dave, in search of the door the key would unlock.

Dave went around to the back of the asylum building, where a number of ramshackle buildings rested against the main wall, looking as if they needed support. He went to the farthest building which was solid compared to the others, turned and waited for the three men to join him.

Adam ran his eye over it; it was small, all the windows were boarded up, the front of the building had a peak and the marks of what used to be a cross embedded into the framework.

'The chapel?' Adam asked.

'This is it,' Dave agreed. 'Can't say I spent any time here

myself, but some did… Joe did.' He shook his head. 'Don't mean to offend if you're the religious types, but you'd think after praying long enough and nothin' changed, you'd get the picture…'

'No-one's listening?' Nate asked.

Dave nodded. 'Yep, pretty much. I've seen a lot in my years of nursing that would make you question your faith, but sometimes it just gets people through,' he said, with a shrug. He turned around, pushed the key into the lock and smiled with satisfaction when it clicked.

Dave pushed the timber door open with his hip and entered. It was a small room, the pews had long gone, but the altar was still evident and the only remaining window, with stained glass intact, was high above the back of the altar out of reach of looters and vandals.

Thomas wrinkled his nose. 'Stuffy in here… guessing it hasn't been open for a while, hey?'

'Years and years,' Dave said.

'So how did Dad get a key to the chapel?' Thomas asked, as he wandered around.

Dave crossed his arms across his chest and leaned against a boarded-up window. 'There was this priest who was a good bloke, Father William Doyle—a Mick—we'd just call him Will, … he used to say "if there's a Father Will, there's a way" all the time like it was the first time we ever heard the joke. Dave smiled at the memory. 'Even if you didn't believe, he'd tell you to come in here to rest or to have some peace. He understood Joe.'

'Why didn't he try and stop what was going on?' Adam asked. 'He must have known.'

'He did try and stop it; he fought the fight for about a year, and then he was transferred out. We didn't see him after that. The next guy didn't bother trying.'

Adam wandered around the inside perimeter of the church checking out the building; Nate turned to Dave.

'What can you tell us? Where did Joe normally sit in here? Where might he have hidden something?' Nate asked him.

Dave sighed. 'I don't know much. Joe didn't like to participate, just watch. He wasn't into past... what do you call it... pasture care?'

'Pastoral care,' Adam said, as he rejoined them.

'Yeah, that's it. Joe would usually sit in the last row in that corner,' he said, pointing. 'But there's something you should see.' He led them to the altar and began to pull down some boarding on the back wall. The men watched for a moment, and then joined in to help him. Behind it was a painting... angels, Jesus rising with the crucifixion marks in his hands, blue skies, radiant light and clouds. It stopped in one corner; unfinished.

'Joe painted this; worked on it for about a year,' Dave said, standing back to take it in. 'Father Will invited him to do it.' He turned to Thomas. 'Your dad was probably the happiest he could be during his time here when he was working on this. The new priest stopped it; that's why it's unfinished.'

'It's amazing,' Thomas said looking up at it. 'Truly amazing. I could never be this good.'

'Where would he have kept his stuff while he was working in here?' Nate asked. 'You know, brushes, paints... arty stuff.'

'Probably in that little back room where the priest kept his stuff, I'm guessing,' Dave said, moving towards a small room. Adam followed.

'The vestry,' Adam said, 'Catholic school...' he said, in response to the looks he got. 'Though this is more like a walk-in closet for a tradie.'

Nate walked over and stood beside Dave and Adam. He

took in the rows of tin cans, brittle paint brushes, roller trays, rolled up wire and rags.

Adam began to move the items, handing a few tins to Nate. 'Perfect place to hide stuff. If the paint tins feel empty, see if you can pry them open.' Adam pulled a small Swiss army knife from his pocket and offered it to Nate. Adam shook out newspaper sheets, lifted trays and pressed against the back wall to make sure it was solid. Behind him, Nate flipped the lids off paint tins and Thomas knocked the lids back on when there was nothing to be found. Adam worked his way to the lowest shelf, the tins sitting directly on the floor of the cupboard, and he passed two large 10-litre tins to Nate.

'Careful, that feels half full,' he said.

Nate took the two and struggled with the lid of the first one.

'Can't get this one, but from the sloshing sound, I'd say it's got paint in there.' He passed it to Thomas to stack with the others. He flipped the lid on the second 10-litre tin and leaned back. 'Found something!' Nate proclaimed.

Thomas came to stand next to him.

'This is it,' Nate said, 'these have to be Joe's drawings.'

Inside the tin, tightly rolled, were no less than a dozen scrolls. Nate passed one to Thomas and pulled one out himself. The ribbons securing them were frail, falling apart as they were slid down off the scroll.

Nate moved to the half-timber altar that remained and Dave, grabbing a rag from the shelves, dusted it down. They held their collective breaths as Nate and Thomas opened the scrolls. In front of them, detailed pencil etchings revealed extracts from life in the asylum.

Adam exhaled. 'This is it, this is what we need... what Rob needs for the case.'

'Look at this detail,' Nate said, his eyes moving over the scene. 'No wonder he was a risky patient if they found these.'

'They're amazing,' Dave said, 'I'd forgotten how vivid they were.'

'This was real?' Thomas asked looking at Dave.

Dave nodded. 'He's captured what was going on.'

Thomas reached for another scroll and unwrapped it. 'This is the shock treatment,' he said. Dave looked away.

Nate opened another scroll and his breath hitched. 'Adam, look at this,' he said. Adam moved beside him. The drawing featured eight men sitting like a jury, a patient in the middle, small and vulnerable. Nate tapped on the man drawn as the judge. The same face of that man appeared on every second juror.

'Digby. That's him without a doubt... judge and jury,' Nate said.

Thomas studied the drawing over Nate's shoulder. 'Who is he?'

Dave glanced at the drawing and his lips thinned into a sneer. He answered before Nate could explain.

'Superintendent Gregor Digby... one of the greatest bastards to ever walk this earth.' His jaw locked and he looked away.

'Superintendent! Makes it sound like a prison not a hospital,' Thomas said.

'It was for most of us... I mean the patients here,' Dave said.

Adam looked at Dave. 'I'm guessing Digby wasn't employer of the year to his staff then either?'

Dave shook his head. 'A cruel, spiteful man.'

Nate rolled the drawing up. 'I think these speak for his time in authority,' he said, and tapped the lid back on the tin.

Adam moved back to the cupboard and lifted the last of the paint trays from the bottom shelf. Dave joined him; taking the trays and stacking them with the tins.

Adam pointed at a timber door in the floor; it's rusted iron ring handle barely visible as it blended with the old timbers and dirt. 'Dave, know what that is?'

Dave shook his head. 'Don't know. Might be best to leave it,' he said. 'C'mon. Let's get it over with,' Adam said.

The two men grabbed the ring but the door came up easily. They stepped back with alarm.

'Crap,' Dave muttered.

Adam drew in a deep breath. Lying in front of them were the remains of two bodies... dusty bones, a skull evident, and another in reverse position, as if they were lying head to toe.

'Joe,' Adam said, in a low voice. The name drew the other two men and Thomas and Nate came up behind them. Adam rose and pushed Thomas back.

'It may not be your father,' he said, pre-empting Thomas's reaction.

Thomas pushed past him and looked in. He dropped to his knees, studying the bones.

'It's my father,' he said, and pointed to a delicate chain that was visible in the dirt. The pendant was a small cross with a stone in the centre. If it were clean, it would reveal a deep red ruby. 'In a photo Mum's got, Dad's wearing this. I'm sure, pretty sure...'

His voice broke and Adam put his hand on Thomas's shoulder as he rose.

'I'm okay,' he shrugged. 'I never knew him. I knew he wasn't alive. But now... he's really dead.'

Adam nodded and looked back to the dusty tomb.

'We found you, Joe,' he said in a quiet voice. Then, he saw another small cross lying in the bones of Joe's hand. It was a half-broken cross; Adam had seen it before that half broken cross… he looked back but Dave Trigg was no longer behind him.

Nate took his phone out of his pocket. 'I'll call it in to the cops.' He moved towards the door.

'I can't let you do that,' Dave said, standing in the doorway. He slammed the door closed.

The men were locked inside, lit only by the small stained-glass window meters above them.

'Dave!' Nate pounded on the door. 'Open this now.'

Adam joined him and they tried their shoulders against it. The door was old and thick and wouldn't budge.

'I don't want to die in here,' Thomas said, backing towards the wall. 'This can't happen to Mum, she won't cope, I'm all she has.'

'No-one's going to die, Joe, um Thomas,' Adam said, mixing his words. 'It's okay, we'll find a way out.' He cased the room.

'They didn't,' Thomas said looking down at the corpses.

'They were buried here,' Adam said. 'Stay calm, we'll get out.'

'Petrol… can you smell petrol?' Thomas asked.

Adam sniffed the air. He could smell petrol and hear it being splashed up against the door; it was seeping in through the cracks. He and Thomas put their shoulders to the door again, pounding hard and fast.

Nate tried to get reception on his phone, but it was weak inside the isolated building. 'C'mon,' he willed it. 'Hey, it's ringing.' The call connected to the police. 'Matt we're trapped…'

*Smoke!* Dave was lighting a fire outside the door. The old timber place would go up like a funeral pyre.

# Chapter 38

Thomas was terrified; his eyes were huge. He ran around the room, pushing and kicking on the timber wall panels, trying to find a way out. Nate stayed on the phone with Sergeant Matt Burns directing him to the location.

Adam grabbed Thomas by his shoulders.

'Listen! Stop… this is what we're going to do. You're going to get on my shoulders and see if you can pull yourself through that window,' he said, looking at the small glass window above them.

'Right, yeah, right, that's good,' Thomas said, shaking. 'I can get you both out then, yeah…'

Adam squatted as Thomas stepped onto his shoulders.

'Grasp anything you can to take some of your weight,' Adam said, as he staggered to his feet. Thomas was in reaching distance of the window. He shoved it to no avail and began pounding his fist on it.

'Here,' Nate called from below, and handed him a small but full paint can. He returned to the phone call. Adam leaned against the wall, trying to support Thomas' weight. He closed his eyes as he heard Thomas hit the window, breaking the glass and shattering it, pieces falling to the floor.

Adam opened his eyes and began to cough with the thick smoke seeping in.

'Need to get down low,' Nate told him, as he began to cough as well.

'Soon as I get him out,' Adam said, his hands around Thomas's ankles. 'You're next.' He felt Thomas pulling himself up the wall and Adam looked up to see him halfway through the window, then hoisting himself right through. It was a fair drop but it wouldn't kill him.

'Watch your back,' he yelled to him, before choking on more smoke. 'Nate, c'mon.'

'We'll toss for who goes next,' Nate said.

'Matilda,' Adam said, the one word that mattered – Nate's daughter's name. 'Get up, quick.'

They could hear sirens now, as Nate got a leg up from Adam, and before Thomas could make it to the door, it swung open and fresh air rushed in.

Mac stood in the doorway. 'Hurry,' he yelled.

Nate dropped back to the ground, Adam grabbed the paint tin with the drawings in it, and the two friends ran out. Outside, they bent over, taking in the fresh air.

Thomas tried to race back in.

Mac pulled him back. 'Are you crazy kid?' he asked, and pulled him further away from the building; the fire was catching fast.

'Dad's in there, and his painting… it'll be ruined,' Thomas said.

Mac glared at Thomas, trying to work out who his father might be.

Nate grabbed Thomas. 'The firies are here, hopefully they'll get to it in time.' Two fire trucks and a cop car were navigating their way through the wire fence and gate.

Adam stopped coughing long enough to explain. 'Mac, this is Thomas, you've met I believe.'

'Ghost tour guy,' Mac said.

'Thanks for helping with my business,' Thomas said.

'Yeah, don't mention it. Kept it interesting for a while there,' Mac said. 'Who's your dad?'

'Thomas is Joe's son,' Nate said.

Mac's eyes widened, and he studied Thomas's face. 'Yeah, I can see that now. Didn't know he had a son... good for him.'

'Mac you better bolt,' Adam said, pushing himself upright. 'Before the police arrive and you get asked for your address.'

Mac nodded. He looked at Thomas and the two men. 'Yeah. I'm guessing you found... well I'm sorry you found Joe like this,' he said, with sincerity.

Thomas nodded, overcome.

'Thanks,' Adam said. 'We let him down.'

Mac scoffed. 'You were kids. He was expecting nothin' from you.'

'We could have remembered him, looked him up when we got older... checked on him,' Nate said, standing with hands on hips, drawing deep breaths. 'We just abandoned him.'

Mac shook his head. 'Wasn't you kids that abandoned him. Plenty of others did. Joe didn't have an unkind bone in that body,' he said. 'He wouldn't want you saying that stuff and blamin' yourself. Anyway, gotta go. I'll be talking to you.'

Adam nodded. 'Thanks Mac, for saving us!' Nate and Thomas repeated Adam's sentiments.

'Sure,' he said, looking a little embarrassed and unaccustomed to praise. He moved quickly from the building to return to his room in the abandoned home.

'No sign of Dave?' Adam asked.

Nate shook his head.

'Why would he do that?' Thomas asked. 'Didn't you say he was the one who tried to smuggle Dad out… now it looks like he was his killer.'

'Joe had the half cross in his hand. Remember where we saw the other half?' Adam asked Nate.

Nate nodded. 'Around Dave's neck.'

'He was scared for his life,' Adam told Thomas. 'Scared of Digby's repercussions… even to this day. So he just kept us blindly stumbling along.'

Sergeant Matt exited the police car with a young female constable as the firies pushed past them and began to quench the fire.

'You alright?' Matt asked.

'We are now, thanks,' Nate said. 'Pretty hairy there for a moment.'

'Want to tell me what's going on?' Matt said. 'From the top.'

# Chapter 39

'These are amazing,' John Liberman said. Joe's drawings were spread out on the solicitor's boardroom table, the corners held down with a variety of objects. Adam and Nate studied the drawings with him. 'We'll get them all photocopied immediately and a back up set done for Rob.'

'That'd be great,' Adam said. 'He'll be blown away to see these after hearing all the victims' accounts... really brings it home.'

'Rob was telling me he'd have at least another six months to a year part-time work with you, continuing to see some of these patients and getting them through, especially if it goes to court,' John said.

'Yeah, I think he's happy for the work; it'll be good to have him around,' Adam said. 'Do you think it will get to trial?'

'They'd be crazy to let it get traction,' Nate said.

'Couldn't agree more,' John said. 'They'll be offering us an independent mediator, I'd say. Especially when they see these.'

'Get it settled and out of the spotlight,' Nate said, with gravel in his voice.

'Yeah, we'll see if your clients want that,' John said. 'I suspect they will.'

'It'll be easier for them,' Adam agreed. He paused in front of a drawing of a man in a straitjacket. His eyes were the largest part of his body, staring straight at the viewer of the drawing, challenging them not to turn away. Behind him, the perspective was uneven to create a feeling of an enormous room bearing down on him. He moved to the next drawing; a person strapped to a bed with several dark figures looming over them; next, a drawing of the river with a body floating in it, and more… everyone as daunting as the last.

'So, can you submit these drawings as evidence?' Adam asked.

'Of the treatment received, absolutely,' John said, 'especially as we have the diary entries as well.'

Nate pointed to the corner. 'Joe signed each one and his agent will have some original works with signatures to show they're authentic.' Nate shook his head. 'You'd think it was the 19th century, wouldn't you? Not a few decades ago… can't believe this stuff happened while everyone else was out there, living a normal life, going about their own business.'

'Doesn't tell you what happened to Joe though, who killed him,' John said.

'Not yet anyway. We'll see what the cops come up with,' Nate said. 'There's a mark on his skull that's not normal… a fracture, a final blow maybe. My money is on Digby or his henchmen,' Nate said.

'Not the nurse? Did they get him?' John asked.

'Dave Trigg, yeah,' Adam said.

'He's too stupid to be a criminal. May as well have left a breadcrumb trail to his door,' Nate said, and rolled his eyes.

'I think he wanted to be caught,' Adam said, 'poor bugger.' He saw the unsympathetic look Nate sported and explained to John. 'He was a victim too.'

'Or so he says,' Nate quipped in.

'I saw a few lines in the newspaper about him… give me the backstory,' John said.

Nate picked it up. 'He told the cops last night that it wasn't a coincidence that he came to nurse at the River Park Hospital. His little sister was a patient there, and it didn't take him too long to realise what was going on with the patients. Digby, the superintendent found out about his connection and did a deal with him. His sister would be safe under Digby's supervision if Dave did some favours for him in return.'

'Surely killing Joe wasn't one of them?' John asked.

'No,' Adam picked up the story. 'But he was caught trying to smuggle Joe out. He told us he hid Joe in his car but I'm guessing that was a cover story to save his own arse. From the story he gave the police, they didn't get that far. He tried to defend Joe against some of the orderlies and he and Joe came off second best. That's when the cross was broken… he thinks Joe might have kept the bit of crucifix to give him later. He didn't see Joe again after that night and no-one would tell him anything about Joe's whereabouts.'

'Then to punish Dave, Digby had his sister moved… and Dave never found out where. He still doesn't know,' Nate said. 'Dave told the cops he hadn't heard from Digby for years, and he eventually had to accept that his sister was dead, but then Digby rings out of the blue a few weeks back…'

'When we started digging around and breathing life into the class action,' Adam added.

'… and he told Dave if he did a few more things for him, he'd tell him where he could find his sister,' Nate finished.

John shook his head. 'God almighty, that's horrendous.

So he's constantly haunted by the fact she could be alive and needing him, or she could be dead and not buried with family.'

Adam nodded. 'He said he couldn't let it go… he had to know. Even if that meant driving Dan off the road and locking us up.'

'He didn't think we'd die though, apparently,' Nate said, cynically. 'It was show and tell for Digby… he said he knew Mac would get us out, and he followed Dan down the range to keep an eye on her… what little good that would have done if she'd gone over the edge!'

'Wow,' John breathed out. 'Sounds like Dave was seriously being fitted up as the scapegoat. So, what about the superintendent, Digby… what happens to him?'

'Time will tell. They've got Dave's testimony, phone records of the calls, the skeletons in the church if they can get to the bottom of that,' Nate said.

'Maybe DNA will identify one of the skeletons as Dave's sister,' Adam suggested.

Nate nodded. 'I'd love to see Digby go down for all of it.'

'Me too, karma caught up with him at last,' Adam said.

Nate turned to him. 'You of all people should know from your work there's no karma. This sort of crap happened all the time when I was in the police service… you'd have to let someone walk when you knew they were good for the crime… if you could just deliver an eye for an eye. In a way, Dave did us a favour or Digby might have walked… the drawings at least show us what went on but not who was involved.'

John sighed and nodded. 'We'll see… I've got a feeling with a good lawyer, Digby could wiggle out of this. His staff, if any of them are around, won't turn him in because I suspect most of them were actively involved unless they do a deal for immunity. As for our clients, the best they can hope for now is an apology and financial compensation.'

'Surely they'll come out of the woodwork to accuse Digby… some of his former staff will have an attack of guilt or conscience,' Adam said.

'Nah,' Nate shook his head, 'you're talking like a psychologist. From an ex-cop's perspective, trust me, people can justify anything and once they've justified it in their heads, they're as good as innocent in their own minds. Justice will only be a band-aid.'

John smiled. 'Nate, so cynical for one so young, Adam still so optimistic.'

'At least we've found Joe. We can bury him now, give him a headstone,' Adam said.

*****

That night, Adam pulled up out the front of a unit block in St Lucia. It was an old block, cream-coloured bricks, iron verandah railings, and surrounded by modern units.

Safety in numbers, he thought, seeing the wall-to-wall units. As he went up the stairs to find her unit number buzzer, the exterior door of the block opened and Kelsey came out. She looked sassy, he thought, confident. He remembered her like that back then.

'Hey you,' she said, greeting him. 'I thought I'd save you buzzing.'

'Thanks, nice neighbourhood,' he said, glancing up the street at the trees lining both sides like an archway. He was surprised he felt so nervous; he attempted to cover it by flattering the street while he wiped his palms on his suit pants.

She looked in the same direction. 'Mm, nice area if you like units, but there are units everywhere now,' she said, with a shrug. 'It's close to work at least.'

'I should get a library card,' Adam said.

'Sure, they'll give them to pretty much anyone these days,' she teased.

Adam laughed. 'Thanks.'

Putting her head on the side, she studied him. 'Am I too casual?'

'You look great,' he said, with a smile, admiring the stylish navy-blue dress and caramel boots she wore.'

He offered her his arm as they strode down the stairs, and led her to the car, opening the door of his Mercedes for her.

'Nice,' she said and lowered herself into the leather seat. She looked up at him. 'Ah, you haven't dressed for me, have you? I bet you've come straight from work,' she realised, amused.

'Are you kidding?' he said, closing her door and walking around to the driver's side. He slid in beside her. 'I've been home for hours trying on everything in the wardrobe.'

She laughed, and his eyes roamed over her face. He reached for the ignition and she stopped him.

'Adam, I have to tell you something… well a few things,' she said, and hesitated.

'Now?' he asked.

She nodded. 'Maybe others wouldn't say this stuff up front, but I'm fairly direct… I don't want to waste your time or mine.'

Adam felt his heart rate increase; he turned in his car seat to look at her.

*She only wants to be friends, she's married, or gay, she prefers Nate to me, doesn't want to go out with anyone who reminds her of the past, can't forgive me for not coming back for her…* he ran through the scenarios in the solid pause.

The atmosphere between them was filled with ice cold air; he wouldn't have been surprised to see the windows mist up.

'Sure, tell me,' he said, inviting her to speak but not wanting to hear what she had to say.

'Okay, let me finish though...' she said, and took a deep breath.

'I like you, a lot, Adam.' She held up her hand so he didn't reciprocate and interrupt her. 'I don't play around, when I'm with someone I'm completely loyal. I'm not sure that I can have children because of what happened... I don't always sleep well and I leave a night light on. I don't like people much... I don't need a lot of company, I don't even have an online presence.'

She watched his face as she slowly delivered each line. 'I know you're only taking me out, not proposing, but no point heading up this garden path if any of that freaks you out because that's me.'

Adam nodded and reached over for her hand. He took it in his, rubbing his thumb over her delicate, pale skin. He looked up at her.

'I like you too, a lot. The rest doesn't bother me at all.'

Kelsey laughed, a surprised, pleased, spontaneous laugh, as she looked at him. She nodded. 'Okay then.'

'Okay then,' he agreed and smiled at her.

And that was his plan, just like it was the first time he met her. To make her smile and keep her safe. But tonight, he'd start with taking her to dinner.

# Chapter 40

It was an intimate gathering on a perfect Brisbane day; standing at the side of the small church, St Francis of Assisi's in West End, a group had gathered to farewell Joseph O'Connell.

'Nice day for it,' Thomas said, nervously looking around; churches were a foreign place to him. 'Why are funerals always in the morning on a weekday?'

'To be inconvenient,' Adam answered. 'It reminds us what's important... you know, stop, think about life and leave the office for a moment.' Adam shrugged, 'Or something like that.'

'Right,' Thomas said, 'yeah, I get that.'

'I'm liking that red shirt with your suit. Nice touch,' Nate said, teasing Thomas in an attempt to relax him.

Thomas ran his hands down his suit front. 'Yeah, I wear black all the time, I thought Dad would appreciate a splash of colour.' He looked to the church again. 'To... you know, bury Dad, do we have to convert or anything?'

Nate followed Thomas's gaze into the church and up the aisle; Joe's coffin sat at the front of the church, waiting for the proceedings to begin.

'Yeah, we'll need to dunk you completely in water before the ceremony,' Nate said, and Adam smiled.

'Just your head actually,' Adam added.

A middle-aged priest, slight of build with salt-and-pepper greying hair, moved beside them and smiled at the men. 'Ignore them Thomas, you don't need to convert. Although, that would be a nice win for the day,' he said with hope in his voice. 'I'm glad you found me,' he said, shaking hands with them all.

'So are we,' Adam said. 'Mac helped.'

They looked over at Mac who stood back from the group, Kelsey by his side, and Rob beside them, casually trying to relax them both.

'Good that Mac found some support too. I don't know that young lady, who is she?' Father Will asked.

'Kelsey. She was a patient for a brief time; Mac came into the library where Kelsey worked some time back and recognised her straight away,' Adam said. He turned back to the priest. 'Been a few years since you thought of Joe too I guess?'

Father Will nodded. 'Nearly two decades... I was a bit younger then. I'd like to say I'm wiser now, but I'm just crankier.'

The men laughed.

Father Will looked at them. 'Amazing.'

'What is?' Nate asked, sobering up with another glance to Joe's coffin waiting inside the church for them to join him.

'The two of you,' Father Will said. 'I saw the illustration Joe did of you both... and here you are in the flesh, all these years later. You have good hearts.'

Adam looked away embarrassed. Nate looked skyward before answering. 'Adam maybe, but if I take claim to that a lightning bolt will strike me.'

It was Father Will's turn to laugh. 'Yes, God moves in

mysterious ways. Ah, is this your mum, Thomas?' he asked with a nod towards the carpark. 'We can begin if it is.'

They looked over to where a small white Mazda had pulled up and a woman hurried from the car. She was adept at caution; taking in the surrounds and the group with quick and subtle looks.

'Good, she found it,' Thomas said, and headed over to greet her.

*****

'Who are all these people?' Donna asked, linking her arm through her son's as they walked towards the church. She scoped the small crowd once more; surprised to see a dozen or so people gathered to farewell Joe.

'Friends of Dad's, he did alright,' Thomas said.

'He did, didn't he?' she agreed. 'Is he here, the nurse who tried to get him out and then killed him?'

'No, but he didn't kill him. He was framed,' Thomas said, and saw the suspicious look on his mother's face. 'Honest, ask Nate, he'll tell you.'

Behind them, Danielle and Jessica pulled up in Jessica's car. Thomas's mother, Donna, turned and recognising Danielle, seemed to relax a little.

Thomas introduced his mother around.

'I'll go in, just come in when you are ready,' Father Will said, Jessica and Danielle followed. Adam moved to Mac, Rob and Kelsey, accompanying them inside.

'Well,' Donna said, as she and Thomas walked in beside Nate, 'you found him. Thank you.'

'We did. I'm sorry it was not how you wanted it to turn out, but I guess the odds were against you having a chance at a normal life,' he said.

Donna smiled. 'You know, we had a moment, and that's a lot more than some people have, I can tell you. Besides, look what we created.'

Thomas rolled his eyes but reddened with pleasure. His mother took his arm and they settled into the front pew.

*****

'I've had the honour of officiating at many funerals, at many baptisms and weddings… all the cycles of life,' Father Will said, in his attempt to keep Joe's farewell comfortable and intimate. 'But when I received Adam's call telling me we could now bury Joe; that Mac remembered me and knew I would want to see Joe off, I felt very grateful. To look around and see your faces, and to know that each and every one of you had a connection to Joe, whether you knew him, loved him, are his flesh and blood, or are now working to get justice for Joe, it is a tribute to the man.

'Some funerals will have people overflowing out the doors, but many of those don't know the dearly beloved. They come for family and tradition. Joe was here for a short time and look at whom he touched.'

He stopped and looked at every face: Joe's wife and son; the two boys he befriended, now men; the people he shared his pain with in the wards; his agent who knew his talent; the solicitor who carried out his last wishes; and the man who had snuck into the back row that Father Will guessed was Joe's brother, Stephen. He continued.

'I remember his talent, but most of all, I remember his kindness… a gentle soul who will find a kinder world in the next than he found here.'

*****

The mourners began to move away from the gravesite where Joe now rested in the freshly dug earth. Nate and Danielle walked Thomas and his mother back to her car.

'When are you heading home?' Danielle asked Donna.

'I'm driving back tomorrow,' she said. 'I'll be back up for Christmas though,' she said, smiling at her son.

Nate looked at Thomas. 'So, what are you going to do with your Dad's gift… the legacy fund which should keep on keeping on? Stay with the ghost business?'

'Funny you should ask,' he said. 'I've been thinking a lot about what you and Adam said… you know about having different skills and tapping into them.'

'Yeah, we're full of good advice,' Nate agreed. Danielle laughed beside him.

'Oh sorry,' she said, seeing his expression. 'Of course you are,' she agreed.

Thomas grinned. 'I've started to develop a game… you know how you both thought my mapping skills and the illustrations were really good, we'll I'm doing some graphics and I'm putting together the ultimate game!'

'Have you played *Final Fantasy 15*?' Nate asked, his eyes widened with interest.

'Yeah, but I like *Destiny 2* better… you know the graphics are really good, and I thought maybe I could work some of Dad's images in too…'

Donna and Danielle smiled and turned to say their goodbyes to Father Will. When everyone had left, Nate looked around for Adam and found him back at Joe's grave. He walked over to join him.

'Kelsey gone too?'

'Yeah, Rob's going to drop her and Mac home. I'm seeing her tomorrow,' he said, and smiled at the thought.

'Good on you, a better fit for you, than anyone we know.'

Nate thought that covered all past and present prospects. He put his hand on Adam's shoulder. 'Ready to go?'

'Yeah. You know what pisses me off more than anything?' Adam asked.

'I could have a fair stab at that,' Nate said.

'There's no justice. Not just for what happened at the asylum to Joe, Kelsey and Mac, and all the others… but in Joe's life. His shitty father was pretty much the catalyst for all of it. Ruined Joe and Stephen's life, the treatment at the asylum just finished it off,' Adam said, and nudged the loose dirt near Joe's grave. He continued: 'Imagine if he had been encouraged as an artist; and if he got to raise Thomas with Donna, without fear…'

Nate nodded. 'Except that wasn't his path, and you of all people know that we all get dealt different hands, it's just how we deal with them. At least he's been found now and he's got a place where Thomas can visit him.'

Adam nodded. 'Yeah.'

'Come on, I'll shout the first round. Rob's going to meet us at the pub.' Nate looked down on Joe's pale timber casket. 'Bye Joe, thanks. Be seeing you.'

Nate dropped his hand from Adam's shoulder and started towards the church car park.

'See you Joe,' Adam said, and began to follow Nate.

# Chapter 41

**Then...**

'Do you think he'll ever come back?' Adam asked, as he swung his leg over the tree branch below Nate and pulled himself up to see further into the grounds of the asylum. He counted three people in the yard, but no Joe.

Nate shrugged. 'It's been at least four weeks now... longer than the last time he went away. They might have moved him to somewhere else.'

'He would have told us, unless they didn't tell him,' Adam said. 'It's kind of weird he didn't tell us if he knew he was going to go away forever.'

'He could be dead,' Nate suggested.

'Do you think we should tell the police... you know that he's missing or ask them if he's dead? They'd know for sure.'

Nate frowned. 'Don't know. If we do they'll want to know why we want to know.'

The boys sat staring at the asylum yard.

'I've got an idea,' Nate said. 'We could write to the hospital and see if the letter gets returned to us.'

'Yeah, we could, but we don't know his last name. There could be like a stack of Joes who live there,' Adam said.

'Want to go to the front counter and pretend to be visitors? We could say we're related but we only know him as Uncle Joe.'

'No.'

'Nuh, me either,' Nate agreed.

'I guess we'll never see him again,' Adam sighed.

'If I was in there... like when we grow up, would you break me out?' Nate asked.

'Yeah, of course. Would you get me out?'

'Yeah, I'd have a really good plan, and once we were out of the gates, we could just disappear... go to Sydney or a place where there's lots of people and they couldn't find us,' Nate said.

'We'd have to go somewhere where they don't have a newspaper because Mum would be all over it... trying to find me. Our pictures would be everywhere.'

'Yeah, forgot about that,' Nate agreed. 'Then we'd go out into the middle of Australia. Bet they'd never find us there. But... if you were married or something, you might not be able to get away to get me out.'

'Nah,' Adam scoffed. 'I'd get you out... we're blood brothers, remember?'

The boys studied the people coming and going in the grounds for a few more minutes.

'Let's go,' Nate said, lowering himself down the tree, branch by branch. 'Bye, Joe, be seeing you.'

Adam glanced to the grounds where Joe used to sit, by the fence.

'See you, Joe,' he said, and turned to follow Nate.

**Next in the series:** *Stalker*

Adam couldn't wait… his Uncle Allan was coming to watch his cricket game this afternoon; Adam's father was always too busy to get there. Uncle Allan believed Adam and Nate would one day be chosen for the State side if they kept practicing… Adam's bowling was really improving.

Adam didn't have an Uncle Allan.

**Thanks and acknowledgements:**

My sincere thanks to B. Michael Radburn who took time out from his own writing to read a fledgling author's work and offer words of support and encouragement.

To Helen Goltz, publisher, thank you for the overwhelming vote of confidence, suggestions, revisions and staying on my case.

To Joanne James, editor, thanks for all your hard work and for making me look better!

And of course, last but first always, my writer's muses – thanks for keeping me sane.

**From the author, Jack Adams:**

I grew up in Toowoomba, Queensland, in a different era, in a disciplined household but yet I seemed to have had more freedom then today's kids. As a child if misbehaving, my parents threatened to drop me off at the Baillie Henderson Lunatic Asylum (now the Baillie Henderson Hospital). The establishment was clearly named before the era of political correctness, but the thought of being left at a lunatic asylum was enough to pull any kid into line.

To put me in the frame of mind for writing this story, I would sometimes take a drive past the relic of Wolston Park Asylum at Wacol, on the outskirts of Brisbane. You can't get too close, but close enough to imagine the sad lives that came and went through its doors.

This book is completely fictional, but my limited research tells me that suffering of this nature is not. It is hoped we are a better society today – more tolerant, more open to understanding illnesses of the mind and body. However, there may be a balance to get right… when people (men and women) in the community are at risk from those amongst us who need help, when women are not safe walking home at night, then our work is not done yet. Maybe it will never be.

302